WHEN ASPENS QUAKE

Published in the United States by The Spartina Company, Ltd.

ISBN 978-0-9898549-2-4
eISBN 978-0-9898549-3-1

COVER DESIGN BY DAMONZA

To my personal cheerleaders:
Thank you for keeping me constantly inspired.

A BOOK AND SO MUCH MORE...

Listen to the Spotify® Playlist @ http://goo.gl/dEtfPf

Explore the world of Cole Mouzon:

Maps, Spotify® playlists and insight:
Robert-Reeves.com

Locations, recipes, characters @ Pinterest:
http://pinterest.com/crobertreeves/

WHEN ASPENS QUAKE

- A NOVEL -

By Robert Reeves

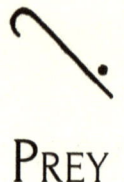

PREY

PROLOGUE

Atlanta

THE BUMPER STICKER on the old champagne Cutlass Supreme in front of her read, "If you're going to ride my ass, at least pull my hair." It had been over a year since Celia Leigh's long blonde hair or anything else had been pulled. Her last boyfriend, Barney, had been over two years prior. Two very long years. And, work and nursing school consumed any time that she had now to find a new lay. There were guys willing, but she was trying to be good – she wanted a husband, not a fuck. Her newly instituted "No Sex For 30 Days" plan was working perfectly, if perfectly meant no boyfriend and no sex. Celia let out a loud huff at her self-induced dry spell.

When told of the house rules, the guys always said it was cool. But… a day or two later and they were gone, too busy for a date. Work, family, a random trip to Africa… Celia found it all funny since they were on-line every time she logged onto OkCupid. That little green dot told her everything she needed to know. They weren't too busy;

they were just too busy to wait for her to put out. She told herself she could do this... she could keep with the plan, but she knew that if given the right guy, the right time... she would be too damn busy for this stupid rule.

Her mental dialog continued as she pulled into her small, vinyl siding adorned apartment building. Rusty iron water stains coated the base of the otherwise dingy white structure. As she parked she noticed a gray bearded man sitting in a weathered blue sedan in her rear mirror. He was obviously watching her. His eyes followed her as she stepped out of her car and gave the man another look. She didn't know what made her more uncomfortable, that he was staring at her or that it appeared he was taking notes... documenting her on some hidden pad on his lap.

Unnerved, she abandoned grabbing her gym bag from the back seat and turned towards the scantly landscaped interior courtyard of the complex. She hastened her steps, afraid she would hear him behind her at any moment. Her head jerked several times in response to noises behind her, only to realize it was a bird rustling in a bush. The keys jangled and dropped twice, before the deadbolt key slid into the lock. The door flew uncontrollably open causing her to fall into the doorway. She rushed to her feet and swung the door closed with a bang, quickly twisting the deadbolt's knob. Inside, she ran into the bathroom and very slowly pushed apart the pink plastic mini-blinds just enough to see out the window that overlooked the parking lot. The car was gone. She looked around the lot several times before collapsing down onto the toilet seat where she put her head in her hands and laughed. "Damn, girl. Chill the fuck out."

Chapter I

Denver

F ALL IN DENVER meant turmoil. The weather had been a rollercoaster of snow, floods, and heat-waves. Labor Day weekend offered no relief from the chaos that had become Cole Mouzon's life.

"You might want to pay attention to me and not that DILF over there." Cole turned away from gazing at the tall brunette man standing at the sideline to see mahogany eyes staring back at him just inches away. A slight scar in the man's brow and a perfectly placed mole between his nose and plump upper lip accented his creamed-coffee skin. His cropped black hair was damp from the stifling heat of the pre-noon September day.

Lifting his own blond brow, Cole responded, "I think you are the one that needs to pay attention to me. You're down by seven, sir." His words were garbled from speaking through his mouth guard.

The man grinned. "Oh, I've been paying attention." A grin appeared across the man's face.

From mid-field, Cole heard the quarterback shout,

"Down… Set…" Cole dug in the ball of his right foot to grip the soggy grass. "Hut!" Cole pushed off and was immediately hit in the chest by "Scar" before spinning enough to get around him to run the assigned "flag" pattern. *Five feet out, then cut diagonally to the sideline…* Scar was back, pushing up against him with his shoulders and solid body, trying to break Cole's run. Looking back over his shoulder just for a second, Cole saw the quarterback release the ball, spinning in a tight pattern in his direction. He pushed his legs harder into the ground with each step to pick up speed and lose his guard. Reaching his arms completely out, he waited for the ball to drop into his gloved hands. The ball appeared in front of him, hands out, still running at full speed… *three feet overthrown.* Before he could respond, he collided with Scar, both tumbling in a knotted pile. Cole's hip ached from slamming into the ground as he stood up. Cole looked down and saw the impact marked by a muddy spot on his white shorts. Rubbing it, he could hear the team's coach yelling at one of the refs about the lack of a flag on Scar.

"What the hell, man? That was pass interference. Where is the damn flag?" The short, mustached ref with his black and white stripped jersey merely looked at the coach and waved him off as he half-jogged across the field.

Cole joined the huddle where the quarterback was trying to rally his troops. Running his hand through his bleach-blond buzzed-cut hair, Jeffery Sloan looked around the circle of players with their burnt umber jerseys. "Good try guys, good try. Cole, you were almost there. A little more speed, okay?" Cole looked at the six-five man and faked a smile. *You try being tackled by a one-ninety, two-hundred pound solid muscle Scar.* Cole looked back to see the Latino guy gazing at him from the other end of the field. "Cole! Pay attention. You are purple this time." Cole looked down to Jeffery's forearm sleeve holder and its squares of various plays diagramed out in different color lines. *Purple, purple... ah, a "chair" through the mid-field.* The huddle broke.

"Come on guys! We got this. Penguin, penguin. Let's do this." The team had devised a plan of making-up play names based on animals to confuse the opposing team. The particular animal name didn't matter, what did was the first letter of the name. Penguin, starting with a "P," meant the quarterback was going to try and aim for the purple player first. Jeffery was going for Cole again.

Cole crouched this time on the left side of the quarterback and next to Alice, the co-ed team's center. From Scar's movement to position himself again within inches across the line of scrimmage from Cole it was apparent that he had been assigned to Cole for the game rather than playing a zone position. Scar leaned in, "Zander here. And, 'sidelines' over there... has nothing on me. I've probably tackled you better than he ever has. Let's show him how it is done." Zander stood up slightly up, turned to the man Cole had been eyeing earlier at the sideline and gave an obvious wink in his direction. From the corner of his eyes, Cole saw Cash Calhoun's crystal blue eyes tighten. Cole bit down on his mouth guard and gave a quick smile to Zander. *Game on.*

"Hut." Cole was off and slammed again by Zander's palms colliding against his chest as he came off the line. Unable to use his own hands to guard against the assault without drawing a penalty, Cole pushed back with his chest, momentarily throwing Zander off balance and to the side. Cole took advantage and ran straight out ten yards, pump-faked with his feet to one side, then made a hard ninety-degree turn towards the sideline. Several more steps and he took another hard turn pointing him again towards the end-zone. He peeked over his shoulder; the ball was already in the air. *Shit*. Cole picked up speed, extending his hands out before him again to cradle the ball at impact. Seconds later it came into view while still looking ahead and dropped straight into his hands. Gripping the leather, he pulled it in, slightly tucking it under an arm while again picking up speed. Feet from the end zone he felt Zander wrap his arms around him, pulling Cole down hard to the ground. Cole reached out with the ball seconds before his knees buckled and slammed into the wet ground. He closed his eyes as he realized he was helpless to prevent his face from skidding across the grass. Cole lifted his head and opened his eyes to see the ball's tip barely inside the end-zone.

Firmly pinned to the ground with Zander on his back, Cole yanked his mouth guard out. "What the hell? Get off me. This is flag football, not tackle." Zander loosened his arms and grabbed Cole's wrists, pushing them over his head and into the ground. He leaned in and whispered into Cole's ear from behind, "I told you that you were going to get tackled. Admit it. You are enjoying this." Zander inhaled deeply and then let loose, slowly crawling off Cole's back.

Cole pushed himself up and mouthed a "fuuuck you" as he walked over to the huddle. The short ref walked over with the yellow flag in his hand that he had been thrown for the tackle. "I suspect you are going to decline the flag and play for the extra point. Am I right?"

"Yeah. We are going for two." Jeremy nodded and

then waved him off to deal with the huddle. The ref shoved the flag down one of his socks and walked off.

"Okay, we need the two points to avoid a tied game, let's do this, guys. There are twenty seconds left on the clock. We've got this." Jeffery once again pointed out the play being called. Cole was pointed to a red line on the play sleeve. *Ten and in. Simple enough.*

Walking up to the line, Zander was back in a position to match Cole's. "Too rough for you? I can be gentle if you want me to. I aim to please." Cole looked up from finding his spot on the line, "I'm sure you do. Aiming and succeeding are two very different things. Perhaps you need to find something a little more at your level. Say, a puppy?" Zander let loose a throaty laugh and replied, "Oh, a challenge. When do we start?" His gaze intensified. Cole shook his head slowly with a smile and he prepared for the handoff. His photographic memory activated and flicked through the prior two plays, analyzing Scar's previous movements. *He favors going to his left.*

"Down... set... hut!"

Zander's block missed as Cole pump-faked and ran past him into the end zone. Almost positioned, the ball was released in the opposite direction by the quarterback and caught by a five-five young twenty-something that bounded like a gazelle between the lineman and into the end-zone without any coverage. Other players circled around and lifted him onto their shoulders in celebration as Cole walked over. "Nice job, Trevor. For a little man... wow can you move."

"Thanks Cole. Nice catch on your end, too." Trevor looked around Cole to Zander standing several feet outside the crowd, his eyes still fixed on Cole. Noticing that

Trevor wasn't talking about his touchdown, Cole leaned in. "I want no part of catching that bad disease. Nothing but trouble." Trevor snickered. "Well, if you don't want him, give him to me. I can think of a few things I could do with that."

The Captain interrupted before Cole could respond, "Come on cheer time." The team collected together, placed a hand into a circle and everyone together shouted, "Good game. Live life Blue Ballin' Y.O.L.O.'s! Goooo... Ginga Ninjas!"

COLE LOOKED BACK to the sideline where Cash was standing with Cole's four-year-old nephew, Billy, on his shoulders. He inhaled deeply as he took in the image of the six-foot man holding the young bowl-cut blond who was clapping in Cole's direction. Cole unclasped the yellow flagged strap circling his waist as he slowly walked in their direction only to feel the strap yanked out of his hands from behind. "Hey, good game...." Cole turned to see Zander standing there, his neck craned and hand extended, clearly waiting for a name. "Cole. And, yeah... you, too." Cole had to admit, the man was handsome, in a "don't bring that home to momma" kind of way. *T.R.O.U.B.L.E.* To Cole, anyone that pretty had lost appreciation for a healthy relationship long ago and Cole wasn't about to try to re-teach him. Cole looked back to the sideline for a brief second. *Well, except for Cash. He comes amply trained.*

Zander responded, "Thanks, well... hopefully I will see you again, soon. I promise not to be so rough. Well, not straight out the gate, at least." With a grin, he walked away in the direction of his team.

Cole turned back to see Cash, his brow furled and his head slightly cocked. "What was that about?"

Cole walked over and pushed a tuft of brown hair out of Cash's blue eyes and then smiled as he shook his head in slight disbelief. "Don't ask. He's a goofball." Cole looked up at Billy, still on Cash's shoulders, as he mocked the word "goofball." He bounced like he was posting on a horse.

Cole extended his arm and clawed his fingers in the boy's face. "Kinda like you, lil'man. Goofball."

Billy laughed as he pulled away; leaning back enough to cause Cash to readjusted his stance. "I'm not a goo-ball Uncle Cole. You are."

"Ha. Yes, I am. Yes, I am..." Cole leaned down to slip off his soccer cleats and knee high rust-orange socks. Midway through struggling with his laces, he continued. "Thank you again, Cash, for coming. I know this isn't what you likely had planned when we scheduled your visit. A nine a.m. game on a Saturday morning is not fun." He glanced at his sports watch. "Wow, it's eleven already. I don't know about you boys, but I'm starved. What are ya'll hungry for?" He squinted into the full sun as he looked up to the two boys towering over him.

Cash carefully lifted Billy by his armpits and placed him standing on the ground next to Cole. "By no means, I want to know more about you, your world. And, this was awesome. I definitely learned you are a crazy fast runner, and a pretty good receiver. I'm impressed." He lifted and rolled his shoulders. "Boy, you are heavy for only being four years old. What do you weigh, like nine-hundred pounds of muscle?" He playfully pinched Billy's bicep as the boy laughed.

"No, silly!"

Grinning, Cole's mind drifted. He wondered how anyone could be impressed with his life at that moment. He was still haunted by his childhood nightmare that had returned just before the killer Poinsett attacked in Charleston. He had met Cash while trying to survive the killer in his hometown just three-and-a-half months earlier, a killer that took his sister's life and left him as a make-shift parent. Even before that, he had been barely hanging on himself, broken from a dark-ending relationship. But, now he was responsible for someone else's mental stability and success. The thought scared him. *How could Jackie think I was ready for this?* Cole snapped himself out of his mental debate with a prolonged blink.

Still fiddling with his shoes, he flashed a smirk. "Ha. It's these jack-rabbit legs. That's what Jackie used to call them. I could kick her clear across a room when she tickle attacked me as a kid on Saturday mornings."

Cole tensed as he realized he had just mentioned his sister's name and quickly focused on Billy. Cole waited for a delayed response but it did not come. *Close one.* Though it had been almost four months since his cousin-turned-sister, Billy's mother, had been killed in the battery by Poinsett, the emotions were still raw. She had been a constant in his life ever since he was adopted by his aunt and uncle when his own mother died. To him, she was his sister. Nothing less. She had been his protector as a child and never stopped, sacrificing herself for him in the WWII battery ruins. Cole refused to not mention her around Billy, she deserved to be remembered. But, he always cringed when he did because Billy seemed to randomly cry at one mention and fondly recall at another. It was a game of dice.

CHAPTER 2

WALKING BACK TO the car, Billy tugged on Cole's hand, "Uncle Cole, can we go see Wilma?"

He looked down to the boy and inspected his Superman t-shirt and navy shorts. He had been addicted to everything Superman since the movie downloaded off of iTunes. His passion had carried over to his attire at some point and there was no end in sight for everything worn having a Man of Steel logo on it. Cole laughed at the sight of the pint-sized superhero.

Cash chimed in before Cole could respond. "Wilma? Who is that?" Cash wagged his hand through the mop of hair at his knee.

Cole responded, "Ha, it's one of the buffalo over at the Arsenal." He then bent down to Billy's level as he first looked up to Cash for approval as to what he was about to say. "Buddy, we can go see Wilma another time. I'm sure that isn't how Cash wants to spend his time, tramping around in a prairie." Cole looked to Billy now frowning.

Sabotage struck fast. "Uh, excuse me. But, I think I might like that, actually. I've never seen a live buffalo."

Pursing his lips, Cole looked askance at Cash as

he stood up. He covered Billy's ears and whispered, "I promise you, it isn't that big of a deal. The feds have set up a large herd of them on the site of a now demolished chemical weapons plant that overlooks the city. We can run out there and chase a few if you want. It's like ten minutes from downtown. But, I'm telling you, it's just grass out there."

Cash looked down at Billy who stared back while mouthing, "please, please, please."

"I don't know about you buddy, but I think I want to chase a buffalo."

Billy bounced up and down. "Yes!" Cash flashed Cole an oblique look with a charming smile.

Cole was helpless against the two boys. He gave in with a roll of his eyes. "… but only after I get something in my belly. You know how I get when I'm hungry." Cole winked at Billy as he bounded into the silver Audi sedan with Cash following behind him to latch the sly kid into his car seat. The back door closed, the man turned and firmly pushed Cole up against the car. The kiss was unexpected and intense.

The time between Cash's arrival and that moment had been awkward, with Cole never knowing if the chemistry they felt in Charleston had lingered enough for this first visit since then to be more than just as friends. Cole felt like he was at a teen prom, never sure if his feelings were welcomed, reciprocated. As with most first kisses, especially those between men, it was awkward as they both wrestled for the lead like two men dancing. Giving in to follow, Cole suspected it was as much for him as it was a message to Zander. *Cash's property.*

TAKER

CHAPTER 3

RUBBING HIS TATTOOED forearm didn't seem to help. It never had. But, it just seemed the thing to do after rolling up the sleeves of his flannel shirt. Smith Gilmer ached in most joints. That's what sixty-four years on the planet does to a man. His birth name was Poinsett, but that had changed several times since the early eighties. Much like his name, the aches didn't come with the package. Rather, both were derived from painful moments... mostly from delivering pain to others. He reasoned it was a small price to pay for playing the game.

The kitchen was small, with dingy white paint and some ivy wallpaper that looked to be an addition from the late-seventies. The pea-green refrigerator hummed as Smith pulled out an old diner-style vinyl topped seat. Smith leaned in before sitting. Spread across the matching kitchen table were several newspaper clippings. Still damp from his shower, he pushed his shoulder length salt-and-pepper hair behind each ear for a better look before he began fiddling with the clippings' edges with his fingers. "Slaughter in Macon" read the headline of one. "Sacrifice Murder" headlined another clipping. *Stupid ants. So very wrong.* Smith could understand the misinterpretation from twits. After all, the bodies were presented in a very formal fashion rather than some bloody crime scene. He always believed that such a ghastly sight was a waste. *Simple minds breed simple lives.* He pushed the papers away as he slowly sat. He rubbed his lower back. Getting old sucked.

His heart pumped hard as he thought of his killings. Murder was art and bodies were his canvas. He had perfected his skills in the thirty or so years since he first discovered his talent. Back then there was a lot more blood, a lot more violence. He was young, inexperienced. That wasn't as true now. Now… he took his time. Studying his future projects was easy since semi-retiring from Georgia Power. But, retirement had come with its limitations. A utilities job provided a reason to be in other's homes. So, his current part-time senior job merely provided a means to an end.

His cherished the killing, but a close second was the watching. He was a meticulous note taker, jotting everything down from their schedule, to appearance, to favorite vices, and they had ample. He needed to know them, needed to know they were the right selection for his art. This took time and patience. "If it's worth doing, it's worth doing right," his mother always said. She was talking about work, but he felt it was apt to murder as well.

A new wrinkle had arisen a year ago that had not been expected, but was nonetheless welcomed. Beth Winters, the bastard daughter from his time in South Carolina, had decided to kill off those he had kidnapped and branded at the beginning of his career. She was never supposed to be part of that game, but she played it well until one of the challengers finished her off.

"Cole Mouzon, Survivor," was in large bold print in one of the cutouts now at the far edge of the table. Smith stretched across the table to grab the clipping. Staring for a few seconds, he drew his finger across the black and white photo of the young man. He had seen the face before. Thirty years had passed since he took the Mouzon boy's mother and him into the marshes outside of Charleston. There he tortured the mother while her boy watched. His body grew hot with anger at the thought of anyone escaping him. He was already on the road out of town by the time he learned only the child survived, the mother dying of her injuries in the marsh. He ran to New York, Texas, and then California, selecting others along the way as he had done the Mouzon boy. He had planted a single seed in each... murder. The time had come to see if those that still survived would bear fruit.

CHAPTER 4

"CAN I HELP you with that?" Cash stood behind Cole, one hand on Cole's shoulder as he looked over onto the stove to ground beef sizzling in a cast-iron skillet.

Cole gave a slight elbow nudge to the onlooker's ribs and smiled. "No, no. I got it. You're in my house, visiting me. The least I can do is cook for you. Sit down. Sorry for all the boxes, but moving day is next week and with work and all, it's all a bit much." Cash withdrew slowly, letting his fingers linger for a moment as they slid down Cole's back.

Cash moved some newspaper from a bar stool seat and sat to watch Cole stirring hamburger meat in a frying pan. "You know you could have just said that this wasn't a good weekend. I wouldn't have been insulted or anything. Who knows, you may have had a math Olympics competition." He let out a short laugh.

The spatula still in his hand, Cole twisted in a futile attempt to look at the white screen-print text on the back of his red T-shirt. He turned back to Cash. "Ha. Ha. Funny. It's from high school. Yes, I'm a dorky nerd. I own it, Mister. And… What? It's been what, four months since

I last saw you. Between your schedule and mine, taking Billy to Florida, all coupled with having to cancel from the flooding here two weeks ago. No, it was time. Not that I missed you or anything." Cole flashed a quick smile before turning back to the stove.

Cash leaned across the kitchen bar counter, his hands cupped together. "Ha. Well, when you put it that way... I guess it was understandable." He pulled back and looked into the living room behind him. "Are you excited to move?"

"Err, I hate moving. But, look around." Cole turned his head to emphasize his words. "This place is way too small for Billy, Dixie and I. Two words. 'One. Bathroom.'" Glancing back to Cash, his eyes were met with intensity and a grin. His eyes popped in his two-tone blue baseball Tee.

Cole's skin went hot as a smile grew. "What? Do I have something on my shirt or something?"

"Ha. No. I just like looking at you. Is that okay?"

Shaking his head, Cole laughed. "Best get your eyes checked, mister. You are clearly not seeing what I am seeing. Case in point... pale." He waved his hand over his left arm to showcase his skin. "It snowed three inches last week, flooded a week before that. Thank goodness it's seventy and sunny today. I'm sure football this morning gave me a nice red neck."

"Hmm, let me see." Cash got off the stool and walked back over Cole, positioning himself against Cole's back. Gripping the collar of Cole's crew neck T-shirt, he pulled it back and looked down it. "Yep, a very nice red neck I must say. Want me to put some aloe on it for you?"

Cole slowly cut his eyes to see Cash still positioned behind him. Cash threw up his hands, "What? I'm just saying. You have a burn. I could be of some use in addressing it, that's all."

Cole grabbed the dishtowel on the counter next to the stove and began winding it to whip. "Uh huh. Trouble, will you gather Billy from the backyard and let him know the sloppy-joes are ready?" The loud pop resonated through the house as it barely caught Cash's jean adorned ass.

CHAPTER 5

I T WAS ALMOST eight by the time they returned from visiting Wilma at the Arsenal and grabbed dinner. Cash collapsed into the couch as Cole readied a reluctant Billy for bed. Thirty minutes later he was in his Superman underoos and asleep in bed. Cole walked back into the living room and snuggled against Cash, lifting one of his arms to wrap around his shoulders as the TV flickered across the dim lit room.

The small house would be missed. Cole had moved there when he first moved to Denver almost two years earlier. The space was small, yes. But, knowing that his killer in Charleston had actually broken-in to try and kill him just a day before he left for the Holy City made the idea of staying unbearable. Had it not been for Dixie barking in the middle of the night before his trip, he might be dead. Guilt flooded in as he wondered if his death would have prevented his sister's. He looked down to the Weimaraner-lab mix sleeping at his feet. Inhaling deeply, he pushed up his mental wall. The reality now was that he no longer felt safe in the home, especially with Billy there. His thoughts were interrupted.

"You know, you look like a pro doing that. You are

pretty great with him." Cash rubbed one of his thumbs against Cole's shoulder and then kissed his forehead.

Cole absorbed the moment before responding. "Thank you. I'm trying. That's about all I can do, right? But, you seem to be pretty good with him as well. He likes you... a lot." He grabbed the thumb on his shoulder and gave it a slight squeeze.

Cash twisted his neck to look down at the head pressed into his side until Cole turned up to look him in the eyes before he began to brag. "What's not to like? Charming, handsome, sporty... did I say handsome?" Cash polished his knuckles of his free hand against his T-shirt in feigned bravado.

Cole sat up and landed a slight slap on Cash's chest with his left hand. But, Cash locked the arm around Cole's shoulder and pulled him back in tight.

Cole gave in, placing a hand on Cash's thigh. "I'll give you handsome. But, I think right now I'm the sporty one of this couple." The word couple echoed in Cole's ear. He hadn't realized that he was thinking as them as a couple until it just escaped his mouth. It felt good, but danger-ous. He was exposing himself to potential hurt again and he grew instantly cold. Cole looked over to Cash grin-ning. He clearly liked that the word "couple" had been used by Cole. *Shit.*

Cole sat back up and attempted to stand as he straightened his shirt. "Want some water, or wine, or something?" He was sputtering in discomfort over his emotions. Exposing himself scared him and a change of topic was the best course for the moment. Cash grabbed his hand and pulled him back down into the couch. "Hush. Do you hear me? Hush. I won't let you do that... I won't let you fall into that abyss that you like to retreat to when things get serious." Cash pushed Cole down, forcing his back into the seat of the couch while he crawled on top of him.

Pinning Cole's arms down by his sides, he went for a kiss, but Cole turned away, his head still spinning with conflicting emotions. Refusing to retreat, Cash started at Cole's neck, slowly kissing down it and across the collar bone. He grew more intense and grabbed the sides of Cole's face, forcing it to face his own. Intense desideration flashed in Cash's eyes just before he rushed in for a deep, slow kiss. Tiny goose bumps tingled across Cole's skin as he released all fear, all dread of what Cash posed. He was safe.

"UNCLE COLE, I can't sleep." The voice came from the hallway to Billy's room. Cole looked at Cash in disappointment and then pushed against his chest to get up. "Coming!" Cash grabbed his hand and let it linger until their hands fell apart as Cole walked away.

Moments later he walked back into the living room with Billy holding his hand and rubbing the sleep out of his eyes with his small knuckles. Cash sat up and made room while Cole sat, placing Billy opposite Cash. Squinting, Billy said, "I want to sit there." He pointed to the small space between Cash and Cole. Looking over at Cash first, Cole lifted Billy and squeezed him between the two. A large blanket that had been lying along the back of the couch was lifted and placed to cover the three boy's legs. An extra tug up to Billy's neck was followed by several tucks. True to kids, Billy found the remote immediately and flicked through the television channels until he landed on *The Incredibles*. Dixie approached and sniffed the gathering before circling a few times and settling at the couch's base.

Billy was discovered asleep within minutes. Looking down at Billy's head on his lap, Cole caught Cash staring at the two. He grinned before nuzzling himself against Cash again. With a faint whisper he added, "Thank you for being amazing. Thank you for being you."

Cardinal Grosbeak.

FRINGILLA CARDINALIS. *Bonap.*
Male 1. Female 2.
Wild Almond.

Drawn from Nature by J. J. Audubon F.R.S. F.L.S.   Engraved, Printed & Coloured by R. Havell London 1827.

CHAPTER 6

"CAN I GET you another 420, hun?" Celia Leigh leaned over the counter of Six-Feet Under's roof-top bar to get a better view of the man chatting up his bearded buddy on the bar stool in front of her. Approximately thirty-two, he was handsome and rugged. She liked his thick arms the most. And, the right amount of chest hair peeked out of his green polo shirt.

He turned slightly and grinned, "I'd love another." Nudging his less attractive friend, "Jim, you want another from this lovely lady?" A loud burp was released as the man side-fisted his chest and turned. His blood-shot eyes widened as he turned to see who his friend was referring to. He took in Celia's tight black t-shirt which revealed ample cleavage to secure a proper tip from her customers. Her long blond hair was swept to the side and over one shoulder. The look was accented by a simple string of small pearls that circled her neck. Her west Georgia accent oozed like sorghum syrup as she smiled and asked, "Darling, you want another?"

"Huh?" The man realized he was staring. "Uh..., yeah. Sorry. I'll take another Sweetwater."

Pulling back to lean into the beer cooler under the

bar, Celia slid open the glass-door top and pulled out two local 420's. She popped off the caps. Cold steam came out of their tops as she handed the two men the glass bottles. The first man craned his neck to say, "thank you ma'am," as Celia moved on to another customer at the far end of the bar.

She was used to the attention. Her mom had run her through all the pageant circles as a young girl. Sweetheart, Carroll County, West Georgia, and Cotton Tail pageants had all agreed that Celia was west Georgia's beauty. She had grown to hate the attention but her mother pressured her to continue. When she could hate the whole dog-and-pony show no more, her mother – Linda-Rae Leigh – announced that she had signed Celia up for another year of pageants for her senior year of high school. That was the last straw. Celia planned her exit with flare. The showcase climaxed with the Miss Bremen Pageant, wherein Celia finally revolted.

Celia has been to the small Bremen, Georgia church auditorium before as Tinker Bell, a Thanksgiving Turkey, and the Mother Mary. But, this time would be different. Wearing a bright red strapped gown during the talent portion of the show, the routine called for her to juggle flaming batons choreographed to Lee Ann Womack's, *I Hope You Dance*. She avoided eye contact with her mother as the CD started to play. The first nail in the casket was, unbeknownst to Linda-Rae, Celia switched the soundtrack to Reba McEntire's, *Fancy*. The entire crowd began to fidget in their gold foldout chairs as Celia twisted and turned to the song about a hooker. But it was their gasp at seeing Celia push off the shoulder straps and pulled down the top of her dress to expose her bare chest and back, that made her start enjoying the moment most. Turning her back to the room on beat as Reba sang, "… here's your one chance Fancy," she revealed a large, tattoo of a flaming phoenix, its wings flared, taking a squat on a princess crown. With one last toss, she threw a flaming baton extra high, intentionally hitting a sprinkler head. Seconds later, the entire auditorium was drenched. Her favorite moment in life was complete when she finally looked to the side stage where Linda-Rae was shaking her head in disbelief, mascara running down her cheeks from the impromptu shower. Popping a fried pickle chip into her mouth, Celia grinned to herself as she reflected. God, she loved that moment.

CHAPTER 7

I T WAS ALMOST 2 a.m. before the rooftop bar emptied out and it was another hour of cleaning and prepping for the lunch crew before she could leave. Wiping down the weathered wood counter that overlooked Oakland Cemetery, Celia noticed what appeared to be fireflies in the old graveyard. Having taken the tour too many times to mention, they were floating somewhere between golfer Bobby Jones' grave and that of Margaret Mitchell. She squinted as she looked closer. She withdrew her gaze slightly as she realized she was actually seeing flashlights. She shook her head and went back to finishing her next day prep. Such a sight wasn't unusual. With Oakland, *Gone With the Wind* fans and grave creepers routinely hopped the fence after hours. *Kids.*

DOWNSTAIRS OF THE single-story building, Celia dragged a bag of trash from the roof-top bar towards the door. A tall man with a black polo and khaki pants threw a white towel over his shoulder as rushed from behind the bar to assist. Celia pulled back as he reached for the bag. "Thanks Gary, but I've got this."

He stood as his shaggy brown hair flopped into his eyes. Sweeping it away with his fingers, "You sure? I mean I may be the muscle here, but I can be a gentleman." Gary flashed a toothy smile. At six-six, he towered over Celia by over a foot and a half making him an impressive bar tender slash bouncer for the restaurant.

She placed a hand high on his full chest, smiled and said, "Oh, I know Gary. And, I recall I still owe you another date one of these days. But, you forget. I'm a pretty tough cookie myself." She released the bag to flex her small bicep.

Chuckling, he responded. "Pretty is an understatement. You are beautiful. And, yes... tough, too. I wouldn't mess with you. As for that date... you know where to find me."

She playfully cut her eyes towards the door and turned while waving a hand over her shoulder and behind her. "Night Gary. Look at the schedule and see when we both have a night off. Until then... stay sweet."

The street was dimly lit by lights attached to old creosote-dipped pine utility poles sufficient to see down Memorial Drive. Celia cautiously walked to the edge of the building, hoping that she didn't come across one of the frequent bums that hung around the area at night. Looking around first, she began to struggle as she tried to fling the trash bag into the rancid dumpster. It was too heavy with half-empty beer bottles. Fighting with the amorphous bag for another minute or so, she gave-up and pushed it against the dumpster's side and then from its bottom until it toppled in.

"Shit!" She jumped as a cat rushed out of the dumpster and into the street. Regaining her composure, her hands were brought to her face as she caught the whiff of stale beer that had leaked through the bag. "Yuck." She wiped her hands on her khaki skirt and crossed the street. As she walked along the red-brick sidewalk just outside the wall of the graveyard her black platforms clapped on the bricks with each step. Her mind drifted to the bartender. *Gary is a good man. Give him a chance. Yeah, but he is a bartender. Not a guy going to school and working his way through bartending. No. A bartender only. Ugh, where is a nerdy Georgia Tech guy that hasn't realized he is smoking hot. That's what I need.*

Rounding the corner of the cemetery toward her apartment complex she was suddenly struck across the face by what felt like an iron pipe. Pain pulsed from her right cheek to her nose and down her neck. Her eyes tried to refocus in the dim streetlight but all she saw was black with white flecks floating everywhere. The second blow came down hard on the back of her head sending stinging pain through her spine. She reached her hand out to stabilize herself. Voices could be heard… two voices, "Get her. Make it clean."

"I got this old man. I got this." She was then shoved and rolled onto her back. A halo of light around a dark shape told her that one of them was leaning over her… staring at her. She pulled in one knee, mentally counted to three and then kicked at the shadow. Contact was made halfway through full extension, landing with a thud against something solid.

"Fuck! My jaw! Fuuuck." Stomping of feet could be heard. "You fucking bitch!"

Still blinded by the pain, Celia rolled toward the street and let out a scream. *Please God, someone hear me. Please.*

She was up on one foot when she felt someone grab a hold of her other thigh, pulling her back into the shadows of the wall. "Do you fucking call this clean? Have I taught you nothing? Get over here, now!" The other voice had her now.

About to lose her balance again, Celia rolled all her weight and locked her elbow out and made contact with the figure behind her. Both fell to the ground and Celia scrambled to get back up. Her throat tightened as she felt someone pulling back on her string of pearls. "Get back over here, Miss Leigh."

Oh my god, they know my name. It's someone I know. Oh lord. "Help me!" But, only darkness came as a final blow to the head made her collapse into the street.

CHAPTER 8

"HURRY-UP, LIL'MAN. WE have to be at Aunt Maggie's by ten for breakfast and for your sleep-over with Perrin tonight." Cole sipped the final drop of the coffee in his large mug.

True to form, Billy came bounding out of his room wearing another Superman T-shirt, this time in white. "Yay! Can't wait! We are going to play Kinect Disney all night. When can I get an Xbox Uncle Cole?"

He put the mug down on the counter and looked at the boy, placing one hand on his hip and cocking his head. "What did we agree? Let's get this move out of the way and maybe Santa will bring you the new one coming out in a few months. Remember?"

Cash added from the couch in the living room, "Oh, the new Xbox One? Sweet. If I were you, Billy, I would wait on that. I've heard it's the best. You talk to it and the games respond to noises in the room." Billy turned to hear more.

Cole shook his head and waved "no" at Cash while standing behind Billy's back. But, it was too late. Billy was excited at this news. "What? Oh, then that is what I want. Does it play Disney?" Cole smiled and dropped his head. He had lost another battle. The topic of the Xbox had been nonstop for over a month and he had told himself that if he had to talk about the machine one more time he was going to personally shoot Bill Gates for the torture.

Looking over to Cole first to see how much trouble he was in, Cash responded, his eyes still on Cole as the words came out slowly. "No clue, buddy. But, I bet if it doesn't, a new Disney game will come out for it."

Cole collapsed into a chair he pulled out from his small dining room table. Throwing his hands up in the air, he said, "Great, just what we need... Billy yelling at the TV to do something. We don't need an Xbox for that; he already does that to me."

Billy turned and jumped in, "Uncle Cole, you yell at the TV when you are watching football. With the Xbox at least it will respond to me. Right, Cash?" He added a slight smirk at the end of his words.

Cole leaned in his chair to get at eye level with his nephew. "Hey, mister. When I yell at Connor Shaw during a Gamecock's game, he listens to me. Why do you think he is doing so well? The one game I missed, he falls to Georgia. Georrrgia." Cole cupped one hand over his forehead in disbelief and then pretended to cry.

Billy pushed his face against Cole's. "Uncle Cole, you are silly."

Cole stuck his tongue out at the boy, fast like a lizard. "Okay, mister. Go pack your sleeping bag and stuff. I need to handle Mister Cash over there." Billy ran out of the room with a long, "Ooooohhhh."

CASH STOOD FROM the couch and walked over to Cole.

He scrunched his nose in guilt and then leaned down to deliver a hug from behind. He whispered, "Sorry."

Cole squeezed the two arms wrapped around him. "Nah, don't worry about that. I guess you owed me one for the elbow I delivered to your chin last night on the couch. Promise it wasn't intentional. Just… well, that nightmare about the marsh. It's still comes with that hand dragging me into the hammock of trees and palmettos."

Cash released his hug and slid down to crouch before Cole with his left hand stopping at one thigh. Looking up into Cole's eyes, his face went stern. "I wondered about that. You gave me quite a wallop. You must have been kicking ass in that dream."

Cole flexed a bicep. Cash pinched it with his free hand. "Yep, see there… money maker."

"Does it still come every night?"

Cole flashed a moue of frustration. "Every night." He paused. "I just don't understand. It was gone after my late teens. Then it came back last February or March, just before Poin… just before what happened in Charleston." Cole stopped himself from saying the female killer's name. She didn't deserve such recognition… such respect.

"Is it any different from then to now? Any change at all?"

"No. It is just there, every night. There is more of it of course since what I saw when MeMe and Penny did that hoodoo thing. But, otherwise… no. It just won't go away."

Cash stood up while keeping his eyes on Cole still seated. He placed a hand on Cole's shoulder. "Perhaps… perhaps I can help you with that."

Cole's eyes grew big matched by a large rictus grin at Cash's insinuation. "Oh! Bring it, mister."

CHAPTER 9

IT SEEMED FITTING to Cole that Maggie's and Harris' home rested on the side of a mountain in Conifer, teetering off a ledge. They both seemed to dangle free, unhindered by societal norms. Harris was an ex-Army Rangers stay-at-home dad that would give Mary Poppins a run for her money. Maggie was a hipster dot-com executive who somehow seemed to balance work and family life like a pro. Their adopted daughter, Perrin, only further accented their dynamic chemistry.

Cole and Maggie had met in college, roommates at the University of South Carolina, in their first year of permitting co-ed living and had been friends ever since. He smiled as she rushed out to the car with her large black and white Labrador retriever mix, Luke, in tow. "Oh my goodness, you are here! It's been forever. Okay, well like a week, but still... forever." She gave Cole a soft hug and then ran over to the other side of the car. Cole opened the back door, Dixie bounded out as Billy pulled at his car seat belt. He leaned in and unsnapped the boy as he heard her voice.

"You must be Cash. I've heard so much about you." Cash extended his hand only for it to be rejected. "Silly, we don't shake here. We hug." She wrapped her arms around him as he looked over to Cole with an awkward smile. The mountain wind picked up her low-back length black hair and draped it over both of them.

Maggie released him and turned back to the house. Waving an arm in its direction, "Come in, come in." Billy rushed up beside her and grabbed her leg mid-step. She looked down just before he released and raced ahead. "Hey, Billy. Perrin is inside watching a 'Tink' movie. Run on up." Billy raced up some wooden stairs and into the large, two story wood-sided house. From the top of the stairs she looked down to the two men ascending. "Cole, I see you have boots. Cash? Ya need a pair?"

Cash looked over to Cole slightly confused and then back up. "Uh, do I need boots for breakfast?"

"Ha. No, not for your bacon and eggs. But, for horse-back riding you will. Those Pumas won't do at all." She looked him up and down. "You look as endowed as Harris. You can borrow a pair of his."

Cash and Cole broke out laughing. Cole responded, "Told ya, Maggie doesn't hold back."

Greeting them at the top landing of the steps to the front door, she added, "And, why should I? Look at me. Do I look like a conformist?" She smiled. Maggie's cherry print western dress accented her curves while her denim jacket for the morning chill made her quintessentially western and hip at the same time. Bare legs showed just enough between the gap of her dress and the start of her cowboy boots to flash several colorful leg tattoos of wolves.

Just as Cole was about to respond, Harris appeared from around the corner of the home. He was similarly inked across most of his body. Ten years Maggie's senior, his muscled body and shaved head gave the observer the impression that he wasn't to be messed with... which was probably true since he was ex-military.

He walked to the base of the steps and looked up to the three at the top. "Cole, my man. Damn, it's good to see you. Maggie keeps all the good ones to herself. She's always telling me about your lunch dates. How do I land a lunch date with you, sexy man?" Shaking his head in feigned disappointment, he walked up the steps and gave Cole a tight hug. He then turned. "Cash I presume."

"Harris?" Cash shuddered on how to respond to the intimidating figure reaching in for a hug as well. Cash looked back to Cole for direction before the hug was delivered. Released, he whispered something into Cole's ear about his spine being realigned from the hug as Harris continued talking.

"Damn Cole. Do you ever date the average guy or just these models? You modelizer, you." Harris slapped Cole hard on the ass and started walking into the front door. He saw a quick wink aimed in Cash's direction.

Cole's mouth dropped for a second before he could catch up. "Uh, Harris, I am not a modelizer, sir. I just happen to be very fortunate in who is attracted to me. And, you make me sound like a hooker or something. This is the only guy I have ever brought to your home." Cole laughed.

"The question is, how many have you taken to your home lately? Player!"

Before Cole could respond, Maggie jumped in, pushing between the two men. "Stop it Harris. Cole is no player." She turned. "Cash, you've got a good one there. But, are you good? That is the better question." She lifted an eyebrow and smiled.

Cole smiled back at his reputation being saved. "I promise you, he is good, Maggie. Probably too good for the ol' modelizer over here." Cole stuck his tongue out at Harris who returned the gesture.

INSIDE THE HOME, Maggie pointed them to the spare bedroom where they could deposit Billy's things. Cole returned and walked into the kitchen where Maggie was making fresh guacamole. With Cash still upstairs, Maggie pushed for details. "So... is it going well? I mean, this is the first time he has been out here, right? How's the sex?"

Cole laughed. "Uh, yeah... this is his first time here and we haven't had sex. Well, not yet." The grin grew slowly.

"What?!?" Harris jumped in, flicking a spatula in the air as he spoke. "You mean to tell me that two sexy men have been under the same roof for a night or more and haven't gone at it? Are you sure that you are gay? Cause, I can tell you... I'd wear that boy out. And, I'm straight."

Cole closed his eyes in playful disbelief of what he had just heard. Harris and Maggie didn't have a judgmental bone in their bodies. They freely talked about sex of any type like it was discussing the weather. Such freedom was foreign to Cole's southern sensibilities. He deflected. "Well, Harris, I know tons of guys that would love to take your straight card, you big ol' bear. You just let me know." Cole dug into his pocket and pulled out his phone to suggest he was going to look a few prospects up.

Harris's loud "roar" rattled the house. Maggie quickly interjected as she waved the knife around in the air that she had been using to cut a green chile. "Uh, that bitch is mine. I earned that card. No man or woman is taking that shit without a fight from me. And, I will cut either one of you if you think otherwise."

Both men backed off laughing.

"Did I miss something?" Cash walked slowly into the room. Cole wrapped an arm around Cash's waist and he around Cole's neck. They looked into each other's eyes and smiled. "Hey mister."

Maggie turned and looked up to Harris. "See, now why don't you love up on me like that?"

Harris eyed the knife still in Maggie's hand. "Well, perhaps if you weren't threatening to cut me, I would get close enough for a hug." He then softly pushed down her hand and slipped in for a kiss.

Maggie shouted loud enough for it to reach the TV room across the house. "Perrin... Billy... come and get your breakfast before it gets eaten by this bear and his two otter friends!" Harris threw his hand up in disbelief at Maggie's lack of acknowledgement for his kiss. Maggie cocked her head towards the TV room's doorway and then went to investigate, smiling at Harris. Mid-step, she blew him a kiss that he caught and then promptly pasted to his butt. His nose crinkled with a defiant smile.

Catching Maggie's middle-finger bird from the corner of his eyes, Cole followed her to determine the holdup. The song, *Happy*, met their ears before they entered. Inside, the kids were dancing hand-in-hand to the Pharrell Williams song blaring out of a small radio, giggling as they hopped up and down, from side-to-side. Perrin's brown afro-puffs bounced against her shoulders and pink tank-top. Billy's eyes greeted Cole with a look of invitation. "Uncle Cole, come dance!" Looking over at Maggie first, the two adults nodded and started hopping hand-in-hand together like the two kids and then switched off to grab a smaller partner.

"What is the delay...?" Harris peeked through the door with Cash standing behind him. He laughed as he walked further into the room and then began to wiggle his butt like he was twisting. Cole followed with exaggerated movements only to feel embarrassed as he noticed Cash was watching, smiling like a Cheshire cat. He toned-down his movements and grimaced. Lingering at the door for a second longer, Cash rushed in and joined, sandwiching Billy loosely between them. Cole grabbed Billy's hand and then Cash's with the other. Cash completed the circle with Billy's hand until they all swished back and forth in a ring. Maggie and Harris were doing the same with Perrin as the song finally ended, Cole collapsing to the ground to exaggerate his exertion. His tongue was pushed out and to the side for further effect.

The two kids giggled more in excitement of the impromptu dance marathon party. Billy paused to extend a hand for Cole to get up, struggling with a pull. Cash grabbed the other arm and pulled with a slight jerk that caused Cole to jump up rapidly and crash into the man's chest. Cole hugged him and then kissed his cheek before letting go and turning.

A whisper came out of Perrin. "Mom, can boys kiss?" Her eyes were big as Maggie leaned down to respond.

"Yeah, isn't that wonderful? They like each other." Maggie turned back to Cole who was now red with embarrassment. She glowed warmly. Harris similarly smiled.

Perrin relaxed and looked up to Harris. "I'm hungry."

"Well, if we are done dancing, breakfast is ready, kiddos."

Perrin skipped out of the room, with Billy not far behind.

"Was that okay?" Cole winced.

"Are you fucking kidding me? That was perfect. She needs to know that's cool."

Harris placed a hand on his wife's shoulder and looked at Cole. "Cole, we love you. And, yes, that was fucking awesome. Just the way it should be. Natural."

Cole turned his eyes to Cash who just smiled back as they walked back to the kitchen.

THE TWO KIDS waited for their plates to be loaded and promptly returned to the TV room to finish their movie. Cole watched the two leave and then turned back to Maggie. "Wow, Perrin is getting tall. What is she like four-and-a-half feet?" At almost five years old, Perrin was almost six-inches taller than Billy at four.

Maggie handed out plates as she responded. "Yeah, she is growing fast." Maggie looked around to make sure the kids were now out of ear-shot and then continued. "But, you wouldn't know it by the way she acts. Can you believe I caught that little shit coloring on her bedroom wall yesterday? I about lost it." She shook her head as she almost laughed and then slapped her palms on top of the granite counter island. "I wanted to cuss her out, but you know how the therapists all say you shouldn't do that." She furled a brow in frustration and then exhaled. "So, because I'm a 'mom' now and supposed to be little-Miss-Susie-sunshine and all that jazz, I sat her down and talked to her with reason and logic. Yuck. Can you imagine me doing that shit? What happened to me? I'm a fucking mother. I didn't sign away my right to raise a little hell when I want, did I?" Maggie laughed and turned to Harris as if he was to answer.

Getting no response, she turned back to Cole and Cash, saying warmly. "I do love that little fart, though. She melts my heart. Who would of thunk it, right? Me. A mom." She crossed her hands before continuing. "Damn, I need a drink. Mimosas, boys?"

CHAPTER 10

"AS THE OLDEST cemetery in Atlanta, it was established in 1850 on six-acres of land and originally called the Atlanta Cemetery. It wasn't until 1870 that it was renamed Oakland because of all the oak and magnolia trees. It is also one of the oldest historical plots of land in Atlanta having survived Sherman's burning of the city in 1864 during the Civil War. Designed in a Victorian-style and a true garden cemetery, many of the trees are original, though several were lost during a tornado that swept through downtown Atlanta several years ago. If you will follow me, I will show you one of the original magnolias, estimated to be over two-hundred years old."

Stepping directly behind the late-forties tour guide, a strawberry blonde young girl flicked her hair and then nudged her mother. "Mom, this sucks. Really? A graveyard tour? Why couldn't I have gone with Dad and Stewart to the World of Coke or the Aquarium? There is nothing here but bugs and dead people." She curled her lip in disgust as she looked around. By the slight peek around her mother followed by a flash of disapproval, the tour guide had overheard the conversation. She curled her lip again, this time at him.

The mother shrugged her shoulders at the man, as if to say, *kids*, and then turned back to her daughter. "Gail. How hard is it to spend just a few hours with your mom? Seriously. I asked one thing of you on this trip. One! Am I that horrible of a mom? Huh? I take you to soccer practice. I take you to the mall. You stay clothed, with nice clothes, I may add. I never got name brand things as a girl. That Kate Spade bag you're toting? Your dad didn't get that for you. So, if I ask you to spend a little time with me, then I think I deserve that. Don't you?" She paused. "Don't answer that."

"Mom. Seriously? I heard that speech on Desperate Housewives. You were sitting right next to me. Uh, be original."

The mother raised a hand in protest and turned away. "No. I won't hear anymore. Let's get through this tour so I can see where Margret Mitchell was buried and then you..."

"Mom!" The girl went stiff.

"Gail, let me finish. ...then you can spend your time with your Dad or whatever and leave your mom all alone thinking about how she has a..."

"Mom! Look! Turn your head and look."

"Margret Mitchell?" The mother excitedly turned to where he daughter was pointing and then let out a wailing scream.

CHAPTER 11

BREAKFAST WAS SCARFED down quickly before everyone set out on the horses from the pasture adjoining the couple's home. Maggie bailed on the excursion by her fourth mimosa, having decided she needed alone time, free of kids. So, Harris took the lead with Perrin and Billy riding together alongside him. Cash and Cole took it slower following behind across the mountain's face dotted with blue-gray sage and ponderosa pine.

"Wow, I can see why you like it out here. Look at all that snow on those mountains." Cash's head turned wide as he took in the bucolic mountain views before stopping at one particular mountain capped with snow.

"I think that is Pike's Peak, but I'll have to ask Harris." Cole patted the side of his appaloosa's neck.

Cash turned back to Cole. "You look comfortable on him. How long have you ridden?"

"It's been years, actually. Not since I was really young. Back then I wanted to ride in the summer Olympics."

A brow was lifted. "Oh? Why did you stop?"

"Money. My uncle injured his back and horses

just weren't a luxury we could afford anymore." Cole paused. "And, you? This clearly isn't your first time." He admired the view of the man straddling a bay colored horse.

"Nah, I did some polo in Charleston. But, got bored by high school."

Cash looked back to the mountains. "Do you ski much?

"Oh, I try. Last year the snow kinda sucked. But, as you can see, it started early this year. So, perhaps I'll get up there with Billy this year. I'd love for him to learn young. Their low center of gravity makes it almost impossible to fall at his age. Great training grounds for a future skiing Olympian."

"Oh? I'm surprised Colorado hasn't ever hosted the Olympics."

Cole let out a short laugh. "Uh, yeah... Denver won't be seeing the Olympics anytime soon. They put it up last year to host and the U.S. Olympic committee said a very loud, 'De-nied.'"

"What? With all these mountains and how active this place is? It just doesn't make sense to me. I mean, don't you have the Olympic Committee headquartered down in Colorado Springs? Why wouldn't they have it here?"

"Oh, cause Denver burnt that bridge long ago. Back in 1970 Denver actually won by a landslide the hosting rights for the 1976 winter Olympics. But, a few years later the costs to host had tripled and the people here didn't want foreigners, from other countries or other states, messing up the state's beauty and environment by tramping all over the place. So they told the International Olympic Committee, 'Thanks, but no thanks.' Well, that pissed them off so much that when

Salt Lake City asked to host it instead, the IOC said, 'Hell no, 'merica.' Since then, if Denver even drops-off an application, the IOC and USOC stamp it denied without even opening the envelope."

Cash's horse swatted its large tail, striking his leg. He looked back up and grinned before continuing. "Damn. That sucks. So how in the world did the USOC end up headquartered here?"

"Consolation prize? Political connections? No clue, but supposedly Colorado Springs grabbed the headquarters rights from New York City after the USOC had Congress step in and shut down the NCAA's claim over amateur athletes and their money in the late-seventies."

"Well, it was that or Baton Rouge, Louisiana. They were the only two cities to apply against New York. Swamp or mountains? I think mountains win out, wouldn't you say?"

Harris had slowed to join the conversation before Cash could respond. "So... how are you liking it out here so far, Cash? Somewhere you might want to live?" He gave a wink to Cole, as though he was helping him out. But, Cole's face flushed with Harris' prying.

Cash sputtered before answering. "Well, actually... I've uhm, applied for a job out here. At C.U.. Boulder? They are looking for a history professor and I figured I'm due for a change. It's tenure track which is what I'm looking for. So, we shall see." Cash looked over to Cole for a reaction to his disclosure.

Cole just stared, not knowing how to respond. He liked Cash. But, the thought of Cash changing his life to be close made him feel uncomfortable. He hadn't thought that far into the future. Their relationship they had barely formed in Charleston... this, whatever he wanted to call it, was being taken day-by-day and Cole wasn't prepared to think much further than that at the moment. Cole forced a smile to avoid sending the wrong message. Things just became serious.

COLE COULDN'T PUSH it out of his head what Cash had said on the red dirt trail as he tried to say good-bye to Billy back at the house. Turning it over and over again in his head, he himself said it was "… just an application. No big deal." But, that wasn't very convincing. A flood of doubts crashed into mind. *He doesn't know me. He can't be serious.* Cole pushed up his wall to redirect his thoughts to the moment and exhaled.

Crouched down, Cole hugged his nephew. "Okay, buddy. I'm going to miss you. Be nice to Miss Maggie and everyone. Mind her and Mister Harris, you hear me?"

He smiled back. "Yes, sir."

"Now, say good-bye to Mister Cash. He flies out before you get back tomorrow afternoon." Cole stood and pushed Billy in Cash's direction.

The boy looked up to the towering man. "Awe. Are you sure you can't stay a little bit longer? You said you would go fishing with us."

"Don't worry buddy. I'll be back soon… fingers crossed." Cash glanced over to Cole. "Maybe in a month for Halloween. Would that be cool?"

"Yes, sir! I'm going as Iron Man. Woosh! You want to be the Hulk?"

Cole interrupted. "Uhm, perhaps he wants to be Thor, Billy. Why don't we see if we can get him here for that first." Taking a deep breath, Cole's mind flashed to

Cash dressed sleeveless with a red cape flapping behind him. Cole inhaled the thought before mentally shaking it off. Thor had dropped a time-bomb and Cole needed to figure out how to handle it.

CHAPTER 12

GAIL AND HER mother had been pushed behind a yellow taped line now formed around a giant red-leafed tree. The stout Atlanta PD officer standing next to her was talking on his phone in a hushed tone, trying to cover the receiver with one hand as his other rested on his side holster. The words were broken, but she could hear most of what the officer was saying. "Agent Leas… been another killing… matches the profile you have been chasing… May. Yeah. Same… same style. Posed and all. Uh huh. Okay, I'll have my team forward you their pictures for your review… flight down here. Tomorrow? Yeah,… should work. Have a safe flight." Pulling the phone away from his ear, he turned to Gail who was sitting on a stone ledge.

"Sorry about that, ma'am. I just had to make a call. Now for that statement." He removed the pad he had previously shoved under one arm before placing one foot on the stone wall that the two women were sitting. Pad and pen in hand, he leaned in to start the interview. "So when did you notice the body again?"

Gail stared at a crumb stuck in his broad mustache. Unimpressed, she responded, "Officer Emmick, right?

My mom and I were talking while the guide was walking us down the path towards one of those monuments. What did he call it Mom? Confederate Dead?" Gail looked back to her mother who was still trembling, unable to speak a word. "Uh, Mom, it's just a dead body. Whatever." Gail turned back to the officer, rolling her eyes. "Anyway, I looked over her shoulder while the guide was yapping about that thing and I saw it, just there. Hanging. All red and such. At first I had no clue what it was, but then realized it was a body. It looked fake. You know like one of those mannequins or something. But, after taking another look it was pretty obvious that it was real. I don't think I've ever seen a body so white before. Not that I've seen that many dead bodies, but look at it, she is like vampire white." The officer followed Gail's hand as she waved in the direction of the tree.

Suspended spread-eagle by yellow rope between two large branches was the nude body of Celia Leigh, milk white except for a very large scarlet tattoo of a flaming bird on her back. He had been told that wire had been used to pose the neck and head in a half-cocked position. And, Emmick had worked homicide for the Atlanta PD for seven years and knew dead bodies shouldn't be that white. She had been drained of blood.

Turning back to Gail, he said, "Did you or anyone else go over there?"

Gail tightened her eyes. "Do I look stupid? I've seen enough CSI to know better than to get near that thing. And, no one else would look at it, much less walk up to it."

Letting out a slow exhale in obvious disappointment with the girl's attitude, "Well, good. Is there anything else that you think I should know?"

Gail stood and grabbed her mom's hand reluctantly. "No. Can I get my mom out of here, I mean look at her. What a mess."

Looking over to the mother, Emmick responded, "Sure. We have your information if we need anything else. Take care of her."

Love

CHAPTER 13

PULLING DOWN THE tail of his black v-neck sweater, Cole ground his teeth before he spoke. "Eek, first date. That's kind of big time, don't you think?" He then winced slightly before relaxing to look around to avoid eye contact. The openness of North, a high-end restaurant in the affluent area of Denver called Cherry Creek, was accented with white leather seating and blaze-orange tulips. Seated at a table against the floor-to-ceiling glass windows that look onto the street, Cole had a momentary shiver. He was unsure whether it was his nerves or the cold night temperature radiating off the glass. Either way, he forced a smile and finally looked back to Cash.

He was seated across the table in a fitted blue sweater that made the gold flecks in his otherwise azure eyes pop. He warmly smiled back. "Only if you let it. I mean, it isn't like we have never hung out alone before."

"Yeah, I mean… I know. It's just… well, you know… different. Our meeting was certainly unconventional. I was home being hunted by a crazy lady, make that two crazy ladies, and had just met you and learned of your brother Mark who, unknown to me, had been kidnapped… unknown to me, when I was kidnapped. Wow, that's a mouthful. Might need a venn diagram or flow chart for that story." Cole paused. "Since then, sure… we have talked on the phone and FaceTime'd every couple of days or so, but I haven't seen you in four months. And, Billy has been around since you arrived Friday night."

Cash's smile disappeared. "Is that okay? I mean… are you still cool with us hanging out and seeing what develops?"

Cole leaned into the small wooden table and looked into Cash's eyes. They still sparkled as much as the first time he saw them at their meeting at Cash's office in the College of Charleston. "Cash, you are amazing. Here I am telling you that I'm nervous and you think I'm no longer interested. We wouldn't be sitting here if that was the case, you get me?" His head tilted to one side as he waited for agreement.

Cash smiled again. "Yeah, but I don't think I got you quite yet, but I'm working on it."

IT HAD BEEN a long four months. Though they had hoped it wouldn't have taken so long to see each other, life happened and got in the way. Billy needed priority first. Then work, storms, and the new duty of being a parent made scheduling a nightmare. Phone calls, texts, FaceTime… they were like dry water, never completely quenching the desire to just be near someone, to have them present. And, though the feelings had not failed, they had not grown much either. Distance stalls desire.

Ultimately, Cash got tired of excuses and announced he bought a ticket, pick him up at the airport or he would sleep there for the weekend. Either way, he was going to be in the same state as Cole for the first time in "too long." Billy being present from pickup till this moment kept Cole's emotions under tight control. *Be cool, Cole. Cool. He may not look like what you recall. – Lie. You FaceTime that man and he is always gorgeous. – He may not be feeling it anymore. – Dumb. The man is flying 1700 miles to see you. – Well, that chemistry may be gone now. – Hmmm, true. But, you have to try. Take that step forward. You promised.*

"You know your food is going to get cold if you just keep staring at me all night."

Cash's words caused Cole to look down. He had zoned off and totally missed that the waiter had brought his plate. "Hmm, well. I really came for the salted butterscotch pudding."

"That's all?" A subtle wink was delivered.

With a soft laugh, Cole responded. "Okay, perhaps your company, too. After all, this is like the first adult conversation I have had in a few months. I miss it."

Cash sat back as the conversation diverged to more serious topics momentarily. "How is Billy? He seems to be handling everything pretty well."

Still fiddling with the fork on his plate, Cole answered. "Yeah. He has his moments, and his therapist has certainly helped him and me to address his mother's death directly, to not bottle it up. But, it's still hard. The key is keeping him busy. Friends, school, horseback riding lessons – anything and everything to keep his little mind from dwelling on the loss. There is something to be said for that saying, 'an idle mind is the devil's playground.' Billy is best when he is remembering to live life. I'm slowly learning that lesson, too."

THE CONVERSATION CONTINUED on various top-
ics, family, jobs, and life in general – avoiding the obvious topic of "them." "I do wonder if I'm cut out for this,
a sentiment Mom... Ava... seems to agree with." Cole
looked down and fiddled with a fork more before starting again. "Not that I blame her, you know. I mean... A
single man suddenly handed a child to care for?" Cole
pinched a smile at one corner of his mouth. "I wonder if
I'm doing right by Billy in not letting them care for him."
Cole looked up for a response.

Cash pushed out a lackluster smile and then leaned
in to look eye-to-eye with him. Cole looked down. "Cole,
your sister believed that you caring for Billy was in his
best interest. It's going to take a while for your folks, even
you, to accept that. You are going to mess up, that's just
part of parenting."

Looking down, Cole shuffled in his chair before a
weak attempt at deflecting the topic. "And you, 'Fort
Knox?' How's life in Charleston? What did all your
potential dates say when you told them you were flying
here for the weekend for a date with a wreck with a kid?"
Turning his eyes up to finally meet Cash's, Cole grimaced
as he mentally crossed his fingers that the conversational
trigger he just loaded did not backfire.

With a soft smile, Cash answered. "Hmm, first...
there are no others. Second, I am not 'Fort Knox,' sir. You
are. I never know what you are thinking, feeling most
times. And, finally... you are not a 'wreck with a kid.' You
are pretty damn amazing. You do know that. You don't
believe it most times, but you know it. Ignoring your
looks, and... they are hard to ignore, you flourish where

ninety percent of people fail. Though you like to hide it, your heart is in everything you do, everything you say. It makes you uncomfortable, and that's why you change the subject like you just did, but… you are all heart. I love that. So, what did I tell everyone back in Charleston about where I was going? I told them I was going to tell someone that I love all that they are about, all that they are and then hold my breath that they feel even half of what I am feeling now, sitting right here in front of you."

Cole's eyes locked with Cash's, forcing him to put his hand to his chest. His heart was galloping out of control. Warmth tingling up into his neck. Seconds went without blinking as Cole fought back the initial response to recoil behind his mental wall where he felt calm, in control. *Breathe, breathe….*

Cole was saved from the moment as Cash said, "I didn't say that you had to respond. I just believe in putting it out there. Life is too short to hold back on such things. Sorry if I just made things awkward." Cash maintained eye contact. His words were calm and bought Cole just enough time to relax, but he still didn't know how to respond. He leaned back slightly in his chair with obvious nervousness that what he had just said had landed with a great thud. His face flashed fear as he watched Cole pinch his eyes closed, forcing single tears at the inner corners of his eyes. They opened and looked to the door.

"Okay, can you say something, anything? I'm dying over here, now. I'm sorry. I shouldn't…"

Cash stopped speaking as Cole turned back to him and extended his arm across the table and grabbed his hand. Cole still refused to speak as Cash looked down and then back up now with a renewed smile.

"Dessert?" The waiter said as he walked up. "We have a wonderful butterscotch..."

He was interrupted. "No. I think we will pass. Check please." Cash kept eye contact as Cole addressed the waiter who slumped over the table and slowly grabbed the empty plates before walking away. They stared at each other in silence until the bill was returned and paid. Softly, Cole grabbed Cash's hand and led him out of the restaurant and into the car parked on the street.

CHAPTER 14

COLE DROVE THEM home in silence. He could hardly catch his breath as the car door finally opened. It wasn't until they walked into the house that the tension released. Cole grabbed the collar of Cash's white button-down and pushed him against the wall. Cash's stubble felt like sandpaper against his cheek as they kissed deeply. Cole pulled back for just a second to look into his eyes before pressing in for more. He could feel Cash's hands busying themselves with unbuttoning his shirt as he broke to catch a breath. Cole reciprocated, pushing his hands through the small tuft of hair between his pecs as soon as it was exposed. He pulled back, grasping one of Cash's hands and led him to Cole's bedroom, where they wrestled with each other's belts until their pants were peeled off.

Cash pushed Cole into the high four-post mahogany bed and then they both jumped in like a kids at a sleep over, laughing. Cash grew intense again and grabbed Cole's face to firmly push his lips against his own. Cole exhaled as he felt his body tingle with desire for more of Cash… all of Cash. A moan escaped before he was able to refocus. He opened his eyes as Cash's lips worked their way down to his hips. Cash pushed, signaling him to roll over, wherein he started kissing the nape of his back between his shoulder blades towards the crease of his ass.

His briefs were pulled down just as lips pressed against his left cheek and then the right. His body trembled again, but this time with slight hesitation as to the reality of what was about to happen. Cole hadn't been with anyone since his ex more than two years prior and intimacy unnerved him. He was vulnerable in the moment. Cole held his breath for a few seconds until the panic of letting someone get so close to him, have such control over him, passed.

Cash pulled himself up along Cole's now nude body until his hips were pressed between Cole's thighs. Cole pushed his hips up into Cash's groin as his hair was grabbed, pulling his head back. He gave in, accepting his role for the night as he was kissed deeply. His body was Cash's.

CHAPTER 15

C OLE WOKE UP as he always did, in a deep sweat, heart racing. He couldn't shake the childhood nightmare that hunted his sleep.

"You okay?"

Cole looked over to the man looking back in drowsy concern. "Awe. Sorry about that, sir."

Cash gave a thin smile back. "That dream of yours?"

Rubbing a knuckle in one eye, he responded. "Yeah, some ol' same ol'. Sorry if I woke you."

A kiss landed on his cheek. Cash collaped back down into the bed. "At least you didn't hit me this time." He laughed as Cole kiddingly sulked.

The sunlight peeked through the curtains catching those flecks in Cash's eyes again. The memories of the night before flicked through his mind like a graphic slide show as all moments of his life did. Perfectly preserved, whether good or bad, Cole's memory captured life frame-by-frame for instant recall. It was haunting, but also comforting. Cole flushed with heat as his mind hit the moment where Cash climaxed the night before. A grin crossed his face as he looked over to Cash now rolled face down into a pillow, his bare back and ass exposed. His body was Cole's.

"I HATE THAT you have to go back this afternoon. I was just getting used to this… you know, you being here and all." Cole grabbed Cash's hand under the table as they sat at a patio table outside of Root Down, an eclectic restaurant that overlooked downtown Denver.

"Oh? You aren't ready to get rid of me?" Cash smiled.

"After last night? Uh, that would be a big, 'No!' I'd like to keep you around much, much longer." Cole tightened his grip on Cash's hand.

"Good. Cause I filled out that application with CU, so I'd hate to get it and then learn you didn't want me here."

Cole felt guilty for his previous response to the news. "No. I'd like that very much. It's just not something I'm accustomed to… the thought of you in my life. It will take a little time to accept it. You might have to pinch me every now and then to make sure I appreciate that you are real and not some figment of my imagination."

"Was last night and this morning a good pinch?" Cash tightened his eyes and grinned.

Cole leaned in to whisper in his ear. "A very wonderful pinch. That or the best wet dream I've ever had."

"Hmm, we will just have to keep doing it until you realize it's real."

Cole perked up. "Oh! Then I will always believe it's a dream cause I never want that to stop."

WALKING ACROSS A white pedestrian suspension bridge into Confluence Park hand-in-hand, Cash broke the stroll's silence. "So, we haven't really talked too much about what happened in Charleston. How is that? Everything okay?"

Cole pulled them off to an overlook over the water before responding. "It's as good as it can be. I mean, I told you about Billy and helping him through his emotions, the loss of his mother and such. Not much more there."

"I know. But, what about what Winters was trying to do, her attempt to find the guy that took you and my brother when y'all were kids. Any update on that?"

Cole felt nervous. He didn't know how much to say, how much to tell, without coming off as obsessed. Of course he was, but that didn't mean he wanted Cash or anyone else to know that he had been personally researching and digging for any information on The Taker, the man that had kidnapped him and tortured his mother. He just needed to know. Like wanting cake even when full, it was instinctive and resisting the urge just made it worse. The need to understand who took him and why, demanded to be met.

"Well, the FBI hasn't really been very helpful since May. I've been cut out of the loop." Cole looked back to Cash's eyes and knew that he suspected there was more there. Cole tried to look away, but Cash grabbed his chin and turned it back to look eye-to-eye.

"Mister attorney, that isn't what I asked. Remember, I'm the guy that agreed to withhold information from the police in Charleston so you could face Poinsett alone. So, I know that you aren't about to take no for an answer from the FBI." Cash finished his cross-examination with a grin.

Speaking like a guilty child, Cole responded. "Okay, so maybe I've looked into it a little bit. She was on to something, Cash. And, I think I owe it to my sister and Mark to find this guy. That is, if he is still alive."

Cash turned to stand with his back against the bridge's railing like Cole and then looked over. "Cole, promise me you will leave that alone. That you will stay away from that. I understand. I really do. But, all those secrets and darkness have already taken too many wonderful people. I don't think Jamie or Mark would want you in any further danger. And, more importantly, I don't want you in danger. So, please... please just leave it alone."

Cole felt his mental wall go up to protect him from the guilt creeping upon him. "Cash, I'm okay. There is no risk in just investigating it. No one is chasing me. No one is trying to kill me anymore. My research is just paper, that's all." Cole lied. He cared for Cash and valued his opinion, but not on this.

"Cole, promise me that you will not go chasing after whatever you find in your papers. Think of Billy. Do you want him in danger?" Cash's face went pale as he realized what he had just done. But, it was too late. "Excuse me? Do not preach to me about the safety of my nephew. I have been given the authority to know what is best for him, not you. Okay?"

Cash rushed to calm the situation. "Cole, I'm sorry. I didn't mean to suggest otherwise. Please... I'm just worried. I care for you and don't want anything to happen to you. Or, Billy."

Cole looked into his eyes for a few seconds before he

calmed enough to speak. "I know you do. Look, let's just not talk about this. I promise that I won't get myself in trouble. And, if I do, you can come along for the ride." A smile appeared at the corner of his mouth. "Now, come on. Your flight is in like two hours and we still have to take the shuttle back to the car before I can bawl out my eyes watching you leave."

CHAPTER 16

"AGENT LEAS, AGENT Meadows. You were to meet me in the lobby thirty-five minutes ago." Frank Meadows looked at Leas in his towel. "Long night?" Without responding, Leas inspected his new guest. Navy blazer, khaki pants. The old school impression was accented by his gray hair, cropped tightly. A lean man in his late fifties looked back at the younger agent with cold indifference.

He had lost track of time. *How the hell did it get to be seven a.m. already?* Not responding to the older man, he turned and rushed to his wrinkled pants he had just laid on the couch thirty minutes earlier. Meadows walked through the open hotel door and looked around to notice two empty bottles of Knob Creek lying next to the trash can. He sat on the arm of the small couch in the room and watched impatiently as Leas hurried around the room to dress. The untouched bed was noted.

"You know this is a smoke-free room, right?" Meadows held up the no-smoking placard as he looked at the filled make-shift soda can ash tray next to Leas. "I suspect that is especially important to the people here at the Ellis, since this hotel is famous for the deadliest hotel file in U.S. history back when it was known at the Winecoff. This place single-handedly caused the advent of the fire code. Hundreds of people frying-up and jumping out windows from fifteen stories can have that sort-of result."

Halfway through buttoning-up the shirt he arrived in Atlanta wearing, Leas looked over. "Am I going to have to hear you rattle on about bullshit like that the entire time? Because, if I am, I'm going to need something to drink."

Meadows looked back to the bottles. "I suspect you have had enough to drink for now. I'd prefer to not smell your sorrows."

"Man, fuck off. I just got in late last night. Okay? Let's just get going. There is some crazy to catch and the faster that happens, the faster I get to ditch you."

LEAS STILL COULDN'T accept that he was now bootstrapped to a partner. He hadn't had a partner in over fifteen years and the idea that he now had to be babysat pissed him off. "Just understand one thing, Agent Meadows, this is my show. You listen to me and do what I say. You got that?"

"Agent, I've been around the block a few times and I get your response. But, let's get this clear. You may be some type of serial killer expert, but I don't answer to you. I got dog walking duty because you can't seem to do your job." Meadows looked up to the taller agent to connect to his eyes. "I suspect from the whiskey oozing out of your pores that if you spent less time in the bottle and more on your files I wouldn't be here. But, I am and we are just going to have to make the best of it, aren't we?"

Meadows wiped his mustache intensely as if he was rubbing Leas' scent out of his nose.

Leas' tanned skin turned a dark shade of red with anger as he cut his eyes away from Meadows and back to the graveyard crime scene. "Well, mister profiler, what do you see?"

Meadows looked up to the branch where two days earlier Celia Leigh's body had been discovered. The FBI had been notified of the murder because it loosely matched two others in the city that had been found over the past sixteen months. Leas had been sent to the events in Charleston back in May to chase down the killer but had failed to move the case forward. With a new body, came new emphasis on the case... and Leas.

Leas' affinity to whiskey had been known for some time by the agency. He had been ordered to participate in counseling, but he attended the sessions just to keep his job. When D.C. learned of the events of Charleston and his utter failure to control the situation until the last minute, a decision had to be made: fire the guy and lose one of their best serial murder experts, or put someone on babysitting duty. Meadows got the job of sitter just days before he was about to announce his retirement. After reading the files and several long discussions with his wife, he decided to take this one last case. He had only been playing nanny for forty-eight hours and was already having second thoughts.

Meadows pulled out a small black leather covered pad and began to walk the scene. "Good god, man. What kind of old school is this? What are you like ancient?" Meadows ignored Leas' comments as he worked a large circle around the scene. "Oh, come on man. Are you serious? The scene has been sitting for two days, police everywhere. Do you really think you will find anything out here?" Leas waved his hand in the air to get Meadows' attention. Yet, he refused to respond until he finished his walk of the scene.

Stopping under the tree where the body had been tied, Meadows looked up to the branch where the body had been tied and said, "Behavior reflects personality, agent. You should at least know that." Meadows kept his eyes busy focusing on the branch as Leas responded.

"Don't give me that Behavioral Science Unit horse shit. Profiling is about gut feeling, not some classification scheme invented by the FBI."

"Agent Leas, I agree with you. Gut feelings have a place in all this. But, to make sure you have the information necessary to have an accurate feeling, you need to try to understand the killer. Take his scene for example. If we consider the four crime phases of a murder's behavior into account, specifically the body disposal phase, we know that this killer... or killers took great care in selecting the scene. They wanted the body to be found. They wanted the body to celebrate something. That question feeds into the antecedent phase. What fantasy or plan is driving the killer? You're the serial murder expert, that's your domain. What does the way that body was displayed tell you about the killer?" Meadows finally looked back to Leas to wait for his response.

Leas rolled and stretched his neck as if preparing for a fight, trying to suggest to Meadows he thought it was all a waste of time. But, he personally agreed on the scene. The killer was saying something, celebrating something and wanted everyone to know. "This isn't his first murder displayed like this, so... we know it is likely more a celebration than a warning. Warnings are usually displayed differently and singularly suggest that someone run. This one isn't like that. There is no horrible gore; it's more an admiration for the body, her lines... her tattoo."

"Impressive, Agent. They say you are decent at your job when not tipping back the bottle." Meadows let the comment sink in before continuing. "Bodies... they always talk to us. You just have to figure out what they are saying. Like the three we currently have. Organized. Structured. Planned. Whoever this is feels justified or righteous. He takes pride in his work. He is patient, too. Selects them with care. Tell me agent, what is special about this one?"

Leas looked at the photographs of the body he had in his hand. Turning through them he stopped. "The tattoo. The phoenix."

"What's special about that?"

Leas rolled his eyes knowing that Meadows already knew the answer. "Well, birds usually represent many things. Freedom, renewal... like releasing doves at a ceremony. Grace, beauty with birds like peacocks. Or, strength, authority as with eagles."

"So which is it here? Freedom, grace, or is he exhorting authority?" Meadows was playing professor, prying Leas to think more analytically about the case.

Scratching his head, Leas responded, "There was nothing about the body that screamed authority. The pose was wrong, looking away. Plus, the girl was too soft, too angelic. Her killer is either signaling a rebirth, perhaps his or... theirs, or he is honoring the victims, celebrating their beauty. That's my two-cents, now can we go?"

By the furled brow and smile on Meadows' face, Leas was correct.

CHAPTER 17

I T HAD BEEN a week since Cash returned to Charleston, but to Cole it felt like a decade. He was letting down his guard, letting the man in and as uncomfortable as it was, it felt good. Cole didn't just feel cared for, he felt craved... desired. His experience with Jeremy... the drugs, the suicide... had struck hard at Cole's confidence that he could ever trust, much less find love. Cash was the first person to challenge Cole's doubt.

He snapped out of his thoughts and looked on as movers scattered here and there. Boxes littered the turn-of-the-century two-story brick house on Park Hill, with more being randomly placed as Cole looked over with dread. House shopping was exciting. Moving was a pain. "Just put those in the living room for now if you don't mind. I'll find a place for them later." Cole's OCD kicked in as he watched the large, sweaty man shuffle by and deposit the box in the middle of the living room. Cole wondered if the man put any thought into the idea of placing it against the wall so it was out of the way from the other mover's traffic but stopped himself from saying anything. *Best to just do it yourself.*

Cole's mind worked on logic and economy. He was

constantly analyzing his movements and tasks to minimize waste. If he intended to cook a meal, he mapped out
the movements around the kitchen first to minimize his
movements and time. *At which point did he grab the eggs
three feet from the stove versus turning on the coffee pot two
feet away? What is more time efficient for fastest delivery,
turning the egg and then grabbing the plate, or grabbing the
plate before pouring the coffee?* He knew the mental process
in itself wasted time, and then there were the moments
where all the thoughts log-jammed, causing him to freeze
in place trying to sort out a new, more efficient path. The
logistical hoops of his mind drained him, but it was the
only brain he had. So, he reasoned he was stuck with it.

Cole's mind was still fixated on the mess before him
when a woman walked into the front door. "Excuse me,
are you the new neighbor?" The woman's silver-gray
hair suggested she was much older than her face would
suggest.

"Uh, that would be me." He extended his hand.
"Cole."

She shook it and responded, "Hannah, Hannah
Mills-Rodriguez."

Cole chuckled, "That's a mouthful."

"Yeah, it was that or take my wife's name. And, I'm
too progressive for that. So we compromised."

"Ah." Lesbians were unpredictable to Cole. They
either loved him or hated him. He could never figure
out why some were so stand-offish toward him, but suspected it had a lot to do with the inability of some gays to
do much more than make a nice cocktail. He progressed
slowly. "Glad to see there's 'family' in the neighborhood.
I'm still pretty new to Denver. So, I'm still trying to figure
out the different areas."

Hannah lit up and spoke like she was discussing a juicy secret. "I knew it! I told Nancy... that's my wife. I told her that you were gay. You were dressed too nice for a straight guy in Denver when we saw you walking the place the other day."

Cole laughed. "Ha. Well, someone once told me I was either gay or from Charleston because those were the only two explanations for the bright colors I routinely wear. I told them, 'Both.'"

"Ha! So, you're from the South, too? I love it! Glad to meet another southerner. I grew up right on the border of Louisiana, a small town called Orange, Texas."

"Very nice. Always happy to meet another sweet tea drinker."

"True, but mine is usually in the form of Fire Fly vodka now."

Cole stared at her in surprise. "What? That's from Charleston. Or, it was. In fact, I think I have some around here. Want to join me for some?" Cole looked back towards the home's front door.

"Fuck yeah! It's after ten a.m. on a Saturday."

Cole turned and opened the screen door. "I'll be right back." Inside the home he began digging through one of the boxes for the liquor. The delivery of a text vibrated on his phone in his pocket. He pulled it out. Garrett Cummings, the parent of little Richie was texting to ask if Billy was gluten-free. He rolled his eyes and wanted to punch in, "he eats dirt" but stopped himself. Gluten-free was obsessive in Denver with it rarely not being available. There were whole restaurants in town that offered nothing but the stuff. He wondered if recreational pot brownies came gluten-free just as his hand struck gold. Sweet tea vodka. Cole raced around to find two mismatched glass jars and filled them with ice and some water before returning to the front porch.

A BLUE-HAIRED LADY in her pink night gown and matching slippers was shuffling down the sidewalk at the end of his pathway looking nosily at Cole and Hannah. "Pay no attention to that old bird. She's just a mean ol'bitch. Her name's Betty."

Cole looked at Hannah with a lifted brow. "Any particular reason?"

"Oh, plenty. But, mine is personal." Cole handed her a jar and poured some tea vodka in as they looked on at the lady now sweeping her massive driveway. Hannah continued. "I moved here from Texas in the early eighties and bought my place next door pretty soon after that in 1988. I was told that Denver was a pretty relaxed place back then, and for the most part it was. But, that didn't stop this neighborhood. See, unknown to me when I bought my place, Denver still had 'zero zoning' in place. Know what that is?" Cole shook his head as he sipped his tea.

Hannah continued, "Well, the 'living in sin' law, as they called it, was put in place in the 1950s to prevent black families from moving into white neighborhoods. Then in the sixties, it was changed some to prevent hippie communes from taking up in this neighborhood. Finally, in the eighties, when AIDs came on, they used it to keep out the gays. The laws pretty much said that only families could live in these homes, and a family was defined as two married people. Well, I guess cause I'm a big'ol lipstick lesbian or something, the realtor forgot to ask me about that. So get this..." She slapped Cole's leg like a joke was about to be told. Lifting her glass in the direction of the lady, she resumed. "That damn woman comes over one day after a girlfriend spent the night and asks me if the woman was kin. I was like 'Hell no. I don't know what kind of family you come from, but I don't sleep with kin. She's my girlfriend.'"

Hannah winked. "I knew damn well what she was asking, but just wanted to get her skirt going. Anyway, she tells me that I better not have her over again because she will have me ticketed." Hannah stopped to look at Cole in his eyes to reenact her shock at the moment. "So, I was like, 'Ticket? What the hell kind of ticket are you going to give me, ma'am?' She proceeds to tell me that only immediate relatives and spouses are permitted to stay in the home more than one or two nights. I'm like, fuck my life. How's a girl supposed to get laid with that shit? Thank god some straight white couples, including one a few blocks over, had been suing over that shit for like fourteen years and ended up getting City Council to strike that bull-shit off the books after I had lived here almost a year. But, that old coot doesn't care. Be careful of her, she will have the water department knocking on your door if your sprinklers are on for even a second after the time permitted."

Almost instinctively, the old lady turned and gave a mean eye in the direction of Cole and Hannah. Hannah lifted her jar and yelled out, "Yeah, fuck you, too. Why don't you stay out my bid-ness!" The old lady waved an angry hand at them and then walked into her home. Hannah leaned in and asked Cole, "That's how you say 'business' in the South Carolina, right? Or, so I've heard on The Real Housewives of Atlanta."

Cole just shook his head in disbelief. "Yeah, pretty

much. Just like that." He admired Hannah's brass but cringed at its delivery. Yet, somehow he knew that Hannah was going to be the best neighbor ever. They raised their makeshift glasses. "Cheers to Betty."

MENTOR

CHAPTER 18

"WHAT'S UP OLD man? You writing that squiggly stuff in that notebook of yours again?" A young mocha skinned man plopped down on a worn bench next to Smith, looking out from his front porch of his Cabbagetown area bungalow on Savannah Street. Atlanta was cooler than usual for late September, but the air was still sticky. He had moved to the area after leaving Charleston. The name sake of zealous cabbage cooking Appalachian laborers who first moved into the mill town of Fulton Bag and Cotton Mill, its streets were narrow and in disrepair when he arrived. *A perfect place to go unnoticed.* But, like most neighborhoods in Atlanta, the past decade of high gas prices and park-and-go traffic had caused a revival of inner-city communities, transforming the area into a "quaint," "hip" community, complete with hipsters, local corner stores, and pastel painted shotgun homes.

"Old man. Old man, are you listening to me. When are we heading out next?" Smith looked back to the man sitting on his porch for a second and then turned back to his journal. "Patience, I said. You know how this works. Everything has its time. Everything has its place.

Otherwise... well, just be patient. Dammit." Kendrick Monroe was a kid that somehow Smith had adopted without knowing it. Since last April he had been unable to shake him. The fact that he lived five feet away in the next home didn't help. He had moved in with his parents four years ago. Almost immediately it was apparent that things were not well in the home. Opened windows told him that Mr. Monroe liked to drink and then hit. Marsha, the mother, wore heavy bags under one or both eyes most times from the strikes. The boy didn't fare much better. A broken arm last year would have had him removed from the home if he was a minor, but at twenty-two, he was on his own in the State's eyes. To his credit, he never struck back... until the end.

"Don't you have work or something?"

"No, man. I have off. Don't have to show up at Lowe's till noon tomorrow. I'm pumped for another one. Aren't you? I mean, the one two weeks ago was kickin'."

"Listen here. You are a part of this because I allow you to be part of this. I can end this like I can end you. Do you get me, 'man'?" The words were delivered with steely coldness. Smith had grown fond of Ken's presence and assistance in the game. But, he had no tolerance for anyone or anything that interrupted his plans.

"Sorry. I didn't... You know. I'm just on a high since the last one. When are we doing this again?"

Smith shook his head in frustration. "Soon, but I've got business to take care of. You need to trust that I've got this under control. You go around stringing up people too often and you'll get caught. Do you want to get caught? Huh?" Smith looked over his shoulder to see Ken's response.

"No. But, I can handle myself. You know that. I have..."

The old man grew impatient with Kendrick's insistence. "No you can't. You go off half cocked like some kid in a candy store and you are going to get us both caught. Remember, I'm the coach here. Listen to me and everything will be okay. Don't, well... you will be next. Now, did you get everything I asked for from work for next time? We might move it up."

Shaking off the sting, Ken responded. "Yeah, duct tape, rope, heavy wire and paint brushes. That's all, right?"

Still writing in his journal, he spoke without looking up. "Bucket?"

"Oh, yeah. Bucket...check."

"Good. Now go away. Go help your mom or something. I've got business for the next week or so, but when I get back we will lock this in." With a wave of his hand he brushed off the man. Alone, he jotted down a few more strokes into his journal. Only one word was discernible, "Mouzon."

Chapter 19

TWO WEEKS OF moving had worn on Cole and Billy. Antsy like a dog left home alone too long, Billy had resulted to making up way too many imaginary friends for Cole's comfort. The last straw was when he named one of them Snooky. The chosen escape was horseback riding lessons. Billy had been to a few before the move, and Cole decided it was time to get him back into a stable routine.

Driving up to Vail, Cole recalled pictures of his mom on horseback that adorned Granny's walls, ribbons hung at their corners. From what Granny said, Libby loved horses as a little girl and convinced a neighbor to teach her western riding in exchange for raking pine straw around the stables. Granny told him of how she would save up nickels and quarters for gas money to drive Libby to Aiken, South Carolina to compete. The ribbons flooded in. It was only after getting pregnant with Cole that she stopped.

Riding lessons had been Cole's brilliant idea to give Billy an outlet. Cole had ridden himself off and on since childhood, Granny's way of reminding him of Libby... reminding herself. Though Jackie was never a horse lover, the result had appeared the same in Billy. He had developed a passion that pulled him though the tough memories of losing his mother. Pulling up to the property, he was out the door before Cole could turn off the car's engine, racing to meet Lori Tinnison, the stable's owner.

She ran her fingers through his wiry blonde hair as he walked up. "Well hey there, Billy! You ready to ride today?" She patted his head.

He sat in a dust filled depression to pull off his shoes and responded, "Yes ma'am. Is Jessica here today?"

Lori smiled, looking down at the boy now struggling to pull on brown pint-sized Justin ropers that he had saved for over the past three months to pay half. She looked around the yard and responded, "Yeah, she is around here somewhere. One of the cats had kittens, so she has been playing with them near the back end of the stables."

"Jessica, huh?" Closing the car door and walking up, Cole had a large grin on his face. "I thought you came for the horses."

"Oh, I did Uncle Cole." Billy, half standing – pressing his foot into a boot, looked back to Lori, "I get to ride Kahlua today, right?"

"You sure do, Billy. But remember, you have to help prep her before you can ride. I think one of our new volunteers, Lance, is in the stables starting that now. You need to go and help."

Half out of breath from the ordeal of getting on his boots, Billy responded, "Okay! Uncle Cole, are you going remember my snack pack?"

Billy ran off towards the stables with Cole shouting behind, "I got it mister, don't you worry."

Lori followed Billy with her eyes before turning back

to Cole. "Don't you love them at that age? Everything is exciting and new. They tackle it all with so much energy."

Cole smiled, "You can say that again. He is a ball of energy. I struggle to keep up."

Wiping her forehead with the back of her leather gloved hand, she replied. "Ha, if you ever figure out how to, you let me know. Between Jessica and her brother, James, I think I get ten minutes to catch my breath. But, how are you dealing with it all... I mean, this is all pretty new to you, right?" Lori looked down and kicked at the ground, knowing she was touching on a possibly sensitive subject. A small cloud of red dust floated a few inches before falling again.

Cole lifted up his cap and scratched his blonde hair. "Yeah, it is. I mean I wanted kids, but actually having them is drastically different... life changing. Other than the fact that I constantly feel tired and incompetent, it is wonderful actually. If you have any advice on how to fix those issues, I'm all ears?"

Lori placed a hand on Cole's shoulder. "Sorry to tell you, but tired and confused are par for the course when it comes to parenting. You get used to it eventually. But, if you are looking for advice... Remember to also take care of yourself. Go to the gym, have adult time on occasion, perhaps a weekend away. Parenting is a twenty-four hour job and you're always on call. But, remember to take time to recharge, cause those little boogers will wear you out otherwise." She laughed.

"I appreciate the insight, I need all the advice I can get." Cole looked around to see several unfamiliar faces walking around the property, obvious parents of other riders. "Looks like you are busy today. What's up?"

"Oh, we host therapy sessions a few times a month. So, a lot of them are here for that."

"Therapy?"

"Yeah, kids with Down syndrome, emotional issues, etcetera... they come here and ride the horses with our trainers to give them something new to process, to give them a break for the routine therapy they may do at home."

"Wow, does it work?"

Lori turned towards a fenced in area with several horses being ridden by kids with helmets and trainers walking alongside the horses. She pointed at a child closest to the fence. "See Matt over there in the blue polo? When he first started coming here he threw horrible fits and we couldn't get him on the horse. Four months later, we can't get him off the horse and I'm told by his parents that his behavior at home has improved dramatically. He's like a new kid." Turning back to Cole, she continued, "Don't ask me what it is, but I see it every day. Even in adults. Put them around animals and their behavior totally changes."

Cole watched one of the kids atop a horse being led by what he presumed was one of the volunteers. They then both walked over to the fence rail and leaned in to watch the horses working. "Well, I've definitely seen the impact in Billy. He just seems like a happier kid since coming here."

"Yeah? So he's dealing with his mom's death well?"

Cole paused to think about how to respond. "Well, I don't know what is 'well,' but he certainly has fewer sad and angry days compared to when it first happened." He paused. He was constantly impressed with Billy's ability to move forward. Somehow he had discovered a way to choose happiness over gloom over his mother's death. He beamed happiness.

"You know, kids are amazingly resilient. And, Billy is an angel."

"Thank you. He is pretty amazing that's for sure. His ability to heal is definitely inspirational." Cole mimicked Lori, kicking at the dusty red clay ground. "Okay, well I've taken enough of your time. Let me see how Billy is coming along with... Kahlua you said?"

"Yeah, her stall is toward the back. I think Lance is back there working with her. Older gentleman, cowboy hat, jeans, boots... can't miss him." She smiled knowing that the description described pretty much everyone present.

CHAPTER 20

THE HEAVY SCENT of straw filled Cole's nostrils as he walked into the large ponderosa pine stable. A row of ten or so stalls lined either side of the building. Whiffs of saddle soap and leather were caught as he worked his way towards the back end where one of the doors stood open. A sorrel colored Morgan snorted as he walked by, clearly not happy with Cole disturbing his morning meal of oats. A white and brown spotted paint was being handled by a woman in the next stall. Cole was about to stop to watch when he heard Billy's voice.

Cole found Billy leaning over with a large hoof between his legs and giggling. The hoof's owner was a large brownish horse that dwarfed even Cole. Cole turned to the silver haired man standing next to Billy, supervising the cleaning. "Here you go Billy. Take this pick and get all that hay and stuff out from the crevices. Make it all nice and clean now. We can't have Kahlua walking around like that." Cole couldn't help but notice the man was built for his age with more muscle than most young men.

"Yes, sir." Billy walked around and grabbed another

one of the horse's large hooves and began working on it intensely.

Smiling with pride, Cole said, "Wow, I can't even get him to clean his room and you have him picking hooves. What am I doing wrong?"

The man looked up to respond, "Little Billy seems to be an expert. You must be doing something right." A slight grin crossed the man's face as Cole chuckled. The man continued, "This your boy?"

"He's mine if you are about to say something good. Otherwise..." Cole let out chuckle. "Yes, he's my nephew." Cole looked longingly at Billy, seeing his sister in the boy's face. Billy was busy using the brush end of the pick to finish his task, unaware that his uncle was staring at him.

Cole leaned in and ran a hand across a white patch of hair between the horse's two ears. "And, is this the famous Kuhlua?"

The old man patted gently on one side of the horse's neck. "Yep, this here is Kahlua. She's a good'ol horse."

Billy looked up. "I get to ride her today!" He walked across the stable to a small wooden table with a saddle on it. Struggling to get his arms around it and lift it, Cole walked over to help.

From the corner of his eye he caught sight of someone working just outside the stable's open doors. Cole squinted in sudden recognition. *Zander.* Shirtless, jeans, shoving hay from a large pile into the back of a small truck bed, Cole took in what resembled some smutty romance cover. The man was hot. There was no doubt about that. His muscles were thick and defined with his pecs lying like heavy armor plates on top the man's rippled core. A flash of his back revealed a very large black tattoo that looked Mayan or some other ancestral style. Cole couldn't make out what it was supposed to be before his appreciation for the man was interrupted.

"Uncle Cole... come on. Mr. Kennedy needs the saddle." Billy was looking up at him impatiently. Cole had totally forgotten that he was standing motionless in the stable still holding the heavy saddle by its horn.

Cole's attention had been noticed, "You know ol'Zander, do you?" The old man grinned as he took the saddle and slung it over the horse's back on top of a small saddle pad.

Cole felt foolish that someone had noticed him ogling the man outside. Caught, Cole hung his head in embarrassment. "You can say that. We play in a football league together. That's about as much as I know."

"Oh, that boy is a good one for sure. I've been here for about a month and a half now and from what I hear, he comes out here every weekend to volunteer with the horse therapy program. Been doing it for years, they say. Don't really know too much about him myself other than he is a hard worker, always steppin' in where the stables need help. Supposedly, he even donated feed money one year when there wasn't enough funding for the program. You oughta go say 'hi.' Lil'Billy and I got this all under control. We will be ridin' for the next hour or so. Go on now, go make a friend."

"We got this Uncle Cole." Billy smiled with overflowing anticipation.

COLE KNEW EXACTLY what Mr. Kennedy really meant. *Go get you some.* Still stinging from the awkwardness of being caught admiring another man, Cole decided to test the waters cautiously as he walked away from Billy and Mr. Kennedy to finish their prep. Cole exited the stables' back entrance and walked to a fenced arena where small kids with helmets were riding, each with an adult walking alongside to assist. Cole tried to play it cool, placing a boot on the lower rail of the arena's wooden fence. But, true to his klutzy form, the boot slipped off and landed in a large mud puddle next to a galvanized tank of water. Cole momentarily lost his balance and looked in any direction but Zander's to avoid the sting of his embarrassment from being seen.

"Cole?" *Shit, he saw.* Slowly turning, Cole was met with Zander standing, pitchfork in hand, looking over with a huge grin on his face. He lifted a chin, "You need help over there?"

Cole looked down to his boot and jean pant leg now covered in mud spatter. He shook his head and laughed. "No... no. I'm good. Just figured I better break in these jeans to fit in. Can't be too dirty out here in all this dust and... well, mud I guess."

Looking back up, Cole saw Zander push his black hair out of his eyes. "Well, from the looks of it, you're doing a good job of 'fitting in.'" He laughed. Cole joined in, unable to hold back the hilarity of his own stupidity.

Trying to get the subject off him, Cole asked, "So what are you doing out here besides trying to seduce all the housewives with your outfit?" Cole swept his eyes up and down. Zander's body was still holding Cole's attention even with the distraction of looking like a fool covered in mud.

Obviously deciding to play into it, Zander placed his hand behind his head like he was at a muscle competition and compressed his abs slightly. He was teasing Cole and knew that it was working. Grinning to one side, he said, "I have no clue what you are talking about. And, if I was trying to seduce anyone… it wouldn't be housewives." Zander winked. The man was cocky; and it was obvious he loved the game. He relaxed and threw the pitchfork onto the top of the haystack. Grabbing a flannel shirt hanging from the tail of the old white pick-up truck, he walked over as he slipped it on without bothering to button it. As he approached Cole, he placed an arm against the top rail of the pine fence and leaned into it to face Cole from the side. Cole had to admit the man looked good in this place, this moment. Trying not to repeat his previous mishap, Cole crossed both arms across the top rail and leaned into the fence with his chest, turning to his right to look at Zander just inches away.

"So, what are you doing here Cole Mouzon? I got that right, no?" He spoke in a silken tone. Cole wanted to laugh at the cheesy factor but it was actually kind of hot.

His accent fell off as he spoke with rigid formality like he did during business called. "Yes, you got that right. Good memory. I bring my nephew out here on occasion to ride. It helps… it helps distract him." He caught himself reflecting on Billy and Jackie and immediately stopped, seeing no need to voice personal matters with Zander the model.

Zander continued to speak softly. "Huh. I've never seen you out here before. But… I'm glad to see you here today. I've been meaning to hunt you down." He pursed his lips.

Cole's tone changed. "Hunt me down?" He leaned back to wait for what he suspected would be a good line.

"Yeah, hunt you down for Dazbog, or something." His smile made the 'something' heavy with meaning.

Still trying to avoid his temptation to looking below the collar bone of the man, Cole responded. "I'm always up for coffee. You just let me know when. But, 'something...' – 'something' sounds like trouble and if you didn't notice at the game two weeks ago, I'm currently seeing someone." The idea of dating someone was still difficult to accept since it first came up during Cash's visit. But, in this moment, it felt right... safe.

It was Zander's turn to lean back in contemplation. "You mean that hip-tatic guy that was there? Wow. I'm disappointed. You could do so much better." He paused and cut his eyes back to Cole playfully. "Like me for instance. I've never even seen the guy before that game. Does he not go out?"

Cole laughed, "Yes, he goes out... in Charleston." Trying to continue, Cole saw Zander gnaw on the word 'Charleston' as if he was trying to figure out how to pronounce it, but looking more like a horse fiddling with a bit in his mouth. Cole shook his head and rolled his eyes. "Anyway... he doesn't live here. So, that is why you haven't had an opportunity to realize that he is the better man."

Zander leaned in closely, brows raised. "Oh really? If you gave me an opportunity I am sure that you would come to see I am right." The dry wind blew. He smelled like straw and hormones. Cole wondered if anyone had ever tried to bottle the scent. Cole inhaled deeply and then let it out.

Zander pulled back and turned his head. "See that horse over there with the brown and gray spots? Thrasher. Part Clydesdale, part quarter horse. Twelve hands of muscle. They said he couldn't be broken. But I did it. And, I can break you."

Cole looked at the massive horse in the adjoining pasture before catching the last part of Zander's sentence. His head pulled back, and his eye-bows lifted. *'Break' me?* Head down and shaking in disbelief, Cole responded, "You, mister, are trouble. And, I am sure all of your little fans love that. But, as you can see, I don't have the luxury of trouble anymore." Cole cocked his head behind him, waved over to where Billy was now riding and then turned back. He grimaced at what he had just heard himself say. He was old. A parent. And, that meant to him no more 'trouble.'

"Oh, you have me all wrong. I'm not trouble. I'm pleasure... fortune... passion. You should always have those things in your life even if you are a parent."

"Ha. 'Things trouble says.' Ojos que no ven, corazón que no siente. No thank you." Cole smiled at being able to spit out the Spanish saying he had learned during a trip to Columbia without stumbling.

Zander was clearly impressed. "'Eyes that don't see, heart that doesn't feel?' Where did you hear that?"

"I know all about the lore of latino pleasure, passion... the wondering eyes. It's like a hot iron, scalding one moment and just as fast, ice cold. I don't subscribe to the idea that what I don't know won't hurt me. If you are with me, you are with only me. You can say I have trust issues." Cole winked.

Zander laughed. "Well, good for me that I'm not some philandering latino. I'm Native American." He smirked. "Born and raised here in Colorado. Have you heard the lore of the Ute? Our irons never get cold." Zander placed his hand on one of Cole's hips as if he was going to pull him in. "Go out with me... this weekend."

Cole looked down to Zander's hand. "Got plans."

"Next weekend."

"Got plans."

Zander tugged Cole's arm. "Three weekends from now. Come on." He flashed his brown puppy eyes.

"In Atlanta." Cole tried to avoid contact but couldn't help grinning. This was likely one of the few times Zander didn't get what he wanted.

Zander turned his head away slowly and then swiftly back. "Wait... for Pride? I'll be there. That can be our first date." His eyes went bright.

Shit. "Uh, no I'll be there with the guy you saw. Moved from there two years ago, so otherwise catching up with friends." Zander mouthed a playful "damn" and then dropped his head. He kicked up a small cloud of dust with one of his boots.

Cole pulled away from his touch and then broke out laughing at all the symbolism that flashed through his head. "As I said, T.R.O.U.B.L.E. Coffee I can do, but anything else, sorry Charlie, I'll have to pass. But, I have plenty of friends that would love to get burned by your iron if you want their numbers."

Zander licked his lips longingly and then stood up from the fence. "In all honesty, I think that's what makes you most attractive. You have your shit together and you know what you want. I am a good guy. You will learn that eventually. I just hope its sooner than later. But, for now, there are horses to be fed. So long sexy Cole Mouzon. Until our next rendezvous." Zander turned and walked away as he slipped his shirt back off and looked over his shoulder to catch Cole taking in the view.

Cole took another deep breath hoping to catch the remnants of Zander's smell while enjoying the view of the tanned man walking away. *Trouble.* How he missed it.

Chapter 21

COLE HAD BEEN alone watching Billy for a while without interruption, but that ended when a brunette in her mid-forties in a long jean skirt walked over to obviously snoop at what she had seen earlier. "So, you know Zander?" She flipped her hair over one shoulder as she talked causing a silver charm bracelet on her wrist to jangle.

"Uhm, yeah... I mean, a little, just through sports."

The woman looked at Cole suspiciously as though she was evaluating his worthiness for conversation. "Sports? Oh? What kind? I didn't know he played any sports." She looked back behind her to the crowd of women she had left. They were all watching. It was obvious she was feeling him out for information on Zander... and him. Cole didn't like snoops and he certainly didn't like ones that came off as making a challenge.

"Yeah, you know... football." What Cole really wanted to say was "sex" to really fluster the woman, but he couldn't bring himself to do it and he certainly didn't what to get that reputation in some country stable where his nephew rode horses. He played nice.

"Oh my goodness, I forgot to introduce myself. I'm

Dora-Lee. And, you are...?" The woman extended her hand hungrily like a witch handing a child an apple. Cole looked at the hand and then extended his own hoping he didn't regret it. "Cole."

Clasping his hand, she pulled him in close and began to whisper, "So, Cole... what's the story with that Zander? Is he single? He barely speaks a word to any of the woman around here, but he was chatting you up like crazy." Cole caught sight of a large diamond engagement ring and wedding band as looked back up to eye his interrogator. Peering over her shoulder he could see the gaggle of women still gathering across the horse arena, waiting in anticipation for Dora-Lee's report. Salivating like cougars over a maimed deer, they craved details... dirty, sultry details.

Cole cut his eyes back to the woman still grasping his hand. "Uhm, you know... I really don't know him that well. We just happen to play in the same football league."

"Oh come on Cole. You've got to give me more than that. Have you ever seen him with a date?" Cole suspected that date or no date, single or not – this crowd didn't care. They would take Zander any way they could find him and if that meant attached, so much better for the hunt.

HE SMILED AT what he was about to do. "You know. I've never seen him on a date. But... I can say that I've heard he likes the hunt... that he likes women to be aggressive, forward with him. He plays all strong and silent until the woman makes the first move. But, once that happens he takes control. So, if one of your friends is looking to get with him I would recommend they be forceful, don't take no for an answer. He will love that." Cole laughed inside as he set his trap. Zander deserved a bit of grief for being so cocky. Cole just hoped that he was around to see this play out.

Dora-Lee grinned with excitement. She had real news to report to her brooding friends and couldn't wait to fill them in. "Well, that sounds fun... I mean, interesting. Thank you Cole. And, by the way... are you single?"

Cole smiled politely, "I'm taken. But, thank you. That Zander though... he is free as the wind."

Finally releasing Cole's hand, Dora-Lee stepped back and turned. "Thank you Cole. I hope to see you out here again soon."

Cole turned back to see Zander jumping into the back of the now fully loaded truck. Oh, what he would give to see Zander's face when this all played out.

CHAPTER 22

"UNCLE COLE, LOOK!" Looking across the arena, Cole saw Billy atop Kahlua alone at the reins. Galloping at half speed, he looked like he had been riding for years as he posted perfectly with the horses. A sense of pride and amazement filled him. His nephew lost his mother to a crazed killer just four months ago and yet, he had been able to maintain his youth, his ability to enjoy life. He was an inspiration to Cole every time he started to think that losing his sister was just too much to bear. Who could have ever thought that a child would teach an adult such a huge lesson as that – life goes on, continues.

"He's doing awesomely, no?" Lori had snuck up beside Cole while he reflected on his nephew.

"He is indeed. Reminds me of his mother. Things always came so easy to her. There wasn't a task, a sport she couldn't conquer." Cole smiled to himself at being able to reference his sister without feeling sad. It felt good.

"Oh? Billy was saying it was you that helped him on a, what was it... yoga ball... at home to work on his posting?" She gave a slight elbow to Cole to emphasis the obvious compliment.

"Well, I couldn't have him coming out here and getting frustrated. I wanted him to enjoy the experience. Plus, it was pretty hilarious to see him hopping around the house on that thing. Kids... got to love them."

"Agreed. They are pretty amazing. From what I gather you are doing a knock-out job for being a new parent. It's obvious that it comes naturally to you. He's pretty lucky to have you in his life."

"I think I'm the lucky one. He reminds me every day that life is about exploring, learning, celebrating. Somewhere along the way to adulthood we seem to lose focus on those things. He has reset those as priorities, not luxuries, in my life."

"Wow. Listen to you over there. Let's talk again when he hits his teens and see what you say." Lori let out a short laugh. "Seriously though, I agree with you. Kids remind us that there is a lot more to life than worrying about work, bills, or money." She looked over to Jessica still playing outside the stables, now with another young boy in tow. "Now, don't get me wrong. There are days I want to wring her neck for all the sassing I get. But, she's a good kid. And, Billy is wonderful. Enjoy him, Cole. They grow up way too fast."

"Message received." Cole offered a captain's salute playfully before she started again.

"And, let me just apologize now. I saw Dora-Lee over here chatting you up. They are like a bunch of vultures out here. I'm sure whatever she was drilling you about was horrible to deal with. Excuse my language, but they are a bunch of catty bitches."

Cole's brows raised. He was shocked at the term, not the sentiment. It was obvious the women were reliving their high school or sorority days every day though they were decades removed from either. Cole and Lori laughed. "Don't worry, they don't get to me. I actually thought it was funny. They are some real snoops." Cole remembered the trap he set for Zander and laughed again.

Placing her hand on Cole's forearm, Lori said, "Oh, you don't know the half of it. They are constantly using the stables as their hunting grounds for new men. Anytime a dad comes out here they pounce like the ratty cougars they think they are. Unfortunately they have succeeded enough times that they have no reason to stop. If I could, I would throw them and their kids out of here, but I need the money from their kids' private lessons to support the therapy program. Honestly, some of their kids are actually decent. Must take after their fathers or something, cause they sure don't take after their mothers." She shook her head at the situation. "Anyway, I hope they didn't draw too much blood."

"Nah, I'm good. Promise. You probably know better than anyone. The front-range and highlands of Colorado were filled with real mountain lions and bears that occasionally attacked hikers and joggers. Those are the beasts I worry about... *now*. Not some old pride of mischievous cougars. I think I can handle them."

Cole grinned back at Lori to show his lack of concern. Inside, the "now" churned his emotions about Charleston, Jackie, and The Taker. That last piece remained unresolved. All indications suggested that The Taker was gone... perhaps even dead of old age. Either way, he hadn't come for Cole, Poinsett had. So there was no suggestion that The Taker had any further interest in Cole since taking him as a child.

Lori patted Cole's shoulder. "Okay, well I need to

help get the therapy kids wrapped up. Billy should be finished in fifteen minutes or so. If I don't see you before you leave, come back soon, okay?"

Cole looked around to see Billy still riding with little assistance. "Sounds like a plan."

Walking off, Lori added, "Oh, and Cole. Be careful. Those kitties like to scratch." She threw out a leather gloved hand in the direction of the cougars. He looked down and laughed before returning to watch Billy. *I'm sure they do. I'm sure they do.*

CHAPTER 23

"UNCLE COLE! DID you see? Did you see? I was riding all by myself?"

Placing a hand on Billy's shoulder and kneeling down, Cole responded, "You better believe I did, lil'man. Way to go. You'll be jumping gates and riding barrels in no time. But, for now... we need to get back to town. It's almost supper time and I have to figure out something to make or we are both going to starve." Cole sucked in his cheeks to mimic a starving zombie and put his arms out stiff in Billy's direction. "And, you know what happens when Uncle Cole gets hungry.... Braaaains...braaaains...." Billy ran around Cole to hide, giggling the entire time.

"Uncle Cole, no! You can't eat my brains."

Playfully deflated, Cole stood and said, "Awe, but I like brains... and broccoli, but mostly brains." A smirk crossed his face as he walked toward the tail of the small SUV and lifted its gate. "Well, come on then. Let's get to the store and make something or else brains it is. Jump up here and kick off those boots."

Billy ran around and pulled himself up into the bed of the car and sat, legs dangling over the lip of the rear bumper. Cole pulled off the miniature cowboy boots smiling to himself at just how small they were. Billy turned and crawled through the car to the backseat and buckled himself in. Shoes would apparently have to wait till home.

Cole was just closing the driver's door when Billy yelled, "Oh no! I forgot my ribbon. I have to have my ribbon. I graduated to level two today!"

"Huh? Ribbon?"

"Yeah, Mr. Kennedy gave it to me. It's green. Can you go get it, pleeeease?" Cole looked around to the stables.

"Yeah, I guess I can. Where did you leave it?"

"I put it on Kahlua's bri... bul... uh, bridal."

Trying to keep from laughing at his nephew's attempt at the word, he responded. "Okay, stay here mister. Here is some goldfish crackers to keep you from craving brains." Cole winked at Billy as he stepped out of the car towards the stables.

Towards the back end of the building he rounded the corner to Kahlua's stall.

"OH! SORRY, WASN'T expecting you here." Zander, his shirt back on and buttoned just a few at its base, was leaning over a saddle on the hay floor, Kahlua chomping on oats in the corner.

"Mister Cole. You didn't get enough of me before, huh?" A mischievous grin crossed his face.

Cocking his head, Cole responded, "Uh, no. My nephew left his ribbon on the bridle. It. Is.... Green." Looking around Zander's torso, Cole saw the bridle hanging on the wooden wall. "And... there it is. If you don't mind...." Cole pushed past Zander, but not without noticing Zander looking at Cole's ass passing by him.

Zander looked up as Cole reached the bridle and pulled off the green ribbon. Cole's back still turned, Zander said, "You know. I have a bone to pick with you. Seems someone encouraged one of the Stepford Wives that I like to play hard-to-get? You wouldn't happen to have any involvement in that, would you?"

Still looking away, Cole smiled at his accomplishment. "Me? Oh, no. Wouldn't have anything to do with that. I mean, I wouldn't dare...."

Without notice, Zander forcefully grabbed first the left, then the right bicep of Cole and then pushed them up over Cole's head and into the stall's wall until he was pinned with Zander pressing his body against him to secure the maneuver.

"Wouldn't dare, huh? Me thinks you jest. I suspected you liked to play during the football game. Game. On."

Cole looked back and forth at the grip Zander had on his biceps and then at the face just inches away, but not before looking at the chest revealed by the spread of the unbuttoned flannel. "I have no clue what you are talking about." Cole raised a brow with a large smile crossing his face.

"Oh, you did it and you are going to be punished for it. I think you like to be punished. And, punished you will be. I bet that hipster man back in Carolina doesn't punish you like you deserve." Zander moved in, feigning an attempt to kiss Cole's neck. Cole caught a whiff of Zander's smell again and closed his eyes before stopping himself from getting caught-up in Zander's type of trouble.

Taking a deep breath of strength to stop the pleasure,

Cole attempted to push Zander off, but it resulted in Zander actually landing a kiss on Cole's neck. Zander decided to take advantage of the opportunity and softly landed two more. His lips were soft. The sensation of being touched rippled across Cole's body, causing goose bumps. Cole caught himself again and wiggled more until he broke Zander's grasp. Cole turned the tables on Zander, pinning him as he had done Cole. But, Cole kept his distance, maintaining space between their two bodies.

"That was your one pass, sir. Try that again and I will take this knee to your jewels, got me?" Cole smiled while tightening his eyes.

Zander looked down but stopped short of ever landing at Cole's knees. "Hmm, so you like it rough, huh? I'm cool with that." He looked up with the last few words with the look of an evil child on his face. He wanted to play with the new toy that was Cole and nothing was going to stop him.

"Look. Are you hot? Yes. But, hot isn't enough for me. So, chase someone else's tail. I'm not interested in...."

Zander interrupted. "So you think I'm hot, huh?"

"You know you are. But, you also know that all you want is play and that isn't for me. Not interested. Got me?" Cole released Zander's arms and backed away.

"You know, I may just surprise you. I'm a lot more than hot body." Zander smiled at his own compliment. "I might just have to demonstrate that to you. If you are worth the work, that is."

Cole shook his head and replied, "I'm not worthy. Please don't waste your time. I think it's better spent on someone else, perhaps one of those ladies out there." Cole chuckled at his attempt to divert the subject off of him. Such conversations made him uncomfortable. The idea that he was "worth" anything wasn't a notion he had entertained in a long time and he wasn't about to do it with Zander.

Zander straightened his shirt, "Perhaps. But, my bet is still on you. But, I see that I'm going to have to put in a bit more time before you agree with me. Take a ride with me. Noooo... not in that way. I mean horseback. There's a small cabin at the top of the uncompahgre, that red mountain out there. We can chill up there and just get to know each other." Zander winked.

Rolling his eyes, Cole responded, "Uh huh. Whatever. Anyway, I have a starving kid in the car waiting on me to return with this green ribbon. Can't have him going zombie on me." Cole turned and walked out of the stall. "Behave yourself mister. Don't make me have to sic those ladies on you."

Cole heard Zander respond from behind him, "I'd rather have you sic that body on me." Cole smiled and kept walking. Being desired was awkward to Cole. He didn't like it. But, he accepted it for what it was, a compliment, even if he didn't feel it was deserved.

Walking out of the stables, he saw Billy's face beam with excitement. Cole flashed the ribbon and Billy waved back from inside the car. Being loved, that was a feeling Cole could feel without regret and Billy gave him that feeling every moment. But, he wasn't the only person who induced that feeling anymore. Cash flashed into mind. Atlanta couldn't come soon enough.

CHAPTER 24

COLE HAD BARELY walked into his small, government issued office on Monday when his cell phone rang. "Hey Mom, how goes it?" Cole's aunt Ava had always been "Mom" to him since the death of his own mother when he was almost four. The Taker had tortured her while Cole and Mark Calhoun watched. She eventually cut herself loose and they escaped into the marsh's of Charleston. But, she died of her injuries before they were found. Ava and his maternal uncle adopted and raised him as their own. But, with the death of their daughter Jackie at the hands of Poinsett, that relationship had become strained.

"What? What news?... They are saying what?"

Ava had called in a panic. The Charleston news had linked the recent Georgia murders to Cole's kidnapping in some way and they were calling her for information on him.

"No. I don't know anything about that? Well, hell no. Don't give them my information. He's fine, Mom. Billy is fine."

"Look, let me figure out what is going on. I'll call you back. Promise. Yeah, I love you, too."

Dread of the events of May flooded Cole's mind. His skin grew hot. He pushed it out, behind his wall until he was cold and clear again. Clicking through his cell phone, he found Leas' number and punched it in.

CHAPTER 25

LEAS FOUND HIMSELF staring at the music mem-
orabilia covering the walls of Smith's Olde Bar on
the edge of Midtown, Atlanta. Meadows nudged
him as the lanky, goatee-toting bartender walked over.
Speaking loud so as to be heard over a rock band playing
upstairs, Leas said, "I'll take another whiskey." Meadows'
eyes suggested disapproval before obviously giving in
and doubling the order with a head nod. The bartender
tossed the bar rag over his shoulder and walked away.

"Not trying to be your momma or anything... but,
I think you should probably slow down that habit of
yours." Meadows' head was cocked toward Leas as he
spoke. "From what I have seen so far, you can be a decent
investigator when you are sober."

Leas continued to study a Lenny Kravitz autographed
photo card as he took a drag from his cigarette and then
responded. "If you'd seen what I've seen. If you'd expe-
rienced what I have... you might know that – but for
this – I wouldn't be here right now, Agent." Leas lifted his
empty highball glass and shook the small ball of ice at its
base to indicate that he was referencing whiskey.

Meadows paused his response until the bartender

had completed his approach and left with their empty glasses, fresh drinks set before them. "Boy, I'm not faulting you. I know about your loss, your wife." Meadows took a swig of his whiskey and placed the glass heavily down on the old oak bar. "This job... chasing killers... it isn't for everyone. God knows I've seen how wicked man can be."

Leas turned to him. "Yeah, I know about your cases. We all have those, I guess."

"Perhaps, but this guy... what we are chasing now... he seems too like Rader for my comfort. He's a watcher, a planner that is taunting us and appears to have just started back up."

Leas was aware of Dennis Lynn Rader, the BTK killer. He had killed ten over a three decade period, striking only a few years and then pausing for ten years or so between 1974 and 1991. Like many serial killers, he had a signature – his being binding, torturing, and killing... "BTK."

MEADOWS AND LEAS drank quietly for several minutes before Meadows started talking again. "Rader identified and monitored his victims by using his job as an ADT Security systems installer to get into peoples' lives and homes. His murders actually created the perfect situation where he was exposed to those trying to protect against the BTK killer, yet, they were unknowingly inviting him into their homes instead." Meadows took another swig. "This guy is identifying his victims in some methodical way that plays into his lifestyle, perhaps through his job like Rader. We have to figure this out before he can act again."

Leas raised his empty glass to the bartender waiting on the opposite end of the bar and then said, "But, Rader had an obsession for taunting the police. He wrote letters and stuck them in library books, taped packages to stop signs, mailed others to *The Wichita Eagle* and... to you." Leas tilted his head in Meadow's direction in anticipation of his response.

"Yeah... but we have no obvious messages here. If this killer is communicating with us, he isn't doing it directly like Rader. Of course, that was Rader's downfall. We fooled him. He asked in a letter if he sent a disk of photos taken by him of his murders could it be traced back. We responded with an article in the Eagle saying, 'Of course not.' Ten days later he was arrested when it was discovered the photos had been saved off his Christ Lutheran Church computer. I doubt this guy is going to be as foolish." Meadows grabbed the new glass of whiskey before Leas and poured half of it into his own empty glass. He picked up his and threw it back.

Leas begrudgingly watched the man down his drink. "We are missing something. It's the posing or something, I don't know yet. But, he is talking to us... or someone."

CHAPTER 26

I T WAS TWO-FIFTEEN a.m. when Leas was pushed out of Smith's and landed at the Silver Skillet on Atlanta's 14th Street. The tan colored walls and laminate lunch counter looked like an exact replica of the restaurant depicted in the old show, *Alice*. The sign over the counter said, "Service with a smile... most of the time." Leas half expected Flo to walk out of the back and tell someone to "kiss her grits," but DeDe showed up instead.

She clunked the coffee mug down and then tossed over two creamer cups before walking away from the table. Leas stared at her as she smacked large open-mouth chomps on her gum, occasionally moving her tongue to free it from her teeth. She was seventy on her best day, outfitted in a burnt brown with pea green trim uniform.

"Mister, I ain't got all day. You gonna order somethin' or what?" The whiskey induced spinning in his head made it hard to interpret her words. He looked around the empty restaurant to determine the cause for the rush, stopping to stare first at the numerous menu boards. He had no interest in spicy catfish strips, country ham steak, or the tuna fish cold plate His eyes kept moving until they landed on another waitress sitting at the late night counter. The waitress followed Leas' view. "Honey, what you hungry for ain't on the menu."

Leas looked back at the frail, deeply wrinkled woman just as she popped a bubble with her gum. "What's her name?" He cut his eyes back to the late-twenties blond.

Smacking between words, she hesitantly responded. "Babe, she ain't worth the tip. And… I ain't talking about the change in your pocket." The word "pocket" popped out of her mouth like one of her bubbles.

Leas' voice graveled with firmness. "What's her name?"

"Fine, but it's your dick to rot off." DeDe stepped back and shouted across the small diner. "Hey, Gloria, this man wants to know your name. Why don't you come tell him it. And, get his damn order while you're at it." DeDe walked between the front counters and towards the kitchen as Gloria slowly walked over and took a seat next to Leas in the booth. A hand on his thigh told him that his order was about to be filled.

IT WAS NO surprise that Gloria had no panties on. It had just made it that much easier when they went at it in the alley behind the diner. Somewhere between the dumpster and a pile of filled trash bags, she lifted up her skirt and let Leas have his order. Her turning and leaning against the wall with her hands made it all too easy to lift up her short skirt, unzip his pants and feel normal just for a moment. He didn't know whether it was the alcohol or Gloria's promiscuity, but, he couldn't climax in the position. So he flipped her around, cupped her ass, and lifted her. Face-to-face made him uncomfortable so he stared at the dingy brick wall that Gloria's back was being pressed into and up.

Her deep moaning was irritating by the time she asked if he was okay. He put her down. "Look, this isn't going to happen. Sorry."

"Something wrong with your peter or somethin'?" Her Jersey accent grated on his nerves.

"What? No! Fuck. I'm just not feeling it, okay?" Leas stumbled as he tried to zip up his khakis.

Gloria pushed down her skirt. "Fuckin' drunk. Should'a known betta." Putting out her hand, "Give me some money."

"What are you a hooker or something?"

"Fuck you and your hooker, cocksucker. You made me lose a good hour of tips. You owe me for that pity fuck."

Leas tightened his eyes and dug into his pocket. "Here's a ten. You got change?" He grinned.

Gloria snatched the bill out of his hand, folded it and shoved it in her bra. "You're some character, ya know that? I got your change right here." She cupped her breast and then walked into the diner's open back door. Its screen door smacked closed.

IT WAS MARIA'S birthday. Back in his room he finished off the last of the quarter bottle of Knob Creek before forcing himself to shower. The warm water ran over his shaggy salt-and-pepper hair, disguising the tears he had tried to drown in whiskey most of the day. Even with it being years since her murder, he missed his wife. She had been his best friend and grounding rod for all the horrors of his job. With her gone, he spiraled out of control with nothing to reel him in. Every time he found a focus, the world shifted and disoriented him.

The random sex helped and hurt at the same time. For a brief moment he was on auto pilot, just feeling. But, his mind would eventually snap him back to reality. All he could hope for is that it happened after he finished.

Having sex with anyone but Maria crushed him when he finally realized what he had done. He felt dirty and dishonest. But, he couldn't control himself. He couldn't resist the pressure that built up inside him.

Stepping out of the shower, the tears were gone, but not the ache. He grabbed a towel and wrapped it around his waist. Staring back at him in the mirror was a hollow man, empty of most emotions but sorry and anger. His body had seen better days, but a steady diet of whiskey and cigarettes kept it lean. Inspecting his hairline, he picked up the phone and made a call he had been avoiding. Cole Mouzon knew.

CHAPTER 27

"COLE, THIS IS agent Leas. You called?" The man's words were terse. He clearly did not want to speak with Cole at this moment. His cell phone in hand, Cole rushed to his office door and flung it closed. The wall shook.

Cole was pissed it had taken three days for his call to be answered and jumped into the call without any formalities. He almost panted as he spoke. "Agent, why is it that I have to learn from my mom, who saw it on the news that you have a suspect matching the description of The Taker? Can you explain that to me because I fail to see how I should have been kept in the dark on this? She called me in a panic, telling me there were 'others.' *Others* Agent Leas? Others? And you didn't think to tell me, the only survivor?" It felt good to get it out. It had been over a day since Ava called him with what she saw on the noontime news. The Taker was back and Cole wanted answers.

"Mr. Mouzon... Cole, I understand why you are upset. I didn't intend for you to find out this way. Shit, I didn't intend for anyone to find out. Someone opened their mouth without even knowing all the facts. You aren't in any danger that we know of, okay? It appears isolated to Atlanta."

Covering the phone's receiver, he dropped his tone to avoid having his whole office hear the conversation, Cole continued. "Not in any danger? How the hell do you know that?" Cole typed on his computer's keyboard with one hand trying to Google any news of the Atlanta murders. "The man kidnapped me… murdered my mom. And, his crazy daughter came after me. Yet, you say I'm not in danger?" Images of Jackie in the old Sullivan's Island battery flicked through his head like an old-time movie strip enraging him. The fractured wall couldn't keep all the emotions out and the sting seeped into Cole's voice. "Fucking answer me, damn-it!"

"I wasn't ignoring you, I was waiting for you to finish. I understand you are upset and you have every right to be. It was my call. I told victim services to not reach out to you, yet." The word 'victim' made Cole's blood race. He had never thought of himself as a victim. Victims are weak. Victims lost. He was neither weak nor a loser. Leas continued, "The murders match his profile, his style, but there is nothing to suggest he is aiming for you. Rather, they are completely unrelated."

Cole calmed slightly upon hearing this. The thought of a killer chasing him didn't scare him, it pissed him off. But, the thought of a killer possibly going after Billy terrified him. Cole was ready to sacrifice whatever he had to prevent Billy from being harmed. If that meant running to a killer, then so be it. If it were true that The Taker wasn't after him, the question remained, *Why now?*

"Agent that does not assure me at all that my family is safe. How did you find him? What is going on? Please, tell me something."

Leas let out an exacerbated exhale. "Cole I can't tell you much more. This is an open investigation. It's not related to you. That's all I can say. If we find him, you will be the first to know. But, for now… please understand I can't say anything more." Leas didn't want to expose himself to this drama anymore than he had to so he added, "Look. I have to go. But, I will call you, promise, if we catch this guy."

"But, Agent…"

"No Cole. That's all I can offer at this point. I'll talk to you soon." Leas hung up the phone before Cole could protest.

COLE PULLED BACK the phone and stared at the receiver before quickly shoving it back into his slacks' pocket. Leaning back in his black leather chair he looked at the white ceiling tiles of the old office. He focused on a small water stain on one of the tiles as his mind began to drift and flick through his thoughts like a slideshow. Every third or fourth slide was Jackie. Seeing her in his mind made him feel guilty. He couldn't stop Poinsett. She had acted too fast. He couldn't save her from that crazed woman. He survived. He got to enjoy her son growing-up, him riding a horse. His eyes went red before he successfully pushed his wall back up to block the pain as someone knocked on the door.

"Come in!" Cole wiped off the tears with the back of his hand as the door opened. Amanda Mercer's head peeked in.

"Everything okay?"

He responded to his paralegal. "Yeah, sorry. Just a bad phone call. Nothing big, promise."

"Okay, I was just checking. I got those discovery documents in the Durango Steel case for you. Want those in a binder to take with you to your deposition?"

Cole smiled, "That would be wonderful. Thank you. Really." Amanda closed the door behind her.

Cole looked back to the ceiling. The change in job had been needed. It helped... a lot. As an U.S. Assistant District Attorney for Colorado he had more manageable hours than private practice. That was a huge factor in taking the job. Billy needed a parent. They walked on eggshells when he first joined the office back in late July. But, now... he was just another attorney in their environmental litigation department. The job kept him sane. He worked normal nine-to-five hours mostly, travelled on rare occasions, but for the most part he was home every afternoon before Billy was dropped off by his sitter, Becca.

The office knew about Charleston, they were the government after all. That didn't seem to faze them much other than making sure Cole didn't use Department of Justice resources to investigate his childhood kidnapping. An employment contract was signed with a specific provision that he would be terminated on the spot if he ever tried.

He didn't blame them. Their suspicions were legitimate. Cole wanted to know who The Taker was, he needed to know. This news fed that hunger. One way or another, he was going to find his kidnapper and make him answer for it all. *The kidnapping. His mother. Poinsett. Jackie.*

FUTILE

CHAPTER 28

COLE SLIPPED INTO the house late Saturday morning and dropped the grocery bags next to the door. Billy was still at a birthday party for one of the kids on his soccer team and wouldn't be home for a couple of hours. After grabbing an Odwalla from the fridge, Cole ran up the steps and into his home office.

There was a new file uploaded into DropBox from Daniel Page, Cole's high school friend. Cole had been asking for help since last May when Jackie died, but Daniel had refused. He, like everyone else, had told Cole to move on, that it was over and that 'It is best to leave him alone. *Leave The Taker alone?* What kind of idea was that? He didn't leave Cole and his mother alone. His daughter didn't leave him alone. Why should he be left alone?

But, Daniel relented and agreed to work his connections in D.C. to locate The Taker only after the news got wind of the graveyard murder. The FBI had a leak again; and the leak was saying it was The Taker killing again. Since then, Cole chased rabbits down holes like a weasel – ravenous and vengeful. No one knew but Daniel. They wouldn't agree, but it was Cole's way of coping with the events of Charleston. He had to know… had to stop this once and for all.

The FBI had horribly failed Cole and he wasn't willing to take that chance again. Until the call with Leas a month earlier, he hadn't heard a word. Even now, with two new murders, Leas and the FBI refused to say anything to him other than that they were looking into it. *Looking into it.*

COLE'S POCKET VIBRATED. *Shit.* "Hey Mom, what's up?"

Her voice was panicked again. "Cole, it's all over the news, still. They say that someone is copying that lady, that Poinsett lady and that its related to your case. I just don't know Cole. Are the police giving you any insight into what the news is talking about?"

"No, the FBI isn't really giving me much. They say the news is just guessing at it this time." Ava had been frail since Jackie's death and this development had just made it worse.

"I'm just so very worried, Cole. I think Billy should come back early. Your father and I will pay to move up the flight."

"Mom, please stop. Billy is okay. I will not let anything happen to him."

"I know, I know… but Jackie… Jackie would have wanted this. He doesn't need to be in danger."

Cole pulled back from the phone for a second to compose himself but it didn't help. "What? Are you saying I'm a bad parent or something? If he is in danger I wouldn't take care of it?"

He could hear Ava crying. "I just don't, I mean, we

love you, but... I just don't know what Jackie was thinking in naming you guardian."

Cole caught himself from screaming at her. "What are you saying? That I can't take care of my own nephew? Ava, Jackie chose me to take care of her son and that is what I plan to do. Now, I need to go. I'll talk to you later." Cole slammed the cell phone onto the desk and closed his eyes to calm himself. He had only called his mother Ava a handful of times in his life and they all related to him losing his temper. Visualizing his mental wall, he pushed it up until calm came over him again. He didn't have the luxury of a temper anymore.

SETTING ASIDE HIS conversation with Ava, Cole returned to his lap-top and double clicked on the file delivered to his DropBox; images of the graveyard crime scene file had been delivered. *Damn, Daniel and his source are good.* Cole had seen the Atlanta PD report, but the FBI's file was being tightly guarded. For now, these photos would have to do. The first images were of knots and rope. The rope was common yellow poly found at any Home Depot or Lowe's home improvement store. Several photographed knots showed the rope was new, not dirty. Cole opened up a browser, typed "knot types" into Google and scrolled through till he found an image of a Boy Scouts of America knot tying guide. Studying each one he learned that most of the knots used were called, "two half hitches." They appeared sloppy... rushed. The one holding the body erect from a higher branch was called a "larks head." It was tied perfectly, with care. *Why the difference?*

Cole thought for several minutes with no answer. *Rabbit. Hole.*

THE LACK OF relevance frustrated him. He moved on to looking at the overall scene, studying all the pictures, looking at them from every angle, every view. He had visited the graveyard only once during a law firm summer associate event, but the images were still vivid and workable. Closing his eyes he imagined crime scene images and then pushed then out into his mental space until they were superimposed over his own tour images. He walked the scene, trying to decipher the changes between his visit and the crime scene. The comparison was made difficult by the change in seasons, summer versus fall, and time between the two sets. Things had grown, decayed, broken in the time since he last visited the graveyard. He knew a tornado had taken down trees, too. All this made the comparison impossible.

Stepping forward in his mind to the scene, he saw the body hanging there nude, spread out, in a clearly posed position. *But why this pose?* Standing there for a moment, something else caught his eye. He printed out the pictures and rushed out of the house to pick up Billy. The murders had a meaning.

CHAPTER 29

I T WAS ALMOST five by the time Cole finished his research and rushed over to the birthday party to pick up Billy. Cole was still thinking about the photos he had just seen. Too many pieces were still missing and it drove him crazy. He parked the car and walked through the host's backyard gate.

"Hey, Gwen. Sorry I'm late. Totally lost track of time."

The red head waved a consoling hand. "Not at all. There are still tons of kids here. I think he's over here." Gwen walked around a large bush with Cole following. "Billy, your uncle is here to pick you up."

Billy ran over from playing with several other children at the birthday party. "Awe. I'm not ready to go. We are playing tag."

"Sorry, buddy, but we need to get home. Tomorrow is a school day and I have some work to do on top of feeding you. So, gather your things so we can leave."

"No!" Billy ran off toward the other children.

Cole looked at Mrs. Simms. She shrugged with the obvious appreciation of what was about to happen. Cole walked over and kneeled next to Billy who was playing with one of the girls. "Billy, you have been here all day and had a good time. Let's not spoil it with bad behavior. I asked you to get ready to go. Please do that."

"No! I don't want to go." Billy ran off toward another child.

Cole inhaled deeply. He hated personal conflict and did not like having it with a four-year old. Cole approached Billy and grabbed his arm, only to have Billy yank it away. "Billy! That's enough. We are going home now. Please say goodbye to your friends and tell Mrs. Simms thank you for inviting you."

"No! You aren't my dad. You can't tell me what to do."

Cole inhaled again and then wrapped his arm around Billy by the waist, Billy kicking and screaming as he was lifted and headed to the car. Keeping his calm, he thanked Mrs. Simms as he passed by.

"Of course, Cole. Look, he's been playing like crazy all day, jazzed on sugar and cake. He's just tired, that's all. Lord knows my three have had their moments."

Cole smiled back at her and proceeded to the car. Billy continued to fight with Cole as he tried to get him locked into the child seat. "I hate you. I want NaNa. I hate you. I HATE YOU!" Then the tears came. Lines of dirt formed on Billy's face from the tears' path. Cole tried to wipe them with the tail of his t-shirt, but Billy pushed him away. Stepping back to watch his nephew cry, Cole caught his breath. Perhaps Ava was right. Perhaps he wasn't prepared to be a parent.

CHAPTER 30

STANDING BEFORE A small group of Atlanta PD officers, Meadows and Leas looked out of place in their navy blazers. The chief was a large man that barely fit in his black uniform. "Quiet down, y'all. Let's get this thing started. Let's let these fellas talk so we can all get out of here and find this guy." The three men and woman before him sat down in their plastic chairs. The chrome feet scraped across the linoleum floor. "Okay guys. All yours."

"Thank you, Chief Williams. You've all read the report we prepared and handed out yesterday so you know a little about what the background is on the recent murders in the state: Macon, Athens and Atlanta. We think it's bigger than that. Or, at least there are some signs to suggest that the recent events are linked to some old crimes throughout the country back in the eighties." Leas paused and looked over at Meadows who was holding a large banker's box.

"You've got the memo on those, too. As you can see, there were several kidnappings and killings back then that involved the kids being kidnapped, their parents murdered. The kids were all found alive but with brands. Small, no larger than a watch-face and a 'P' in the middle.

No one really had a clue why or what they meant. We still don't know, honestly." Meadows continued to stare at the gathering as Leas spoke. "Anyway, as you read in the memo, the kidnapping cases converged last May down in Charleston. A woman, Beth Winters, went after them under some delusion that her father was the original kidnapper and killing them was the only way to draw him out. She killed three, perhaps four, before being stopped in Charleston while trying to go after the Mouzon boy discussed in the memo."

Meadows stepped in. "After the Winters woman was killed we discovered she had been using her mother's old home down in Clyo, Georgia as a kind of base. This box contains the materials we found in the home." He lifted the cardboard top off the box and placed it to the side before pulling out a stack of papers. Holding them up in the air he continued. "She was doing research on a guy, Laurence Poinsett. Seems she linked him to the murders and kidnapping. She also thought he was her dad, but that's pretty hard to confirm since we have little to no record of the guy other than he was an electrician in the Charleston area around the time of the Mouzon kidnapping. He disappears after that. All these papers here don't really help on that end. She seems to have hit the same roadblock we did as to who the guy is." He laid the papers down on the table and then dug back into the box.

"Where she did succeed in her research was in linking up some unsolved murders. Unfortunately, she took her impressions to the grave." Meadows looked over to Leas judgmentally. Leas looked back at him with indifference. Meadows had already honored him with his Monday morning quarterbacking opinion that Winters could have been taken without killing her. Leas, of course, disagreed that the situation inside the old fort on Sullivan's Island could have been diffused without Winter's dying. She was about to succeed in killing Mouzon. Taking the shot was the only option. Leas turned away from Meadows' judging look as the book was being pulled out of the box.

"So, what we have left is this." Meadows struggled as the two-inch thick, large book was lifted into the air. A watercolor of a white marsh bird adorned the cover.

"Audubon? What the hell kinda shit is this?" One of the officers shouted out.

"Freedman, shut up and listen to these guys, okay?" The Chief chastised the interruption.

Meadows cracked open the book and stood it up to stand on its base, the cover facing his audience. "Officer, good question. That's where you come in." He floated his hand over the book. "We don't know the significance of this book, yet." He withdrew the final content of the box, a slip of paper in a plastic evidence bag. "This slip of paper was tucked into this book. There are two words, 'Franklin Tree.' The guys indicate it's a type of flowering bush but how it helps us, that part just isn't clear. If could be totally unrelated since Winters had a background in botany, specifically plant poisons. We just aren't sure at this time."

"What makes you think that has anything to do with the recent murders here?" The young female investigator leaned in as she waited for an answer. Leas admired her curves and deep chocolate skin as Meadows responded.

"Because, there is also a date next to the words. The date matches the date of the Macon murder. She was obsessive over finding the man called The Taker, the kidnapper and possibly her father. Somehow, she was linking that man to the recent murders. She had found him here in Georgia."

CHAPTER 31

"EXCUSE ME SIR, you wouldn't happen to know where I can find this crazy handsome guy, about six, six-two, brown hair and amazing green eyes, would you?" Cole smiled as the man turned and extended his arms and wrapped them around Cole's body. He felt a slight nuzzle at his neck as the man dug in for a tight embrace. Cole dropped the handle of his roller-bag and returned the embrace. "Hey sexy. I missed you, too!"

It had been over a month since Cole had last seen Cash in Denver.

Cash pulled loose and smiled. "I thought you would never get here. My flight landed an hour ago. Then I saw yours was delayed. So I grabbed a beer and started grading some papers."

"Awe, I know. I'm sorry. I guess there was a storm somewhere that delayed my flight from getting into Denver and thus, delaying take-off. But, I'm here now. That's all that matters, right?"

Cash gave a sideways smile and said, "I guess. I'm more disappointed that I had to stop drinking to come meet you."

Cole elbowed him as he grabbed his bag and began

walking towards the escalator to the airport train. "Well… don't let me stop you mister. I'll be dropping off my luggage at Pam and Lance's." Cole stuck his tongue out as he continued to walk. "Ann is joining us for dinner tonight. Can't wait for you to meet all of them."

Cash picked up his pace to join Cole, "I guess I can meet your friends. I mean… if they have figured out how to deal with you than I need to get some insight."

Letting out a loud laugh, Cole looked over. "Deal with me? Oh really? I see how you are. As soon as you get around my friends you're going to join forces to give me shit. Okay. Just remember… what's good for the goose is good for the gander. I shall spare no one."

THEIR LUGGAGE COLLECTED, Cash leaned into Cole as they stood on the monorail from the airport to the rental car facility. "That airport is huge." Cash was looking out one of the windows behind them.

"Well, it is the busiest airport in the world. And, they want to keep it that way even if it means just adding to that thing like Lego's."

"Why not just build another one? I mean most large cities have two."

Cole laughed, "Oh, believe me the State has tried, but Fulton County and Atlanta have killed any attempt to share their profits from this place with another County. The State purchased property in the north-west corner of Atlanta, up in Paulding County, just for a new airport. But, when it became a good time to build, Atlanta burned down that idea faster than Sherman burning Atlanta. So they just keep adding to this monster."

"Well, it appears to be running pretty smoothly."

Cole shook his head in agreement. His thoughts had drifted to Billy at Maggie's. Since Billy had become part of Cole's day-to-day life he couldn't imagine a moment without him. They were both survivors of a horrible night that was too slowly fading. They became tethered together in an instant and Cole missed his presence.

"Uhm, did I lose you?" Cash had his head half-cocked looking to see if Cole was paying attention.

Blinking a few times to refocus, Cole responded. "Yeah, I'm here. Sorry. Was just thinking about Billy. I hope he has a blast at Maggie's. Remind me to grab something for her and Harris before I head back."

CHAPTER 32

"OH MY GOD! You're here!" A five-six, Asian woman bounded out of the front door before Cole and Cash could even get up the steps of Pam and Lance Hemmer's brick Buckhead townhome. "Hey baby! I've missed you. And... this must be Cash." Pam turned back to Cole as he was walking into the home. "Damn, boy he's hot. But, you..." Her finger ran up and down in the air. Cole looked down at his outfit.

"What? No like?" Cole looked over to Cash for support but he offered no help beyond a grin.

She pulled at the base of his brown and blue striped tank-top. "Horizontal? No, gurl. That ain't cute." His jaw dropped before she raced in for a hug.

"Gurl, you know I'm just foolin'."

He shook her joke off. "Pam, Cash. Cash, Pam. Where's your man? Still at work?"

"Ugh, you know it. That damn place is killing him." Pam looked back and forth to the two men and flared her palms in exacerbation. "I mean, really? Why the hell do they need to work him so hard? It isn't like the patients are going anywhere. They are in fucking comas."

Cole shook his head in humorous shock at Pam's

comments. Lance was a nurse at Grady Hospital's ICU and worked mostly with the comatose patients.

"Damn woman, have a heart." Cole smiled as he playfully chastised her.

"Actually, I think she has a point. They aren't going anywhere." Cash jumped in.

Wrapping her arms around his high neck, Pam dangled as she added. "Oh, I like this one Cole. He's a keeper. I can see he doesn't take any of your shit." She pulled back from Cash and pointed her finger at Cole. "If that one gives you any shit, just let me know Cash. I'll remind him of all the dirt I have on his ass. Now... let's get y'all settled in and get you a glass of alcohol in those hands. We have a few hours before we are meeting Ann and some secret man at Eclipse de Luna, plenty of time to catch-up."

"Pam, have you ever been to Colorado?" Cash was trying to hold the conversation.

Looking at Cole first as if to see if he knew, "Yeah, it was a long time ago... when I was like a little girl. My grandparents were taken from L.A. and held at the Granada Japanese encampment during the Second World War. What was it called? Camp Amache. He said they were pretty lucky that they ended up at that camp versus the others. Some of the stories from the other camps are horrible. But, according to him, Amache had Japanese as police and a football team that was all Japanese. They even had a Japanese Boy Scouts troop. So, before my granddad died he wanted us to see the place. Now, it is nothing but prairie and cactus but for a single building from what I recall. Talk about a grand tour of the West. *Want wahh.* Boring." Pam's sound effects made Cash laugh. "Okay, go settle in while I bust out some wine."

"SO, I MET this one when he volunteered for some charity event hosted at Fernbank. I'm head of special events for the museum and this boy was riding my ass like he owned it the entire night. Leave it to the queens to demand perfection." Pam had started spilling the beans on Cole's prior life in Atlanta to Cash and he was eating it up. Every few minutes he would look across the L-shaped couch to Cole sitting on the other side of Pam and he would just give a slight grin. "Anyway, I knew as soon as he started commenting on one of the guest's outfits that we were going to be besties."

Pam turned back to Cole. "Do you remember that hooker? Wearing a v-neck that dropped to his navel... child, pleeeeease. It's a party at a natural history museum, not your twink social."

"Uh are you talking about Finn or a guest? Cuz..." Cole tried get in a few words, but Pam kept talking with no room for interruption. "Oh my god, Finn." Pam's eyes got big as she slammed her hand down on the couch. "It could have been him. I had to yell at that boy the other day for his outfit. Gurl, this isn't 'To Catch a Gay.' There will be no cookies served here. Pants and button-up, please. Anyway, that was what? Eight years ago? And, I can't tell you how much I love this boy. He's been through some tough times and yet he always comes out better. I thought Jeremy's death would be the end of...." Pam caught herself venturing into sensitive territory. Looking back at Cole, she changed the subject. "But, enough about that.... Cole has told me about Charleston, so I know that much. But... what are your intentions with my boy?"

Cole's eyes widened in disbelief that Pam just asked

that. She was forward, direct and he loved that about her. But, putting Cash on the spot wasn't what he had planned for this trip. Cole looked over to Cash who looked back in a look that said one thing, *Help*!

Then a loud squeal of a laugh came out, "I'm just messin' with you. Damn boy. Relax!" Pam slapped Cash's folded knee that had been resting on the couch. "You clearly haven't had enough wine. More white or are we ready to move on to the reds?"

Cash exhaled in relief. "Uhm, I'm enjoying the white for now. What is it?" Cole moved across the couch to nestle against Cash in an effort to apologize for the awkward moment, as Pam responded.

"It's a sauv-blanc from our trip to Sonoma this past summer. We ordered a couple of cases of stuff and they just got delivered two weeks ago. So I'm excited to try those too."

"Oh, well if you're busting out the good stuff, fill'er up woman!" Cole raised his glass as Pam returned with a newly opened bottle.

"I'll take more, too. But first, can you direct me to your restroom?"

Pam pointed Cash in the right direction and sat back into the couch next to Cole, watching Cash walk away. When she heard a distant door click closed, she leaned in. "Okay, spill it. What's the scoop? That man, by the way, is fucking hot. If you aren't hitting that I will. And, I have a husband."

Cole shook his head. "You may have some hurdles to cross to get in those pants. Then again, I've seen you single. It isn't pretty to watch a hyena eat its prey."

Pam elbowed him in the ribs. "Ouch woman, that's bone there."

"Gurl, spill it. Have you been touching his bone?"

Cole's eyes widened, "Woman! You know I don't talk about that! What happens in my sex den is for me and only me to know."

"Ugh, you are no fun. Help a married woman out. Give me something to aspire for… Okay, just wink twice if you have done it." Pam rattled her feet up and down on the coffee table in excitement to Cole's response. "Oh my god. Was it hot?!" Again, her feet bounced in excitement until Cash's glass of wine started to tip off the table. Pam rushed in and grabbed it just as Cash walked back into the room.

"Did I miss something?"

Pam and Cole grinned large, guilty smiles. Cole shook his head as Pam added, "Nope. Just catching up." She scooted across the couch to make room for Cash to sit between them. He looked back and forth between the two as he sat, knowing that whatever they were talking about involved him, likely naked.

CHAPTER 33

ECLIPSE DE LUNA was packed as usual. The Spanish tapas restaurant was flat and expansive. Seated in one of the side rooms, Pam asked, "Cash, I don't recall... Did you get a chance to meet Ann in Charleston?" Cash looked back to Cole seated beside him as if to seek an answer, but Cole was talking to Lance across the table. "Uhm, I think she was already back here by the time Cole and I met. He mentioned her, but we actually haven't met, yet."

"Well, speak of the devil...." Pam looked up behind Cash and Cole to where Ann was standing. Cole looked around and immediately stood up to give the blonde woman behind him a hug.

"Woman, I have missed you! Not that we don't talk all the time, but you know what I mean."

"Hell yeah I do. It isn't like there is anyone else like me in this world." Ann turned to a man standing behind her. "Cole, Pam... this is Enrique." The tanned man stepped forward and waved "Hi" to the table. Cole extended his hand to welcome the guy who had the look of intimidation on his face that often occurs when first meeting your date's friends.

"Well if we are introducing people, this is Cash. Cash, Ann." He stood up and extended his hand. She pushed it down and gave him a welcoming hug as though she had known him forever. "I have heard so very much about you."

Cash responded to Ann. "I hope all good."

"Oh, I don't think Cole knows how to speak bad about someone. All these years of hanging around Pam and I, you would think that skill would have worn off on him. But, he has been a total disappointment in that area. We keep him around nonetheless to balance out our sins. Right, Pam?"

"Hell yeah! Someone has to be the light to our darkness. Yin and yang, baby!" From the slight slurring of words Cole could tell the caipirinha Pam raised in salute to Ann was kicking in after the firm base of wine from earlier. Lance leaned over to Pam and whispered what must have been a "slow down babe" based upon her repulsion to the unheard comment. "Have a seat next to me! What do you do Enrique?" Pam patted the seat of the chair next to her and waved the man over. Ann laughed and pushed her date past her so that she could sit next to Cole.

Whispering into Cole's ear, Ann asked, "So, you look good. Are you doing okay, babe? I miss you."

Cole whispered in kind as he watched Pam interrogating Enrique. "I'm good. Promise. You know, every day is a new day. Billy keeps me so occupied with his needs, caring for him, that I forget to feel sorry for myself. So, that's good, right?"

Ann leaned in closer. "Awe, how is lil'Billy. I miss that bugger. Is he growing? Damn, you're a parent. That clearly isn't cramping your style. That man is smokin'. Lord. He gives me the vay-purs!" Ann added a heavy southern accent to the word vapors to emphasis her mimicking of the old term. She cut her eyes to Cash and then back.

Cole let out a solitary laugh. "Uhmm, he gives me the vay-purs, too." Cole looked around to see Cash looking at him from the corner of his eyes. A small spark of energy passed across Cole's body. He was desired and it felt good. He loved those moments of silent attraction. He was drawn to Cash, pulled toward him like a stretched rubber-band pulled forcefully, ready to snap. The feeling felt warm and homey but invigorating. He craved Cash alone in those moments.

Cash rested a hand on Cole's right thigh underneath the table and Cole grabbed it and squeezed tight. He could feel Cash circling a thumb across the back of his hand telling him he was there, beside him.

PUSHING THROUGH THE bar crowd on their way to the restroom, Ann grabbed Cole's hand. "So, give me the scoop. Is the sex hot?"

Cole rolled his eyes. "You women! It's all about sex for you, isn't it? I should be asking you about your Latin lover. How is Enrique in the sack?"

She brushed her long blonde hair to the side. "Oh my god, it's crazy. He does this thing...."

Cole rushed to cover his ears. "Ahhh. Stop! I was kidding. I don't want to hear that." Cole paused for a second. "Okay... perhaps I do. But, not here... in the bar. Yikes." Cole looked around. "Just tell me this. Is it something I need to figure out how to do or get done to me?"

Ann shook her head up and down dramatically. "Yes!!"

Cole smiled at her. "You never change; and I love it. Crazy as hell."

Wrapping her arm around Cole's as if to snuggle, she asked, "So, is everything okay? Seriously, you can tell me. Who's ass do I need to kick. I still feel bad that I wasn't there to help. Cole, I know you've heard it from me a thousand, billion times, but, I am sorry about Jackie. She was one kick ass lady. I know you miss her. How is Billy doing with it all?"

Typical of Ann, she sowed too many questions and statements together to be answered in a single response. So, Cole took them apart.

"Billy is actually doing amazing. He's a tough kid. And, me? I'm doing okay. It's not my first rough time, you know that. We are healing. Thank you for asking."

"Did they ever find the crazy dad of that Poinsett woman? I mean, is that shit out there somewhere, too?" A guy passed by and stared down Ann's deeply cut black top. She followed his eyes until they met. "Yes, they are real. No, you may not touch." She turned back to Cole.

He laughed and then worked to respond without being too serious. "They've totally cut me out of the loop. It's like I was useful while Poinsett was after me, but now... well, they have no use for me. So, I have no clue. I know they went through all her research and stuff at that place they found, her mom's old place near Savannah. From the news reports it was some dump but for a room inside that had photos of me and the others plastered everywhere. I want to know more, Ann. I need to know more." Cole cut himself off at hearing himself sounding almost desperate.

He withheld the truth, that he did know more. Since May he had done his own research on what he had learned about Poinsett and her father, The Taker. He wasn't about to tell Ann or anyone else that he had started his own crusade to discovery his past... the truth. They would all complain, say he was risking his life. He could hear their responses, "Let the cops do it." But, he couldn't. The knowledge of his past had been delivered like an anvil dropping from the sky, heavy and sudden. His need to discover the entire truth and find his mother's killer came with the same weight and speed.

He had never been a patient person and couldn't think of any reason to be patient now. If The Taker was still out there... still alive, he needed to be found now before the answers were lost. Cole remembered his promise to Cash back in Denver. He had to be careful. The idea of luring a killer out of hiding and subjecting his family to another threat was unacceptable. So, his investigation consisted purely of a paper chase for now. He didn't know for how long he could resist the urge to actually chase his killer. One way or another, The Taker would be found.

CHAPTER 34

AGENT LEAS HAD discovered the young female officer's name just moments before she was naked in his bed. Jasmine was her name. Sitting up against the hotel bed's headboard he looked over to her bare buttocks laying next to him. He took another drag of his Marlboro and then twisted it out into a half soda can. "Baby, you've got to get up. It's past midnight and I have an early morning."

The woman turned and spoke in a groggy voice. "Yeah, I've got to get home. The husband thinks I'm pulling a late shift. How long are you in town?"

Leas kept staring at the woman's body. "Uhm, yeah... well, I'm here for as long as it takes. If there isn't any development in a week or so, we will probably head back up to D.C. until something new develops. But, that's unlikely. I may be left down here while my partner follows a few leads elsewhere that we are working on." Leas paused at the word "partner." He hated that he had a partner, especially Meadows that seemed to judge everything Leas was and how he worked-up a file.

Leas crawled out of bed and walked across the room to a small dresser with a mirror over it. He looked at his nude body and then noticed Jasmine inspecting him from behind. He turned. "You like what you see?" His face remained unemotional.

She grinned. "Like I told you last night, you may be old, but you are looking damn fine."

Leas smiled and walked to the end of the bed. "Yeah?"

"Yeah."

He proceeded to crawl up the bed and enjoy Jasmine for another hour. Sleep was overrated.

Chapter 35

COLE COULDN'T DECIPHER if he was awake or dreaming when he first opened his eyes. Cash's arms were wrapped tightly around him. Cole exhaled. The dream had woke him in the middle of the night before he was able to capture several more hours of sleep without interruption.

Turning his head he could see Cash's eyes were still closed, his mouth slightly ajar. Cole looked down the body behind him and replayed the images of the night. That body lit by a distant street lamp outside the window, moving through the sheets with intention. A ripple of hormones and heat ricocheted across Cole's body as he thought about Cash naked. Grinning, he lifted his head to sit up in the bed while trying to avoid waking Cash. Slowly he maneuvered into place. Cash rustled slightly until he readjusted, resting his head on Cole's lap. Cole noticed a small, moist spot on Cash's pillow and laughed to himself quietly. *The boy drools.* Looking down the man's firm body again, he saw the black boxer-briefs torn off in the night had returned. Cole rubbed the bare back lying beside him.

Reaching over to the nightstand, Cole grabbed his

iPhone and saw it was just after 8am, 6am his time. Four texts from various people had come in the night and early morning, three of them looking to see what the plan was for the weekend in Atlanta. The fourth was just a phone number – no name was attached to the contact. The message, "Welcome to Atlanta." Cole had no clue who it could be from. A "770" number meant it was from Georgia, so he determined it was someone who got a new number and failed to note they never advised Cole of the change. He typed in "thx – who is this" to figure out the sender.

With no immediate response, Cole focused on the rest of the texts, all from the same group inquiring as to lunch plans. The Atlanta Pride Aquarium Party was tonight, so most of his friends were doing half-days at work to prepare. "Joe's on Juniper? – 1?"

A rush of texts responded, with a "No." Clearly that was no longer the place to go for lunch in Midtown, Atlanta. Ultimately, the group settled on Henry's just down the block from Piedmont Park. The new building had been a Thai restaurant until the past year and it had the requisite patio, so Cole was more than willing to see what it looked like now. Moreover, it was convenient with Cash and he moving to the Loews Hotel for the remainder of their stay.

PLANS MADE, COLE returned his attention to the man in his bed. It felt natural now. There is no shock, no pause... no shame. It had been six years since he came out, accepting who he was. Even with the loss of his sister, the loss of Jeremy, he could honestly say he had never been happier with who he was. For the first time he was proud of himself, he had had the courage to reveal to the world and the energy from that decision propelled him through all the rough times of the past few years.

When critics used the same argument, "It's a choice," he wanted to stand up and surprisingly agree. It was a choice. Not about whom one is attracted to, but rather, a choice to be happy. It had taken almost two-thirds of Cole's life to choose happiness, but he had gathered the courage and done it.

It didn't mean the choice to be happy was comfortable initially. It was years before kissing a man, waking next to a man came without residual shame seeping in here and there.

But now, with Cash laying next to him it was gone. Happiness over self-acceptance filled the void of where shame once resided. Cole took a deep breath to remind himself that he was actually there, next to a beautiful man that cared for him.

Cash finally rolled open his eyes slowly and stretched like a waking cat, legs and arms in all directions. "Uhm, well... good morning, beautiful. You're up early for being hours behind." His aquamarine eyes glowed in the morning light. Cole swept away a tuft of hair covering them for a better look. "Did you sleep well?"

Cole smiled, "Perfectly. I was next to you."

Cash returned the smile as he rolled to his back as he rubbed the sleep out of his eyes with his knuckles. His bare chest was finally revealed which caught Cole's eyes for a few seconds. Cole shook off the playful images flicking through in his head before he continued. "The boys are already texting. Finn is excited to meet you." Cole smiled a large Cheshire Cat smile. Finn was an old friend that was notorious for flirting with everyone's boyfriend. He had never dared to try on Cole's dates out of respect and it was all show. He had a hard rule, don't sleep with another's man or else you can't complain when you are slept around on. Of course, since Finn never dated, only slept around, he really never had to try out that rule. But, as he said, "A boy's got's to have morals" even if he did sleep with half the guys in town, gay or straight.

Cash's rolling over in the other direction, it was obvious he remembered Cole's warning about Finn and his flirtatious ways. With his face half buried in a pillow, he responded. "So help me, if I survive this gay Disney weekend I will be a happy man."

Cole rubbed the man's back to comfort him. "Awe, it won't be that bad. You're a country mouse in the big city, that's all. I promise I'll be there to take care of you."

CHAPTER 36

WALKING DOWN TENTH Avenue, Cole felt at home in the city he had left almost two years earlier. Things had changed, but like the South overall, the city clung to its old ways like a Bible. As they stepped onto Henry's front patio, Cole pointed out the red brick Margret Mitchell house with its white Tudor trim a block away that stood out amongst modern forest of glass pane towers. Cole wondered the view seen from Apartment 1 back in the early 30's when the author wrote "Gone With the Wind" at a small diner that now overlooked a parking lot.

"There you are! Oh my god, you look all rugged and stuff. That cow town seems to be growing on you, Cole." Finn Lasiter spoke in rapid succession, rattling out words like a machine gun. The pace of his words was emphasized by his twang acquired by some small town in Mississippi. Cole had met him when he first moved to Atlanta and Finn had proved his friendship more than once. He may me flighty and constantly on the hunt for a husband, but it was Finn that Cole called upon discovering Jeremy's body slouched in a tub. And, it was Finn that cared Cole back to health.

"Finn, Pam says hi and... that your shift at the museum starts at eleven tomorrow, so don't drink too much."

"Err, I love that woman, but she needs to back off. I was late one day... one day in the past five years." Finn looked around Cole to eye Cash. "And, hello there... Cash I presume. Damn. You look as good as your namesake. I bet you spend just as well, too." Finn gave a wink at Cole and then placed his thin arm around Cash's waist as he pushed him towards the corner table where two others waited. Approaching the black metal-topped table, Cole couldn't help but notice the cocktail glasses almost empty. He had apparently missed the memo that tank-tops were in order, each wish a different shade of pastel.

Cole stopped at the table and the pulled out one of the metal patio chairs. "Have y'all been here long? Looks like the party got started without us." Cole looked over to the pink tank-topped man closest to him. "Jordan, it's been forever. You're looking great." Cole smiled as the man stood to give him a hug.

"Cole Mouzon. Damn boy, it's been too long." Pulling back, he added with a wave of his hand, "And, yes... I do look great, don't I? I am the fabulous Jordan after all. Can't say the same for you... Did you gain weight or something? Honey, you need to drink your calories, not eat them."

Cole smiled as he noticed Cash pulling out a seat for him and then looked back to Jordan. "Yes, I'm sure it's hard to be Atlanta's Lady Chablis, but it seems to work for you. Still as ashy as ever."

Jordan recoiled in his chair. "Oh, I know you didn't. Throwing shade at one in the afternoon. At least let me get a drink or six in me to prepare myself."

Cole was sure Cash was taking this all in, wondering where in the hell the Cole he knew was switched with the queen now before him. Cole slipped a hand across to Cash's leg to remind him that he was still there.

"Now, that's the Cole I remember. Sharp wit and ready to tussle." The third man finally jumped into the ritualistic fray. "Cole, you look as good as ever. Don't let any of these bitches tell you otherwise." Mason smiled warmly.

The most mellow and 'normal' of the three, six-foot six Mason towered over the group and was the reason to the other two's madness when Cole was part of the circle. His perfectly unkempt curly brown hair accented the hazel in his eyes as he lingered a little too long in Cole's direction. There had never been anything between the two, but not from lack of Mason trying. Rather, Cole was dating Jeremy the majority of their friendship and once Jeremy died, Cole was in no position to date anyone, even Mason.

Looking over at Cash, it was obvious he'd noticed. A 'that wasn't cool' squeeze of Cash's hand was delivered under the table. Cole squeezed back to apologize. He had told Cash about the friendship dynamics to soften any blows, but actually seeing them obviously still stung.

"So you're like a teacher or professor or something, right?" Finn was speaking rapidly again as he interviewed Cash with obsession.

"Yeah, a professor of history at C of C… the College of Charleston. Been doing that for a while now."

"Oh my, I love Charleston… all 'Midnight in the Garden of Good and Evil' and stuff. So romantic."

Cole was quick to correct Finn. "What? That movie was in Savannah, not Charleston, boy! What kind of southerner are you. Think 'The Patriot,' 'North and South' and Rhett Butler." Cole swung his arm around to point at the Mitchell house, but the table looked puzzled as to why.

"Whatever, same thing, different swamp. Anyway, I bet you have to read a lot, huh?" Finn flashed a pained face.

Cash gave a slight laugh at the question before responding, "Yeah, you can say that. Most history usually is recorded in books or some other written format."

"Books? Books are boring." Jordan had decided to pipe in with his two-cents, throwing up a hand with attitude, as though to be counted. "I use mine for doorstops."

"That's because those tricks of yours are coming and going so fast that you don't have time for a door to be closed." Mason had swiped back at Jordan.

Jordan leaned into the table to make eye contact with Mason. "Don't be jealous. Not all of us suffer relationships like you do. What's his name? Damian? A little devil is what he is... all five-two of him. Honey, I have murses bigger than him." Mason held a stern look on his face refusing to respond to the personal attack. There was an awkward silence for a few seconds.

"Is that Cole? Oh my goodness it is!" A thin drag queen stood behind Cole and grabbed his shoulders. Cole turned and faced Bubba Dee. At fifty-five or so, she looked ageless other than her blonde 1950's styled wig and over applied make-up. His white, sleeveless summer dress hugged his hips.

Cole looked up with pleasant surprise. "Hey Bubba. Long time no see."

"Oh, darlin', it's you that disappeared. You moved to Alaska or something, no?"

Cole laughed, "No, just Denver. So, not too far."

Bubba pushed to Cole's side to get a better view. "Oh, well Denver seems to be treating you well. You know, I've always loved doing shows in Denver. What's that thing y'all do out there, Drag Nation? Always a good time."

"Well, let me know next time you are out there. I'll pack my dollar bills and come to Tracks to cheer you on. Those parties out there are insane. Plus, all those straight boys come out and party there, too. Boy, you know Bubba loves the straight boys."

The whole table broke out into laughter. "Oh, and they love them some Bubba, too."

"Okay, well next time I'm over there, you and me baby. But, don't let me take any more of your time with these queens." Bubba leaned in and kissed Cole's cheek. "Love ya, babe. Enjoy your visit."

Bubba Dee walked into the interior of the restaurant as Jordan said, "Is that Pacey?" He directed everyone's attention to a table directly behind Cole. Cole turned slowly not wanting to see who he suspected it to be. *Shit.*

TONTINE

CHAPTER 37

PACEY LOCKHEART WAS seated directly behind him chatting up another man. Pacey's pudgy, muscular thickness was exaggerated next to his boney guest. Cole hadn't seen him since perhaps once after Jeremy's funeral two years earlier and his emotions were still raw from what he knew about Pacey and Jeremy's relationship.

They had been friends before Cole came into the picture. He had told himself shortly before Jeremy's death that there were no clues to the extent of their 'friendship,' but that was a lie. There were clues. The parties, the clubs and random trips... any fool could have seen what was going on but Cole. He had accepted now that he chose to be blind, to see the truth for what it was. That came to an abrupt stop a week before Jeremy committed suicide.

Cole felt himself falling into a dark well of emotions as he looked at Pacey. The wall was there, but Cole let the emotions lap at him momentarily as the memory played out. It was one of the routine Sunday-Funday brunches... drunk brunches, as Cole called them. Everyone was seated at a long patio table at Wahoo! Grill with Jeremy's and Pacey's seats empty. Something told Cole that they were not at the buffet getting food and for once he had the courage to test his hunch.

Walking into the restaurant's converted home interior he didn't see either at the buffet as he pretended to head to the restroom. Cole felt deflated and guilty. Perhaps Jeremy had just joined Pacey for a smoke. Turning a handle opens more than just doors.

Images of everything were Cole's curse. Perhaps that is why he had chosen to be blind, to avoid an image being burned into his mind like chisel to stone. But, it happened. Jeremy was leaning over the top of the toilet, one nostril pressed. Pacey was behind him, clutching Jeremy's nude ass. A single tear escaped before the old wall went up, making Cole cold to the anger and sadness.

Perhaps he was a fool for what he did next. Any one of his friends would have raced in, attacked, made someone pay. But Cole didn't. He slowly closed the door and walked back to the table. Only Finn picked up on Cole's shift in mood. "Something didn't agree with me. Those damn eggs with goat cheese I guess." By the casualness of Jeremy's and Pacey's return to the table, neither had seen their intruder.

Though it would take a week for Cole to gather the strength to confront Jeremy about the drugs, about Pacey, it took only two more days for Jeremy to take his life. The guilt of those days still lingered in the corners of his mind, tearing at Cole as he looked at Pacey. Cole logically knew it wasn't his fault, but martyrs are rarely logical. Cole had been cold, void of emotion as he disclosed what he saw in the restaurant to Jeremy. Jeremy just kept saying, "I can't lose you," over and over again like a bad record. Cole ignored the proclamation as Jeremy confessed his sins in a last ditch effort to hold things together. There was

Pacey, but there were also others – all centered around partying with coke. Much like Jeremy, Cole's internal dialog was stuck, but his private torment was, "You did this. This is your fault."

"ANYWAY..." COLE HAD pushed up the fractured wall and turned. "How's Kenya doing, Jordan?"

Jordan pulled back from the table, "Why is it that you white folk think that just because I'm black I know every damn sister and brother in Atlanta?" Everyone sat still as they waited for the next sentence. He smiled. "And, she is fine, thank you very much. Saw her at Phipps last weekend. Of course, the topic of you-know-who came up. T.R.O.U.B.L.E. Phay best watch out."

"I heard they didn't invite her back for next year." Finn looked genuinely concerned.

"Yeah, you know how it goes. Same panties, different day. It's all for entertainment, right?"

"What's the plan for tonight? What time are y'all getting there? What are you wearing?" Cash decided to move the conversation to a different subject.

Finn responded first. "Jeans and this new pink v-neck is what I have. That... or, maybe a red one." Finn was known for wearing very low-cut v-necks on an almost daily basis. "I'm supposed to meet a boy there. Want to see?" Finn rushed a hand into his jeans pocket and withdrew his phone. "We met on Grindr. The boy is hot!"

The entire table leaned in to see. Finn pushed his phone out into the center of the circle and swiped through until the mango orange app with a black hockey mask at its center flashed across the screen. With tiles of half-naked torsos and faces loading, Cole noticed that most of them were starred as favorites. Finn tapped on one and it enlarged until the entire screen filled with a young six-pack and blue boxer-briefs.

"Damn! That boy needs to visit me!" Jordan grabbed the phone to read the profile like the back of a cereal box. "Twenty-six. Six-one. One eighty-five. Single. Jock." Jordan emphasized his words by flicking a finger in the air like he was checking off a mental list. "About: 'fun or dating.' Looking for: 'Chat, dates, friends, now.' Lord. He's on-line, just one mile away. Now, baby. Now!"

Handing the phone back to Finn, "What's his face look like? That'd be the question."

"Oh, he's hot!" Finn responded in a rush to seek approval. "Look."

An attractive blond with a faux-hawk was on the screen. "Damn boy. You better get that!" Cole chimed in to assure Finn that his tastes weren't off. "Lucky boy. So, we will see him and you tonight in some dank corner of the aquarium party?" A hopeless romantic, Finn was notorious for trying to find love. Cole had met one too many guys that Finn had fallen in love with during his European trips. He met them by a pool, they hit it off at some French club… then they came to visit for a week-end. All left…leaving Finn crushed. With Grindr, at least his efforts had been state-side over the past year or so.

"If I'm lucky!" Finn smiled at Cole's approval.

"I guess if you're lucky you can do the same with me." Cole looked over to Cash who was still clearly watching the show in amazement.

"Lucky? I think you will be the lucky one." A squeeze of the hand came to assure Cole that Cash was fine.

CHAPTER 38

H E HAD TOLD Cash that he was just running out to grab a gift for Maggie while Cash took a nap and he would join, after his errand. He hated deceiving Cash, but it was obvious that he didn't understand Cole's need to understand his past and the killer that had kidnapped him.

The gates to the cemetery were still open. Walking in he tried to play tourist, slowly making his way to the tree he had seen in the photos. The tree was old, very old with a silver trunk and distinctive vertical and linier wood-pecker lines from its years of being rid of bugs or sap. Standing at least forty feet tall, the tree looked cranky and tired.

Cole touched a spot where he believed the yellow rope had been tied around the trunk, dragging his hand across the flakey trunk as he walked the circumference of the tree. A small aluminum plant tag at the base of the tree identified it as *"Prunus serotina* – Black Cherry."

Looking up to a large, heavy branch, Cole imagined the body that once hung there. *The head was cocked.* Cole tried to determine in what direction, what angle the head was cocked to see if the direction pointed anywhere specific, but it was helpless. There was nothing to be seen. No clue. No anything. Whatever The Taker was trying to tell him or anyone else was lost since the murder.

What a waste of time. Ugh. Cole rolled his head around his shoulders in frustration. He looked back towards the gate and noticed that his weird behavior had garnered the attention of one the tourists. Raising a hand to say "hi," Cole turned and made a lap around half the cemetery before exiting.

HE SWUNG BY Green's on Ponce De Leon Avenue before heading back. Green's was fitting. The liquor store was in the same parking lot as "Murder" Kroger, a grocery store location that had a history of shootings and stabbings in the parking lot. Cole couldn't recall ever hearing of one while he lived in the city, but that was likely more because he didn't watch the news than the lack of bloodletting.

Armed with a bottle of local Wolf Creek wine for Maggie, he returned to the hotel where Cash laid in bed watching college football previews. Cole crawled onto the bed and wrapped an arm around Cash. He was safe.

CHAPTER 39

KENDRICK HAD BEEN in the home many times, but never this room. He didn't even know it existed until the day before when he saw the light shining under the heavy door as he walked around the basement. There had always been a stack of paint cans there, hiding what Kendrick suspected was where Smith planned out future killings. Kendrick wanted to know more, to understand Smith… and Mouzon.

He had seen the name in his mother's *Atlanta Journal-Constitution* two days earlier. The name Smith had in his journal. At first he thought it was a prior kill, but Googling the name on his phone indicated that Mouzon was a survivor. The article listed a woman, not Smith, as the attacker. *Why was Smith so interested in Mouzon?* Kendrick needed to know if he was planning a kill without him. He didn't appreciate Kendrick, thought he was a waste. Kendrick grew pissed at the thought.

So, after watching Smith leave for his usual Thursday errands, he popped the lock on the basement window and slipped in just for a peek. Sliding to the side the old pallet stacked with the half-filled paint cans, the door looked ominous. The large padlock was picked quickly, just as Smith had taught him. There was no handle, just a lip between frame and door. So, he forced his fingernails in and pulled the brown wood door back. It creaked at its hinges, causing Kendrick to pause and look back behind him to make sure no one heard... no one was coming. Certain he was alone, he yanked the door open with more force; he was in.

Feeling around in the dark, he found a junction box hammered onto a wooden stud. He flicked the switch. The room was maybe six feet deep and ten feet wide. A small upholstered chair sat at one end, with a wooden counter and under-shelves running the width of the room. Above the counter were Smith's photos of the killings they had done together. Paper clippings hung here and there. Red pen marks circled various faces and portions of the articles. There were also several watercolor paintings tacked to the studs here and there, all of birds. Kendrick had seen drawings like them before, in Smith's journal.

He had always selected his prey carefully, watching them, documenting their every movement. And, when they were taken down, he demanded their bodies be placed in very specific poses. Smith would direct as Kendrick moved and moved again each body part until it perfectly met the poses sketched by Smith in his journal. There was one clear rule: they had to be alive when the posing was complete. Smith told him that to capture them and document them at their best, life must still be pumping through their veins when he took the final picture of them. It was only after Smith took his picture that Kendrick was allowed to end them.

HE REFOCUSED TO look for where the journal could be located. He leaned down to look over the various dusty objects placed on the old shelves under the counter. Eyeing the last corner of the shelf, he noticed a wooden box, dustless and hidden behind several coffee cans filled with old nails. He pulled out the box, cautious to touch nothing else just in case his search was fruitless. Its small brass latch was flicked open and the top slowly turned up. *It was there.*

Kendrick carefully removed the journal, its cracked, black leather looked like aged skin under the buzzing florescent lights. He set it aside as he inspected several weathered Polaroids that had been placed at the bottom of the journal. They were all of children, each identified merely with a number. It was number seven that made him freeze. It was him, taken several years earlier on his mother's porch. He never recalled posing for the picture and its angle suggested it was taken from the street. Looking back at the others, he noticed the same – all were taken secretly.

Looking up at the wall, he noticed the same elusive angles in the surveillance pictures of Celia Leigh and the other two killings. Smith had selected him just as he had those on the wall. Kendrick shoved the photos into the journal and rushed out of the room without worrying about Smith discovering the intrusion. Apprentice or prey, he wasn't going to wait around to find out where he stood.

CHAPTER 40

THE JOURNAL WAS opened to a page filled with what appeared to be scribbles... some kind of code. The only word that was discernible was "Mouzon." It was the page Smith was working on when Kendrick first saw the journal.

"Hun, that looks like some kind of shorthand. No quite sure which kind though. Let's see if I can locate something to help you out." The old librarian pulled her reading glasses off and let them dangle on their beaded chain as she rushed to a metal shelf toward the back of the large room. Hushed whispers made Kendrick uncomfortable as he followed. Kendrick had betrayed Smith, stealing the journal and invading his personal trophy room. At any moment he expected Smith to rush in for the kill.

Kendrick had been stupid, he knew this. But, the old man had refused to recognize him as ready... just as skilled as him. Smith had taught him all he could and it was time for Kendrick to show the world that he was his own man, for them to fear him, not the old man that just barked orders.

"Ah, here we go. Shorthand. Hmm, there is Gregg, Shelton, Taylor and a few others. May I see your book again? Perhaps the style will stand out." The lady flipped open one of the books to a chart of various scripts and then compared it to the journal. "Well, I think you have your work cut out for you. They all look the same to me. Here, take this book and this other one that discusses a few of the differences between the styles." Kendrick looked at her with a helpless face. "Sorry, baby. You will have to do that work. I need to get back to the front desk. But, if you need anything else, just grab me."

KENDRICK WAS THREE hours into his research and all he had discovered was that the shorthand appeared to be Pitman or Gregg. From what he could gather, the series of squiggles and dots represented a phonetic spelling of words. Kendrick realized that because the symbols represented sounds, if he could find ones with the overall same structure he could locate their meaning by a process of elimination thereafter.

He flicked through a weather book and stumbled across one of the symbols on the journal's page. *Mother-wit: natural intelligence.* Kendrick noted a date under the chain of scribes. 7/25/13. The Old man had noted the Mouzon person's intelligence just two months ago. Kendrick remembered Smith's disappearance for several days in July, but had no clue as to where he went. The man had obviously gone to observe Mouzon. Pushing the pages of the dictionary back and forth he found another symbol. *Affiliate: to adopt a child.* Mouzon had adopted someone's child. Kendrick figured that the child was being seen as a weakness, a liability to be taken advantage of when Smith decided to hunt him.

The thought of taking down this person made

Kendrick's blood race with excitement. He craved the killing. He hated Smith's rules, his constant demand for poses. They were dramatic for sure, but the need to match them to some sketch was stupid to him. Just make them bloody and people will get the message. Smith was fascinated with perfection, limiting his impact on the viewer. Kendrick had tried to convince him to put more gore in the last killing but the old man refused. Kendrick was tired of his rules and was now untethered from their restrictions, free to show just how violent he could be when allowed to run the show.

Refocusing, a very ornate symbol stuck out at the end of the entry. Turning through the dictionary, he located several similar symbols. Only one stuck out as relevant. *Regicide: one who kills a king.*

Mouzon, a king? A king of what? Kendrick tumbled the thoughts through his head with the only answer being that Smith was saying that he was the grand prize. Now *his* perfect murder. Kendrick scraped the security tag off the back of the book and shoved it into his green army jacket. He would finish interpreting the journal later.

CHAPTER 41

C OLE HAD BEEN to The Georgia Aquarium too many times to count. The bulk of those visits came in the six months after Jeremy's suicide. It was Cole's escape from the torture of his guilt and sadness. He would sit in the dark stadium of the Ocean Voyager exhibit with its twenty foot tall, sixty foot wide bay window and watch the whale sharks and other massive fish swim throughout what was then the World's largest aquarium. Somewhere he read that watching fish caused a calming effect, even lowered blood pressure. But, all it did for Cole was make him cry.

He sympathized with the whale sharks, trapped in a nice, but small bowl after having the World's oceans as their home. Their circular movement around the tank reminded him of a stressed dog, circling and circling in a panic. They knew where they were, that they were helpless to escape their new captive world.

During his visits he reflected on his life, his bowl. Watching a manta ray glide by, his reality became clear as a child beat on the acrylic pane. The child startled the ray, woke him to his true reality, and for a brief moment it panicked and sped away. A minute or two later it was back, once again blind to what lay behind the glass.

Cole was the ray. Somewhere along the way to loving Jeremy he had lost sight of the world of love. Much like the fish ignoring their millions of visitors, he had tricked himself into going blind to what was actually going on around him… the drugs… the cheating. As hard as it was to accept, he had chosen to ignore. Acceptance of his own deception would make him the shark, circling in distress. It took months, but he finally gathered the strength to escape the bowl that he had placed himself in and moved to Denver where he now remained un-tethered.

"HEY, YOU OKAY?"

Cole turned to Cash who had tucked his arm around Cole's. "Yeah, I'm more than okay. Sorry, I was just thinking about how happy I am to be here with you."

Cash leaned in and kissed Cole's cheek. "Same here."

Cole felt a slight bump on his back and turned to see Finn with a large grin on his face. "Wow! That line is insane. Glad I did VIP. Of course they kept sending me to the wrong damn line." Finn's eyes looked around to the aquariums full of large silver fish swimming in a mass on either side of the large entrance. Flowing banners of lights shifted colors along the ceiling's edge.

Cole responded after taking in the view himself. "I see you went with the pink-V. Nice. Think its deep enough?" Cole placed his free hand on Finn's shoulder to calm his Chihuahua-esk energy.

"I know! Do you like? This is the one I mentioned… figured it would make the best impact."

"Oh, it will make an impact, alright. I pity the guy

you hunt down tonight." Cash seemed to have relaxed, joining in the faux-cattiness. Cole cut his eyes to Cash to make sure it was still the reserved, quiet man that he recalled. He smiled as Cash winked back at him.

"So... Is your boy here or what?"

"I don't know. He had my number, but he hasn't used it. And, I checked Grindr and he hasn't been on in a few hours. So, I have no clue." Finn flashed a frown before being distracted by a guy walking by. "Hmmm, did you see that? Hot!" Finn rushed off in pursuit, leaving Cole to shake his head at how easily Finn was distracted.

Walking into the main atrium, Cole was struck by the mass of people standing around. The large space was packed. At the center of the room was some sort of wall and trampoline entertainment where shirtless guys stepped off the wall and bounced out a few tricks before returning to the wall's top again. Large make-shift bars were placed at the room's edges with lines of men waiting for their watered-down open bar selection.

"Uhm, let's get to VIP. I'm not waiting in that line." Cole pulled on Cash's tucked arm, leading him up a set of stairs to a higher level that overlooked the atrium. They paused at the upper deck's railing to take in the mass of men and occasional women.

"You know PETA and Tim Gunn hate this event... say its cruel to the animals with all this loud beating music and crowd." Cole looked surprised that Cash knew anything about the event.

"Do tell, Mister Cash. I didn't know you were up on current affairs." Cole smiled as he nudged Cash to emphasize he was impressed.

"You know I'm not all boring. I do watch TV. Yes, even the Real Housewives."

"Well, look at that, I learn something new about you every day. Just when I thought I had you figured out."

"Ha. That is something I will never say about you. I can't figure you out no matter how hard I try."

Cole flashed concern on his face. "Is that a bad thing? I mean, I think I am trying to be open... to let you in." He pursed his lips at one corner as he awaited an answer.

Looking at him directly in the eyes, Cash spoke slowly. "Cole, it isn't a bad thing. It's just I find it hard to read you sometimes. I can't tell if you are being yourself or who you think I need you to be. I get it, I do. You are protective of yourself, your life. But, at some point you have to let me in." Cash smiled in an attempt to defuse any hurt he may have caused. "You definitely keep me on my toes, that's for sure. And, I like that." He leaned in for a kiss, but Cole turned away.

He had been hurt. The wall had gone up somewhere between 'not being yourself' and 'let me in.' Cash had been let in... *Hadn't he?* Cole felt safe around him and felt there was a new possibility for fulfilling love. But, apparently Cash wasn't being made to feel that way – he was feeling locked out. Cole's stomach churned at that thought. Was he doing it again? Locking out someone like he did Jeremy just before he overdosed? Cole's head spun for a few seconds before he envisioned all the emotions, all the discussions gathered into a ball and stored in a box.

Cole looked up at Cash who was feeling the sting of Cole turning away. Cole slid a hand to one side of Cash's neck. "I'm sorry if I have ever made you feel that way. Please know I am trying... trying to figure all of this out again. Know this though... I am trying because you are in my life and I don't ever want that to change. You make me try."

Cash pulled Cole in and gave him a tight hug as he nestled his face into Cole's neck. Whispering, he said, "That is all I needed to know."

They held each other for a few seconds longer before Cole broke the serious moment as usual. "Okay! Now for those drinks! How do you like your water? Splash of vodka or rum?"

"Oh, water is best with a vodka mist of course."

CHAPTER 42

DRINKS IN HAND, they walked back to the atrium floor to join Jordan and Mason who apparently had just arrived. "Where have you been?"

Jordan fiddled with his white button-down as he responded. "Oh, you know. Coca-Cola's pride part was tonight, too. So, Mason acted as my date for that." Cole looked over to Mason who mouthed, "Don't ask," making Cole have to turn away to avoid laughing. Jordan picked up on something. "What? Did you say something Mason? You know I could have taken anyone."

"No. No. I was just joking. You know I had a blast. Between the Ernest & Young and Coke folks, you would think the companies only recruited gays. It was a great event. Thank you again for taking me."

Jordan closed one eye to playfully inspect Mason. "I was about to say... You may be a fine white boy and all, but I can still beat you down."

"Oh I have no doubt."

Jordan turned to Cash. "Damn boy, you are looking nice, too. You Charleston boys do know how to spruce up a place. I'm liking that salmon color tattersall. Might have to get me one of those."

"Well, it came from Ben Silver if you want me to pick you one up."

Jordan pulled back for a better view. "No. I think I'd like to just take that one off of you right now. You wouldn't mind walking around shirtless, would you? Cause, I know none of these boys would mind." Jordan leaned in and brushed his hand over Cash's abs. "What you got? A six or eight pack under there?"

Cole pushed away Jordan's hand. "Uh, I would thank you very kindly if you would keep off my property." Cash looked at Cole with surprise as Jordan swept his neck to one side. "Well, then. If you are going to be all possessive and stuff like that...."

A younger guy with red hair walked by and eyed Jordan with interest, his neck rotating to keep him in view as long as possible as he passed. Jordan cocked his head around Cole to eye the man and let out, "Uhhhh. No. Honey, I make more than you weigh. Keep walking."

Cole shook his head and then rattled the ice in his now empty plastic cup. "You know what, I think I need another drink if I'm going to have to deal with you all night."

Cash reached over and took the cup, "I'll get that for you. Jordan, do you need a drink? We can finish discussing what I have under this shirt. Mason, want anything?"

"Oh, I had a few at the other event. I better pace myself since I drove."

With Cash and Jordan gone, Mason leaned to his side to get within earshot of Cole. "He seems like a good guy. You deserve that."

Cole smiled uncomfortably. Mason had always

wanted to be that 'good guy' for him. Cole didn't know how to respond other than, "Thank you." He tried to switched the topic. "And, you? Any potentials out there? That guy Jordan was riding your ass about at lunch?"

Mason laughed. "No. Not him. I had a great date the other night. In fact, he is supposed to be here somewhere." He looked around the room peering over all the shorter men. "Actually... I think I see him over there. I should... Well, I can wait."

Cole looked up to him still looking away. "What? You better go over there, mister. You know as well as I do that it isn't the sharks in those tanks you have to worry about tonight. Grab that man before he becomes someone's baby seal."

Mason smiled warmly down at Cole. "You are amazing. Always have been. I'll be back. Let me just let him know I'm here." Mason walked away and was swallowed by the crowd.

Cole looked around the room to more flowing light banners welcoming the crowd. , He had been out of Atlanta for only a year and a half, but looking back to the crowd he hardly recognized any faces. Several minutes passed with Cole standing alone before he decided to find Cash and Jordan. Looking around, he located Jordan next to one of the bars talking to a guy without Cash.

"Hey. Where did Cash go?"

Jordan looked around. "No clue. I stopped to talk to... Mike, is it? And, next thing I know he was gone. Think I saw him talking to someone over there." Cole rolled his eyes in disappointment. Like a parent leaving their child with a sitter, Cole felt Jordan had some obligation to watch out for Cash and make sure he didn't get lost... or worse. He walked off in the direction where Jordan had pointed, towards an old shrimp shack display. Halfway through the crowd he saw it.

Pacey was holding Cash's hand, whispering in his ear. Pacey cut his eyes and clearly noticed Cole looking on at their conversation. Moments went by with Cole standing still in the crowd just watching. With a cynical grin Pacey leaned in and grabbed Cash's neck.

Cole didn't know how long the kiss lasted; to him if felt like minutes, hours. All he knew is his face was wet with tears by the time he snapped out of the moment. By then, Cash had discovered Cole has seen it.

Cole walked over, hot with emotions. Pacey was glib and defiant as he said, "Oh. Hi Cole. Long time no see. I didn't know you were in town." Cole couldn't get words out before Cash interjected.

"Cole... I didn't... it wasn't what you think. He grabbed me."

Cole heard nothing but the ringing anger in his ears. He turned to Pacey. "You know, you are a piece of shit. Always know that. You take pride in trying to fuck with other's boyfriends. Is this some sort of game with you or what?" Cole pushed aside Cash who was still trying to grab his attention.

"Cole, sweetie... I get whatever I want. You should know that." A large smile crossed his face as he referred to Jeremy. A small crowd had started to develop around the three men. Finn appeared and tugged at Cole's arm. Pacey continued, "You know Cole... you truly are pathetic. You knew I was fucking him and you just let it happen. You are weak and you got everything you deserved. He always said I was the better lay. Why do you think he kept coming back for it? Just accept it. You can't compete with...."

Cole's response came so quick that not even he could remember how it happened. He remembered his fist making contact with Pacey's face. Pacey stumbling back, falling into the touching pool of sharks and rays played like a stop-motion film in his mind. But, the inertia building up to him cocking back and releasing his punch… he couldn't see or feel it. He was numb.

BREAKDOWN

CHAPTER 43

COLE RUSHED AWAY, leaving Finn to deal with Cash who tried to pursue. Finn pushed him back, telling him to give Cole space. Towards the far end of the atrium, he collided into someone's back while looking back at the large crowd behind him.

"What the fu…. Cole? Is that you?"

Cole couldn't speak. He just faked a pained smile as tears ran down his face. His body buzzed with adrenaline from the fight and he just wanted to escape.

"Are you okay? What happened? Shit. Come with me." Cole was rushed off into a dark tunnel in one of the exhibits.

"Cole. Please talk to me, what happened." With Cole still not speaking, Zander clasped his arms around Cole and held him tightly. A minute went by before Cole was able to push up the mental wall he desperately relied upon in such moments to avoid displays of emotion.

With a weak voice, he asked, "What are you doing here?"

Zander pulled back just enough to look at Cole's face. "Ha. He speaks. I came in town for Pride, to hang with friends. Now will you answer my questions? What happened?" Cole didn't respond. "Dude! You got a problem or something? Move on!" Cole looked behind him to see a young guy staring at them in the corner. Caught, he turned and walked away.

Cole rested his head on Zander's shoulder. "I really don't want to talk about it right now, if that is okay? I just want to get drunk."

"Well, then we need to go somewhere else cause there is no way to get drunk on these drinks. Where to?"

"I don't care, Zander. Just get me out of here, please. I just need out of here."

THE TEXTURED GOLD wallpaper of Aurum Lounge made Cole's head spin after his fifth shot of Cuervo. "Uhm, you might want to slow down there, half-pint." Zander had one hand on Cole's side, keeping him upright on the stool.

"'Pathetic.' That's what he called me. I'm not f-ing potetic." Cole's word slurred as his head swayed. "And... then... then... I decked that cock sucker. That wasn't 'pathetic.'"

Zander laughed, "Damn I wish I could have seen that. Mr. prim and proper knocking him out like that. Didn't know you had it in you, champ."

"Prime'n proper? Whaaaaa? Shiiii... I can be bad, too you know." Cole spied a bartender. "Another one, please. Anyway, yeah... like I was saying... I can be trouble like you Mr. Rico Suave."

Zander tightened his eyes at the challenge. "Oh? I didn't think you had it in you."

Cole mimicked Zander's look. "You're hot."

"Yeah, I think you have told me that before."

"No… no… you're hot. And, I know hot."

Zander leaned in to whisper in one ear. "Well, I think you are kind of hot, too."

Cole picked up the shot glass and chugged it. "Bartender! Check."

Zander paid the tab and assisted Cole into a taxi. "Where are you staying?"

"Fuck that! I'm not going back there!" A loud hiccup came out causing the taxi driver to say, "There is a five hundred dollar clean-up fee if he vomits in my car, got me?"

Zander pressed again, "So where are you going?" With both hands, Cole grabbed Zander's shirt at his chest and attempted to pull him into the taxi.

"Your place."

CHAPTER 44

COLE WAS SEATED on the bed as Zander kneeled before him and unbuttoned Cole's shirt. Untucking it from either side, he worked Cole's arms out and threw the shirt onto the floor. Zander stood and unbuttoned his own with the same slow ease of anticipation. Cole stood as they each tackled the other's belt buckles until their jeans fell to the floor. He pulled back the sheets and pushed Cole into the bed, joining him only after taking a second to admire Cole's body.

Their bodies pressed together, Cole felt hot for the intense heat Zander radiated across his body. Zander laid on top of Cole, facing him as he kissed first his neck, then collar bone, before touching his lips. Cole had never been kissed by such soft lips. As they moved back down his chest, he felt a hand slip beneath his briefs to cup his ass. He closed his eyes as he felt the heat of Zander work his way down. Taking a deep breath of Zander's smell, he lost himself as he felt his briefs pulled down and slipped off.

CHAPTER 45

COLE'S HEAD POUNDED at its temples from the assault of cheap tequila. Rolling over and opening his eyes he realized he was in a foreign bed… with a foreign man. The man had his back turned to him, his tanned body standing out against the white sheets. A black tattoo cupped the deltoid of the left arm and across part of the upper back. *Shit… Zander.*

Cole froze in fear and regret. What happened? Placing his palms over his eyes to concentrate, the night before came back to him in broken bits. The kiss… the fight… the bar with Zander. Cole lifted the sheets to see he was naked. Zander's bare ass was pressed against one of his legs. Cole pushed down and then back up the sheet to take in Zander's ass once more before dealing with what had happen.

He mouthed, *Shit, shit, shit.*

Slipping a leg slowly over the bed, he attempted to make it to his briefs and jeans undetected. He would have succeeded but for getting dizzy from standing so quickly and knocking into the nightstand.

"What the fu…." Zander rolled over to Cole standing, holding his jeans in front of him.

Zander rubbed his eyes. "What are you doing? It's... it's only nine a.m. Get back in bed." He rolled back in the other direction as though the conversation was over.

"I need to leave... I... yeah, I just need to leave. Sorry."

Zander rolled back in a rush. "What? Now? Why? I mean... if you need to leave I understand. But, please don't go."

Cole looked down. "Zander, I'm sorry. I shouldn't have gotten you involved in this. I shouldn't have imposed. I shouldn't have..."

"Spent the night? Cause, that is all you did. What, you think I'm going to rape a guy, even if he is sexy, after he passes out on you? No sirree. Not me." Zander smiled back from the bed. "I'm not saying I didn't want to, but like I told you before... I want you to want it, to remember it. How else will the reputation of my skills ever get out?!"

Forgetting that he was still nude, Cole momentarily dropped his jeans and painfully smiled before catching what he was showing.

"Yes, I did get you naked and I enjoyed every minute of it. But, comatose sex is no fun. No one loves a wet noodle in bed. So, you better bring your 'A'game next time we get naked." Zander threw the sheet off of him with bravado, exposing his ripped body. "You're awake now. Want to tackle this?"

Cole felt sick from the tequila and what he had done. Holding back the flood of tears piling-up behind his eyes, he said. "You know, I'm probably... no, I will definitely regret this, but I better pass. I have a big enough mess on my hands."

COLE WAITED UNTIL he was in a taxi before checking his phone. No messages from Maggie, good. But, there were texts and calls from everyone else. Finn had left two messages and four texts trying to figure out where Cole was and worrying about him. Jordan, five texts that ranted about how much of an ass Cash was and that he had made sure to tell Cash that several times before he disappeared. The majority were from Cash. A brewing sequence of texts and messages started out with apologies, moved to fear of where Cole was, to abandoned hope with the last text advising him he had checked out of the hotel room early in the morning so Cole could collect his stuff without running into him.

Cole broke down in the back of the taxi as Lango the driver looked on. Cole was torn. Part of him wanted to run to Cash, to hold him, to tell him everything was okay. But, it wasn't. He had been hurt and in turn, likely hurt Cash if he knew about Cole leaving with Zander. The thought of telling Cash how the night ended made the tears worse.

At some point before the taxi ride ended, he did the classic flip, convincing himself that it was Cash that had caused it all. He wouldn't repeat the mistake he made with Jeremy. He couldn't ignore the pain that was inflicted. His head swirled with countering arguments. Cole pushed up his mental wall as he paid the taxi outside the hotel. Cash said he left early but that could be a trap. Cole needed to prepare himself for battle should he be in the room.

But, there was no battle to be had. Cash and his belongings were gone. A handwritten note was on one of the pillows. Cole sat on the edge of the bed as he opened the note.

Cole, I am so sorry for what happened. There are a million excuses and explanations I could tell you but I'm sure you don't want to hear them. Please know I didn't want that – I want you. I've wanted you since the day I met you in my office last spring in Charleston. Please know how much I care for you. I love you,

Cash

Cole's eyes released the dam of emotions and went red with tears again. He just wanted to be held. He picked up the pillow and inhaled the remaining scent of Cash before curling into bed, the pillow tucked tightly between his arms. He was alone, again.

CHAPTER 46

"HOLY COW SHIT! You look like a fucking mess." Finn pulled out a chair to sit by him.

Heavy black bags hung under Cole's eyes as he forced a smile and sat.

"Well, I say good riddance. He doesn't deserve you. And, making out with Pacey... that's just all sorts of wrong."

Finn slammed a hand on the table causing one of the Tenth and Piedmont waiters to look over. "Jordan! Stop cheerleading bad decisions. You weren't even there until after it happened. So, you don't know what you are talking about."

"Well... I just think..."

"No, you don't think. That's the problem."

"Jordan, shut the fuck up." Mason jumped in from the end of the table. Cole looked over to see him looking as if he was watching someone die. Cole cut his eyes away before he started to tear-up again. He pushed his wall up, squeezing it tight until he grew numb.

"Fine. I've got better places to be. Cole, always a pleasure. Text me later, baby. Jordan is here for you." Jordan stood up from the table. Cole stood and gave the man a hug before his departure.

"I'm tired of his shit. Sorry about that Cole. But, Jordan likes to stir pots too much."

Mason moved over a seat to sit directly across from him. "How are you? Where did you end-up?"

Cole looked down and then slowly back up, turning to look at both men. "I... I went home with a guy." Cole let his words land with a thud, heavy with meaning, before continuing. "A guy from Denver. I ran into him at the party right after it all went down. He helped me get out of there. Then... got a bit drunk and ended up sleeping naked with the man. No sex... but naked." Cole avoided eye contact as he delivered the last part.

Finn covered his mouth in shock as Cole felt Mason refusing to look away with concern for Cole. Cole looked back up and his eyes were still soft, sympathetic. "I fucked up. The whole night was a mess." Cole grabbed Finn's hand. "I'm sorry if all the drama ruined y'all's night."

Finn relaxed and cupped his hand over Cole's. "Are you insane? That night wasn't going anywhere. You just improved the entertainment. Shit, that punch? I've never been so proud of you. Damn boy, you aren't the little Cole I used to know." Finn chuckled causing Mason and Cole to join in.

"It was a good punch, wasn't it?" Cole grinned.

"Good punch? You knocked that ass out cold. The sting rays were sucking on his face a good minute before they fished him out of the pond. Deserves him right. He's been doing that shit to boys all over town for years. You're just the first to actually knock that bitch out." Finn smiled again. "And, Cole, your boy... Cash... he was a wreck after all that. Mason and I ended-up taking care of him when we couldn't find you. He feels like shit for what happened. Pacey totally surprised him."

Cole swallowed. Several texts from Cash had said as much and Finn was only confirming that Cash was the victim of Pacey's tactics. He felt as his heart sank again; he worked to ignore it. A single tear escaped. Finn rushed in with a paper napkin.

"Hon, it's okay. Everything is okay. Just let him know you know what happened. He was utterly broke when he couldn't find you. He wants you back."

Cold again, Cole spoke in stiff words. "I went home with Zander."

Finn's head perked up. He looked over to Mason for confirmation as he spoke. "Zander... that boy that has been trying to get in your cookie jar back in Denver?"

Cole inhaled deeply to gather his strength to keep his wall up.

A heavy hand rubbed Cole's back. "Cole. It will be okay. This is just a test and you both need to figure out how to pass it. This guy would be a fool to let you go." Cole knew that Mason's words had more meaning than he wanted to offer. And then he did.

Mason pulled Cole's chin up so that their eyes met. "Cole, you know how I feel about you. I know that isn't the way you feel about me. And, I haven't hung out with Cash much... but, he loves you. If you love him, tell him. Tell him it all. And, then I dare him be stupid enough to give you up." Mason's words were firm.

Cole felt sick again. Now he was screwing-up another man's life. Being single and depressed had been so much easier. "Mason, thank you." Cole paused and thought before speaking further. "Just know I do love you and appreciate your support."

"Uh, what about me?" Finn was trying to diffuse the seriousness of the moment.

Cole smiled. "Hell no. Can't even stand you." Cole wrapped his arm around Finn's neck and kissed him on the check before whispering. "Of, course I love you. You're my precious."

Finn pushed Cole's arm off. "Ugh, I am not 'the precious.' Yuck. Get away from me Gollum." The two men laughed.

"Come here." Cole wrapped his arm around Mason. "Thank you, sir." Sitting back into his chair, Cole continued. "Ugh. What a mess. What do I do now?"

"Give him space, time. But, you need to tell him about the cowboy. Then, whatever happens. Happens."

CHAPTER 47

MEADOWS FLIPPED OPEN his black laptop and powered it up. Two days had passed since bringing the Atlanta PD into the loop on his investigation. Winters had linked her father to a book by Audubon and he needed to know what she knew before her death. Computers had never been his friend. The years of computer and internet training had made him barely able to email. He didn't trust the web, but knew it was the easiest and fastest way to gain insight on almost anything.

He typed in the obvious, "Audubon murder" and was immediately inundated with hundreds of thousands of hits. Though it appeared Audubon Park in New Jersey was a busy killing spot, none of the links related to his investigation. The terms "Audubon killings" similarly struck out, with the only victims being swans and swallows.

Meadows rethought his search, focusing on Audubon himself. Wiki offered the best information: illegitimate son of a Haitian sugar plantation owner and a chambermaid raised by his quadroon step-mother. Meadows read each fact carefully trying to find any link to the killer or

Winters. From what he could determine from Wiki and the other websites, Audubon was anything but the conservationist most people believed him to be today. Journal notations frequently cited his propensity to shoot birds in excess in hopes of landing the perfect specimen to paint.

Things began to sound familiar as Meadows read further. As with each body linked to the current killer, Audubon became known for his novel use of wires and line to model his specimens. The bodies were maneuvered into poses by wiring. Moreover, according to what he was reading, Audubon demanded the bird be painted unstuffed, posed on wires very soon after it was killed or while it was still alive. He didn't care if the bird was in agony as long as he got its live plumage right. Audubon noted in one journal entry, "I have ascertained that feathers lose their brilliancy almost as rapidly as flesh or skin itself and am of the opinion that a bird alive is 75 percent more rich in colors than 24 hours after its death." Meadows sat up from the screen. Only the closest circle of investigators knew that the coroner believed the victims had all been alive while they were being posed. Someone was copying Audubon's style... making it their own.

The final fact confirmed for Meadows the link between the old kidnappings and the current murders. According to the biographies, Audubon was the first to use bird-banding in the Country. He used pieces of ribbon on finches and then observed them for years. Meadows thought of the Mouzon boy and the others, all marked and set free back in the 80's. They had been let go intentionally to be observed, studied.

CHAPTER 48

"AGENT LEAS, WELL this is a surprise. Is everything okay?" Based on Cash's response, the call was unexpected. Leas could hear worry in his voice.

"Thank you for taking my call, Mr. Calhoun. I know you are busy with the school year and all, so I won't take too much of your time. I just have a quick history question that I need some insight on and figured, well... you being a history professor and all, you might be able to shoot me in the right direction."

Cash's voice suggested suspicion. "Sure... how can I help you?"

"You see, my partner over here has stumbled on what he thinks is a link between Audubon, you know... the bird guy and all, and some type of writing called Pitman's, uh... Pitman's shorthand. Any insight on how the two could be linked?"

Cash was still trying to process the news of Leas having a partner when he heard the name Audubon. He was immediately concerned, but responded. "Uhm, the Pitman style of shorthand wasn't readily known when he started out, and Audubon didn't use any other version. At most he scribbled. In fact, he was a notoriously poor writer of English because he was of French Creole descent, raised in Haiti. His English was taught to him by Quakers while sick with yellow fever in New York shortly after arriving in the Country. And, his Creole accent was considered uneducated and unsophisticated for the time making his door-to-door sales pitches of his book almost impossible. Think the bayous of Louisiana." Cash paused. "Agent why all the questions? Does this have to do with Cole and Poinsett? Is everything okay?"

Leas paused before answering, "Everything is fine. I just have a case where this naturalist shit has come up again and you were helpful before so I just wanted to get some quick insight, that's all."

"Agent, you're not saying everything. Audubon has connections to Charleston just like the last naturalist. In fact, his relationship with John Bachman, a Charleston Lutheran minister and naturalist, is widely considered the turning point in Audubon's career and the success of *Birds of America*. Audubon visited Charleston a lot to spend time with Bachman and his family. They too collaborated on the *Quadrupeds of North America* book. And, Audubon's sons married Bachman's daughters. Bachman's sister-in-law, Maria Martin, painted many of the plants in the paintings. So, I find it highly unusual that you are calling me. Does this have anything to do with those murders in Atlanta that are being linked by the news to what happened here in Charleston?"

Agent Leas paused. He wanted to be careful to reveal just enough. "Mr. Calhoun, I can't really talk about those cases. I just needed some quick insight." Trying to shift the topic, "Uhm, how are you two doing? I mean, have you chatted with him lately?" Leas had picked-up on the two men's relationship being something more than friendship in Charleston and he wanted to know if Cole suspected anything.

"No. I haven't talked to him in a while. But, back to my question... your refusal to answer says that this is related to Cole. Is he in danger?" Cash's words were rushed.

"No. He isn't in danger. We have just uncovered some clues, that is all I can say. There is nothing to worry about. Look, I need to run, but I appreciate the insight. I would appreciate you keeping this to yourself for now. The news has enough to talk about."

"Of course, but... Cole."

Leas interrupted him, "There is no current danger to Mr. Mouzon. It is under control. Now, I really need to hang-up. And, thank you again."

Leas hung up the phone and looked over to Meadows. "There, I did it. Now fucking leave my room."

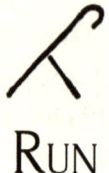

RUN

CHAPTER 49

DENVER WAS SUFFERING another heat-wave as Cole trudged along the sidewalk in a failed attempt to jog, Mr. Probz blaring in his earbuds. "I'm sorry, but I need to stop for a second and catch my breath. I know I've lived here a bit, but the altitude still kills me." Cole leaned over panting as Noel Granger looked on laughing. Noel swiped his hand over his forehead and through his curly brown hair and then flicked his hand to his side to discard the sweat.

Somewhere between the slow-motion parade and coffin races, Cole had met the late twenty-something man at the Frozen Dead Guy Days in Nederland, Colorado, his first year in the state. Like something out of the show *Storage Wars*, Cole had found himself celebrating a cytogenetically frozen dead Norwegian, Bredo Morstel, who had been abandoned in a mountain shed and Cole decided drunk was the best option. Perhaps it was the booze or perhaps it was Noel's animated celebration of a rediscovered dead guy. Either way, they had been friends since.

IT HAD BEEN a week since Cole returned from Atlanta without seeing Cash. The bags under his eyes had lifted only slightly but he still felt the weight of the events.

With his hands on his hips and breathing in deep huffs, Noel responded. "Damn man. It only takes a few months for your body to adjust to living a mile up in altitude by pumping extra blood cells into your veins. Your blood should be as thick as syrup by now. Perhaps if you ran more often…"

Cole let out a laugh and then responded, "Suck it, okay. It's the altitude and not my lazy ass just being out of shape. I work out every day." Noel turned his head and pinched one eye. Cole rolled his eyes. "Okay… every few days lately. Bite me."

"Excuses, excuses. I see I'm going to have to demand you come jogging with me more often."

Cole smiled. His ability to wall-up the events of Atlanta had started to crack and he worried at any moment his wall would break. Since the Aquarium party, Cole had refused to respond to any contact from Cash. He needed space. He needed courage to tell Cash everything. Cole exhaled heavily. Cole missed him, missed his comfort and the squeeze of his hand that always told him "It will be okay." It was not okay. Perhaps it was best that Cash was no longer in the picture, one less person to get hurt.

Cole pushed off his emotions.

"More often? I was kind of surprised you asked today. I mean, how did you get the day off? Isn't she due to fly in this week? Not that I'm complaining. With everything going on lately, well, just… thank you for the invite."

"Oh man, don't get me started. If I had known when I went to Starkey to study household management and become a butler that I would end up dealing with her, I think I would have changed my degree to dog grooming. Divas! I guess I should be grateful I didn't get hired by Celine. She's supposed to be the worst." Noel leaned against a tree trunk as Cole stood up.

"Whatever. You love that job. Damn man, if I could live in Aspen half the year in an empty house waiting on some diva to come visit maybe a week out of every other month I'd say, 'Where do I sign up?'"

"Oh man. Did I tell you what she did last month while she was in town with the babies? She asked me to call a massage therapist to come over. The woman dropped everything and rushed over before Nick got in from the airport and what did she do? She decided she wanted a back rub instead. A fucking back rub! The masseuse looked at me like 'what the fuck' when the woman told her to crawl in bed with her and her kids and just rub her back while she napped. She's a damn grown woman."

Cole let out a heavy laugh at what he had just been told. "What!? A back rub... and with her kids in the bed?"

"Yeah, she just needed it 'to help her sleep.' Please. She has plenty of other ways to accomplish that."

"Well, I am sure she was tired from hocking all her shit on QVC. What 'moment' is she having right now? A bedazzled 'moment?' I'm still waiting for her TRL ice cream cart inspired collection. That was a 'moment' I can't forget." Cole paused and laughed more as Noel just shook his head. "You know, that's what you get for going to that school. If you wanted to avoid divas, going to the number one butler school wasn't your best decision."

"Yeah, but I wanted to live in Denver and see the world. So far all I've seen is Aspen." Noel laughed at himself.

Cole looked off into the distance. "Uhm, what is that?"

Noel looked over across the park to several people with faces covered in blood. "Zombies! Oh my god, I totally forgot! It's the zombie crawl today. Awe, I wanted to do the organ trail."

Cole looked at him in disgust. "The what?"

"The organ trail, you know like to Oregon Trail game, but its zombiefied, so you run around like a scavenger hunt and stop at different locations. Each one has either a challenge like eating bugs or digging through pig guts, or answering a trivia question." Noel dropped his shoulders in disappointment. "Err, I was supposed to do it with Dan my ex. Sucks."

"Well, living in Atlanta with all their zombie craziness and filming of *Walking Dead*, I think I'll pass. I've seen enough brain eaters in my life." Cole looked back and found a spot to sit down in the grass. His butt barely brushed the grass before Noel noticed.

"Uhm, I wouldn't do that...."

Cole was now lying back, his hands behind his head as he listened to Noel. "Do what?"

"Lay in that grass. I wouldn't do that."

Cole quickly sat up and looked around to see if he had failed to see an ant hill, or worse, dog shit. Seeing nothing he looked back to Noel. "What do you see?"

"Nothing man, but this is Cheeseman Park. There are dead people under you. People are constantly finding bones and jewelry and shit here."

Cole remained seated, looking around the park and up the hill to the granite, greek-style pavilion. "Dude, this is a park."

"Uh, it is now. But is wasn't always. Most of these

trees, bushes were planted as headstones at what was once Prospect Hill Cemetery. Over there you had the Chinese area, and there… the Grand Army and Jewish areas. Catholics were buried somewhere over there." Noel pointed in various directions as he talked. He moved from the tree to the concrete sidewalk and sat on its edge, careful to not sit in the grass.

"You're screwing with me. Not true."

"Man, look it up. Google it. You will see. There are dead people under there… something about just plowing under the headstones… removing them and saying 'Ta-da! City, I present you a park.' Someone told me Stephen Spielberg got the idea for the movie *Poltergeist* from Cheeseman. Ask Nancy about it."

"Oh hell no!" Cole leaned in as if to whisper, "But, don't people like make out here and stuff? I mean, that's messed up."

"I know!" That's why you won't see me laying in that grass. No sir. Uh uh. Ain't gonna do it." Noel's mimic of a Christina Aguilera 'moment' was not lost on Cole. The two men laughed.

"SPEAKING OF THINGS not getting done, what's up with that guy back in your hometown?" Noel had changed the subject to the one thing Cole did not want to talk about. Cole had filled Noel in over the phone about what had gone down in Atlanta, but there wasn't much discussion.

Cole looked down and slowly back up. "There is nothing to talk about. It's over." His face was flat. The wall was still firmly in place. But, his mind struggled with hearing what he had just said.

'Over' was not a word he had really associated with Cash since giving in to his emotions in the weeks and months after last being in Charleston. He hadn't fooled himself into thinking it would last forever. But, he had avoided the thought of it ever ending. Cash had meant so much to him in Charleston and their relationship had grown from there. Everything was wonderful until Atlanta. Now... it was over. Hearing that in his head again made him go rigid. He pushed the mental wall up tight, forcing the brewing emotions behind it to crash hard against it.

He was cold and he needed to be. The Taker had been discovered killing again. Even if he had shown no interest in him yet, Cole wanted, needed to find him and understand. There was no option. *Just find him.* Cole needed to know why he had done it, why he had taken Cole and his mother... and Cash's brother, Mark Calhoun. Not having Cash around to distract him was a blessing in disguise. His promise to stay clear of The Taker to Cash drifted across his thoughts.

Then there was Billy. He had already arranged for his care. Granny had booked a trip to Denver several months earlier and would be in town at the end of the week. Cole looked forward to the help. But, more importantly, he looked forward to the flexibility to focus, to find The Taker.

CHAPTER 50

JOGGING BACK TOWARDS Cole's Park Hill home, Noel pushed further on the Cash issue. "But, I thought you two were hitting it off so well. Why would he do that? It makes no sense. I mean, he knew you were on a date, right?"

"Yeah, Noel. He knew we were on a date. But, Pacey is one of those evil gays. He gets off on preying on others' boyfriends. You know, the type that only feels sexy and confident only if they can throw a significant enough wedge between two innocent people so that one sleeps with him. He had it coming, Noel. God it felt good to punch him." Cole punched the air in reenactment. "Then Zander pulled me away."

Noel stopped and grabbed Cole's arm in shock. "Wait a minute! Zander was there? Oh, I didn't hear about this. Damn boy, who isn't chasing after you?" Cole just shook his head.

Rolling his eyes, he responded. "It isn't like that. He was there for the party like everyone else. He just happened to appear just as I was about to make an ass of myself. I mean, it isn't like I don't already have a reputation in Atlanta. But, getting into a cat fight at the

Aquarium Party is not one I want to add to the list. Anyway... I left the party and haven't talked to him since. He saw me looking on. He knows what he did. I have no need to explain it to him."

"Screw that guy! What about Zander? Did you get in those pants? Spill it." Noel was salivating at the gossip.

"Uhm, I don't think so mister. You get nothing. I know you. Why are you so 'obsessed' with me?" Cole's emphasis on 'obsessed' made Noel stumble on the uneven sidewalk.

"I know you did not just...." Noel stood with his jaw dropped.

"Yes, I did. And, what news is there of your dating life, sir?"

"Okay, I'm going to let you defer this conversation today. But, I better get the scoop first. I have followers that are ravenous of all things Cole."

Cole's stomach churned at the thought of gossip about him. It was a given in his world, but it didn't mean he liked it. Stopping at the pathway to his front porch, he turned to Noel. "Deal. You get the exclusive rights to all my dirt. But, only when I say."

Noel smiled, "Perfect. I'll line up my publisher tomorrow."

"Sure thing, Noel. Just make sure you spell my name right. On a different topic, see you tonight at Jake's thing?"

"Yeah, I guess. I mean it's not really my style but I do love to dance. Just promise me that if you catch me singing along to country songs you will shoot me. I cannot be doing that. Ugh."

Cole laughed as he turned to walk into the house. "Sure thing, mister. I'll make it painless, promise."

CHAPTER 51

T HE GROUP OPERATING the Colorado Country Classic dance competition had rented several buses to give the contestants and their guests a sampling of the country western bars in Denver. Jake Danner had been competing for almost three years with his partner and coach, Liz. Cole had met him at a dancing class at Charlie's when he first moved to Denver. Jake spun guys around the dance floor with such precision that he decided to take it up professionally.

"Uhm, are my boots okay for this? I mean everyone else seems to have those black suede dancing boots." Cole looked down to inspect Noel's tan boots with red stitching.

"I think you will be fine. Nice flannel by the way. Didn't know you owned anything other than t-shirts." Noel faked a laugh.

"When in Rome, right? Picked this up at Tar-J after our jog."

Cole nodded in approval as they walked into Stampede. The large wooden bar had what anyone else would consider a circular track with a bar at its center. The wooden floor creaked with every heeled step. The scene was intimidating. Couples of men and women danced in smooth movements in a counter clockwise way around the track.

Jake came up behind them and put his hands on both their backs. "You guys ready to cut the rug? These ladies love to dance, so be prepared to get asked. I'm going to jump out there with Liz to practice a bit." Jake walked away in his tight Wrangler jeans and black wool western hat.

"Shit. We are fucked." Noel was apparently feeling the same way. "I need a drink if I'm going to deal with all this."

Exhaling in dread, Cole agreed. "Grab me a beer please, Budweiser... bottle." The rest of the buses' occupants flooded into the already busy bar and immediately entered onto the track. A memory of Ava and Henry dancing in the living room to country music flashed in his head. The dancing skills in the bar intimidated him, but the place as a whole was comforting.

He slowly meandered to a railing that overlooked the track and found a seat. Noel, dodging dancers circling the bar, weaved his way over to Cole. "So, guess who I ran into at the bar?"

Cole knew whoever it was wasn't good news. He bit. "Who?"

"Look." Noel pointed through the bar and to the other side of the track. Cole moved his head until he figured out what Noel was pointing at. He looked back to Noel and then down to the ground as if to try and hide his face.

"Fuck my life. I don't have time for this shit today."

Noel giggled. "What? The guy is hot. You better jump on that, if you haven't already." Noel raised his chin for a better view. "Oh look, he is coming this way."

Moments later Zander slid onto a stool next to Cole. Tipping a black suede cowboy hat, he said, "Well, if it isn't Cole Mouzon without his sidekick. Are you stalking me?" A large grin appeared.

Cutting his eyes first to Noel and then rolling them to Zander, "I could ask you the same question. I'm here hanging with friends. What's your excuse? And, my side-kick is at a sleep-over." He looked at his watch. "Right about now he is getting his fill of some gluten-free, dairy-free meal and praying for chicken nuggets." Cole couldn't help but notice that Zander's beige shirt was unbuttoned to below his chest.

Zander tipped back his hat and looked at the dancers just inches away. Still looking away, he said, "I come here most weekends and dance. I don't think I've ever seen you here before." He turned back to Cole for a response.

"Yeah, this is a bit far out for me. But, it's pretty cool. So am I going to see you out there cutting the rug?"

"Perhaps. Perhaps if you are lucky, I'll even dance with you."

Cole rolled his head to Noel as if to say, *Did you get this guy?* Apparently Noel did because he leaned around Cole and responded, "I'll dance with you Zander." Cole rolled his eyes again.

"Thanks Noel, but I promised Alison over there the first dance. But, grab me later." Zander stood up and walked around the track to the far end. Every few minutes he would twirl right in front of Cole a brunette woman who Cole presumed was Alison. Her yellow dress would flare out, flashing her boots and long legs.

"EXCUSE ME." A small voice accompanied the tapping

on Cole's shoulder. "Would you like to dance?" The woman could have been no taller than four and a half feet, her hair in a tight ponytail. She cupped her hands in anticipation for Cole's response.

"Uhm, yeah... sure. I'm not great, but I'll try."

The woman's face beamed with excitement. "Oh, don't worry. It's just for fun." Standing up, the woman came to Cole's beltline.

Cole could hear Noel snickering as Cole walked off with the woman. The couple danced, Cole trying to mimic the dancers around him with a rough version of west coast swing. His back ached from all the leaning to compensate for the height differential by the time Chris Brown and Lil Wayne finished up the lyrics to "Forever." The song switched to John Michael Montgomery singing some slow song.

"And you said you were no good. Boy, you did good, real good."

A voice came from behind. "Agreed. Nice moves." Zander had stepped between the two.

"Zander! You know this boy?" The lady craned her neck to make eye contact with the two men.

He grinned. "You can say that. Mind if I cut in?"

The lady waved her arm as if to welcome Zander into a room. He grabbed Cole's hands and began to sway. "Uhm, you do realize we are the only male-male couple on this floor, right?"

"Is that a problem?" He looked at Cole with a certain macho air. Cole looked around the room to see if anyone was staring only to be surprised that no one was.

"Cole, it's the West. The feeling for most people here is they don't care about your personal business. Yeah, you get the odd ball here and there in some rural parts or if you get too close to Utah. But, for the most part your business is your business. Why do you think Trinidad was the sex change capital of the world for so long? The Biber set up shop there and pumped out like four a day, with the community rallying behind him. See, people around here generally don't care." Cole relaxed as Zander spoke.

"There you go." Zander released a hand and spun Cole. He then pulled on the other arm to reel Cole back in.

"Zander, about Atlanta...."

"Yeah. What about it?"

Zander spun Cole again before he could respond. Returned, Cole said, "Uhm, you know that I like someone else, right? I mean, yeah there is a lot of shit there, but that remains unresolved."

Cole switched topics when there wasn't an immediate response. "What do you even do?"

Zander's eyes beamed to match his slight smile. "I work my parents' ranch. Dad got injured about ten years ago, so I've taken it over. Beef ranching." Seeing Cole tighten his eyes, he continued. "Yes, a cowboy. But, don't read that much into it. I'm mostly working at a computer and marketing our free-range, drug-free beef. That's why I live in the city. I do ride the fence with the ranch-hands occasionally, but that is just a few times a month and more for my mental well-being than any need for me to be out there."

Cole matched Zander's grin. "Pretty cool nonetheless. A modern-day cowboy. That's kinda hot." Zander pulled him tightly. They stepped a few more times in silence, Cole's head on the man's shoulder.

As the song came to an end, Zander dipped Cole and leaned in. "That 'it's complicated' status of yours you mentioned a few seconds ago? I know. But, I am here when that is resolved. My money is on me winning out on this little pony." Zander pulled them both back up and slapped Cole on the ass. Cole stood there as a woman grabbed Zander's hand and pulled him back into the flow of dancers. Zander looked back and mouthed, "Mine."

Cole leaned against the railing of the dance floor. The thought of being anyone's property right that moment made Cole squirm. His mind drifted to Cash. He hated to admit it, but missed Cash in his life. Finn was adamant that Cash was the victim of Pacey. He had told him how Cash pled with him to tell Cole that he didn't see it coming, that he wasn't paying attention when Pacey pulled him into the kiss and locked his hand around his neck. Cash was deflated, broken when he couldn't find him after searching the entire aquarium over and over again.

The image of Cash searching made Cole feel queasy. He hated this... the emotions of life. Until Cash and the death of Jackie, he was content to not feel, to have his emotions locked away behind his mental wall. It was fractured now. Feeling made him weak, subject to whims. His wall was failing and its weakness frustrated him in these moments of feeling sad. He just wanted to be cold again.

Cole wondered whether Cash would want anything to do with him when he found out about Zander. Cole had wrestled with whether he really had to tell Cash about what happened that night, but it always came down to disclosure. If they were going to be together everything had to be out there. Cole longed for his hand to be held by Cash. *Shit.* He craved his touch.

Sitting back behind the railing overlooking the dancing loop, Cole turned to Noel. "Noel, I need a drink. A stiff one. It's going to be one of those nights. Let's get this party going." He shoved a hand in his pocket and then slammed a twenty down he had withdrawn on the railing's top.

Noel grinned. "Hell yeah! That's the Cole I know."

CHAPTER 52

ANN LOOKED AROUND the cramped dark wood restaurant to inspect the crowd as she sat. The place was packed for a Thursday night. "Yeah, this isn't my crowd at all."

Cole looked around the large atrium at the hotel's center. "Hey, don't knock this place. If it was good enough for the "Unsinkable Molly Brown" a week after she survived the Titanic sinking, it's good enough for you."

Ann whipped her head back towards Cole. "The who?"

Tilting his head in disbelief, Cole responded. "You know... the Kathy Bates character in the Titanic. Loud. Opinionated. You know, an eighteen-hundreds version of you."

Ann's jaw dropped. She looked down. "Did you hear that Billy, he just said I was loud!"

Billy looked at her and snickered.

"Just calling it as I see it. And, I told you we could have hopped one of the 16th Street buses to a more hip place. We didn't have to stay here inside the Brown Palace."

Still looking around as they walked into some wooden

nautical inspired bar within the hotel, she responded. "This place is like an antique mall, no? Anyway, I'm tired from travel and only here for a night for work. I've got that meeting in the morning at the World Trade Center and then fly right back out. I don't need to be getting all crunk-up and shit." She finally looked back to Cole and smiled. "Plus, I just wanted to see you while I was in town." She placed a hand on Cole's wrist and looked into his eyes. Squinting with inquisition, she asked, "So how are you doing, babe?"

Cole pushed a pained smile to one side and he helped Billy into his oak chair and then sat himself. "I'm good. I'm certainly glad I was able to see you." Cole turned. "Billy, wanted to see you, too." Billy beamed as he looked at Ann and then opened his *Frozen* coloring book. It appeared that the Snow Queen Elsa was going to be donning purple hair tonight.

"Awe, he looks great. You? Not so much." Ann reached out with a finger and touched one of the bags under Cole's eyes. "So, what's the update? You and he working things out or what?"

Cole grimaced. "Haven't talked to him since Atlanta. I just... I don't know how to talk to him, to tell him what happened. When he hears what happened he's gone anyway. So, I don't see a reason to stir the pot."

"What the..." Ann looked down at Billy and then back up. "...F.U.C.K. are you doing Cole? Do you like him or what?"

"Ann, It's stupid, I know. I've only known the guy for like six months but now that I've lost him. I'm messed-up." Cole covered Billy's ears before continuing. "I could tell you I sit on the toilet with all the doors closed and cry pretty every night, but... let's get serious. That isn't happening. But, with all these emotions, I still feel like a crazy chick. Ann, I miss him." Cole lifted his hands and threw them up in abandonment.

Ann laughed. "Honey, you are no chick. But, Cole, if you feel that way you have to do something. Those things you are feeling are called emotions. E-mo-tions. Say it with me."

Cole mouthed the word and then grimaced.

"That's good. See, you haven't felt one of those emotions in a while. You need to get use to it. They are healthy. They make sure you don't pop your top and cut someone."

Cole laughed out loud.

She smiled before continuing. "Okay. Now for Cash. Do you want this man in your life or what?"

Cole thought for a second. "Yes. I love him." His word were slow.

"Then stop... F.U.C.K.I.N.G. it up, you shit." Ann paused, realizing she just cussed. Cole shook his head to not worry. "Granny comes to town late Saturday and he will hear that and more if she gets too much beer in her."

She sat back. "Awh, fun. Anyway... Cole you always do this. You put up that freaking wall of yours, close everybody out and then wonder why you are alone. Stop pushing him away. If he goes away after you have tried, so be it. But, give him the chance to prove you wrong. You are doing yourself no favors by just taking this all on by yourself and ending it before you have even given it a chance."

Cole let Ann's words sink in.

"He's going to hate me, Ann. Nothing horrible happened, but still. That shouldn't have happened at all."

"Will you just shut it!" Ann's voice carried across

the restaurant. She looked around and then continued. "Just stop it, Cole. The guy, from what I can tell, has a good head on his shoulders. And, he is crazy about you. He couldn't take his eyes off you that night at Eclipse de Luna. The man is in love. He will get over this."

Cole looked down to the table. He knew what she was saying was true. Finn had already said as much. The dread of that conversation made him nauseous. Ann interjected while he was still thinking. "Cole, if you love him, you have to fight for him. You two have already been through so much. Fight."

CHAPTER 53

"FINN, THE CATERING crew is finishing up and should be done soon so you can tackle the tables and chairs in the Great Hall." Pam barked the orders as she walked towards the main entrance.

Finn shook his head at Pam's command. "Yeah, it isn't like we don't do Martini's and IMAX every Friday. I got this, lady." The Hall was a large cylinder shaped atrium that housed the museum's showpiece, a large brontosaurus looking skeleton, *Argentinosaurus*, being attached by a t-rex looking *Giganotosaurus*. Standing under the long neck of the larger specimen, Finn felt dwarfed. "When do ya'll think you'll be done?"

One of the workers responded, "Ten minutes okay?" The man wiped his hands down his black pants as he spoke.

"Sure. I'll be back in ten. Let me know if you need anything." Finn climbed the spiral staircase that wrapped around the room to access the upper levels of the museum. The worker's voices echoed into his tiny office off the third floor. Busy tackling supply orders, it was almost twenty minutes before he noticed it was quiet.

Finn threw down his pen and walked back down to the Hall's now dim lit floor.

"Oh! I thought everyone was gone." A dark shadow stood behind one of the dinosaur's legs. "Uh, hello. Can I help you? What else do you have to do?" There was no response. Finn grew frustrated. "Hey, I've got places to be and still need to clean, so if you are done you need to get."

The shadow rushed quickly, knocking Finn in the head with a heavy object and causing him to fall to the cold granite floor. He saw the shadow stand over him for just a second before he was struck again. All went black.

"FINN, ARE YOU still here? I thought I told you to..." Pam let out a screeching wail at the sight of Finn. He was shirtless, suspended between the legs of the larger dinosaur by his hands. Something was wrapped around his mouth. Pam looked around cautiously to see if she was alone and then rushed in. "Oh my god, Finn. Finn! Are you okay?" Several slice marks were cut across his chest in a pattern. Pam had to jump to reach the cloth muzzling Finn. He was weak but alive. She looked up just as his eyes grew big.

"Pam... BEHIND YOU!"

She swung around just before the black shape jumped, hitting her in the chest. His foot slipped off the exhibit's foundation causing him to fall backwards. Pam ran around to the other side of the exhibit, using the legs as a shield. The shape attacked again. Flashes of light told her he had a knife and was slashing through the dark air. Pam jumped back and lost her footing. The shape punched and landed on top of her. The attacker started to choke her as he slammed her head against the floor.

Pam took a deep breath. *Lord help me. One, two – monkey grip.* Pam hooked one hand around his wrist while grabbing his elbow to trap his arm to his chest. Locking his feet and leg with hers she rolled, throwing him off balance until they both rolled and she was on top. She jumped up and ran towards the door. She heard his steps rushing towards her as she rounded into the main entrance.

He tackled her again to the ground by catching her leg. "No! Nooo! Help, Finn help!" He stood and started to drag her back towards the Hall. She took another deep breath, and then released a kick with her other leg, landing it at his extended ankle. "Fuck you asshole." He crumbled to the floor.

Pam scrambled to get up and run as she felt the first slash in her side. She screamed out in pain and fell to the floor. Pam swung her leg again until it connected to the ski mask covered head.

Holding his head, the man barked angrily, "You fucking bitch. You are dead."

Pam rushed to the front ticket counter and slammed the half door behind her. The man, hobbled, jumped through the upper opening just as she hit the alarm, landing on top of her, pinning her to the floor. The space was too tight for her to roll him off of her again. He stabbed as she put up her hand. The blade landed deep into her palm. Pam let out her last scream as he stabbed again. She lifted a knee and landed it into the attacker's groin. He moaned before lifting his hand one final time. The knife dug deep into her chest.

SURVIVOR

CHAPTER 54

"MR. LASITER, I know this isn't the best time, but we need to talk to you. I'm Agent Leas and this is Agent Meadows. We are with the FBI. Do you understand me?"

Finn's entire body hurt. A broken arm, cuts across his chest and bruises made any movement difficult. He was only able to manage a weak nod. He had been told by one of the nurses that Pam was dead, found behind the ticket counter. The thought caused him to tear up as the two agents started to question him.

"We promise not to take too much time. From what we understand you are pretty banged up and we are very sorry about your co-worker. Did you... did she know your attacker?" Finn swayed his head slowly "no" so as to not dislodge the tubes shoved up his nose. The older man took notes as the Latino asked the questions. "Did you see his face?" Another head shake "no." "Did he say anything, anything at all that could help us?" Finn stared at them unsure if he should answer. "Mr. Lasiter, if you are worried or scared, don't be. We can post someone outside your door. You will be perfectly safe. We promise."

"He... he said... 'Tell Mouzon The Taker is back.'"

CHAPTER 55

TRYING TO POUR Dixie's food in her bowl with one hand and balancing the phone in the other, Cole spoke abruptly. "Agent Leas, I don't really have time for this right now. I was told this morning that one of my friends is dead and another in the hospital from an attack." Cole's voice was stern and terse.

"I know."

Cole stood up. "Wait, what? You know what?"

"We know about Mr. Lasiter and Mrs. Hemmer. That is why I called." Leas coughed.

Cole's eyes tightened as he processed what Leas was saying. Pausing a few seconds, he pushed for answers. "Leas, does this have anything to do with The Taker? Tell me now!"

"Cole, we don't know much yet, but, the killer left a message with Mr. Lasiter. He identified himself as The Taker and that you needed to know he was back. Now Cole, don't go...."

"He's back? And the bastard attacked my friends? What? Is he playing with me or what? He clearly knows where I am. My face was plastered all over the TV after his daughter went after me. Why them?" Cole was losing his temper quickly.

"We don't have answers yet. Look Cole, don't do anything stupid. He's clearly trying to lure you out. It's a trap and I need you to stay away from here. No running off like in Charleston. Do you get me? Stay put."

Cole's blood boiled at Leas' command. "Agent, if you did your job this wouldn't have happened. I have to go to Atlanta. A friend is dead and another injured... because of me."

Leas interrupted. "Cole, stay put! That's an order. If I have to arrest you for interfering with an investigation, I will. Mr. Lasiter is safe. I talked to him about this. He understands. If you want us to catch him you need to stay away from here for now, understand me?"

Cole didn't like being told what to do but he also knew that Agent Leas wasn't going to take no for an answer. "Yeah, whatever you say. Agent... so help me. Find him or I will." Cole slammed down the phone. His entire body tingled before growing hot. He would end this once and for all.

CHAPTER 56

COLE WAS STILL fuming from his conversation earlier in the day with Leas as he met Granny at the airport several hours later. He swallowed deep to appear normal. She would be told, but only once Billy was in bed.

Her quick chatter helped to keep his temper at bay. "All I know is they betta have some grits here, cause granny can't have her breakfast sausage without some grits."

"Granny, Granny!" Billy rushed past Cole and into the old lady's arms.

Cole struggled to get out a response to Granny's words without laughing. He watched as Billy was engulfed by the woman's arms. "Granny, you have been shipping me enough grits to feed a horse. The cabinets are full of grits. So, don't you worry, your grandson has you covered." Walking out of the Denver International Airport, Cole kept looking over to Granny. "Uhm, woman, what do you have on? I said flurries, not blizzard." Cole chuckled a few more times as she looked up and down her outfit.

"What? Meme took me shopping. Ya like?" She spun to provide a better view.

Staring at the short woman, he inspected her Russian style shapka-ushanka hat with a faux-fur cheetah jacket that screamed "pimp." Tory Burch style knock-off riding boots accented the look. Cole just shook his head and wrapped his arms around her. "God, I've missed you woman. Billy and I need some of your cooking."

"Oh suga, I've missed y'all as well. Ya look famished. They got chicken here that I can fry?"

Cole shook his head in disbelief. "Yes, Granny, we have chicken here. And, it's pretty decent. If you want to pick some up to fry up I am sure I can arrange that."

"Well, I don't know. All this yankee stuff, ya know. It's like a foreign country."

"Lord woman, Colorado isn't yankee. It's the West. They eat steak and eggs and..."

She continued. "...bull balls. That's what Meme told me. We will not be eating those while I'm here." Granny's eyes grew big and defiant. She looked at Billy in his car seat in the back for agreement.

Cole had no intention of crossing her. "No Rocky Mountain oysters, promise. Now, can I load your luggage in the car so we can get home?"

WITH BILLY ASLEEP, Granny listened patiently as Cole told her about what had happened the night before in Atlanta. She said nothing but held a stern look on her face. Cole couldn't tell if it was worry or anger in her eyes as he talked. But, she said nothing.

Cole switched the topic. "The therapist says Billy seems to be doing well."

Granny's face warmed. "You're doing good, boy. Jackie would be real proud." Granny reached over and grabbed Cole's knee as they sat on the couch watching *Fallen*.

"Thanks Granny, I wish I could agree. I think I'm failing horribly. Just the other day I caught him singing the lyrics to that lollipop song by Maejoer Ali, he thought it was about..."

"I like lollipops, 'nothing wrong with that."

Cole shook his head and laughed, "Granny, the song isn't about sucking a lollipop, but...." Cole swallowed hard at what he was about to discuss with his grandmother. The word came out slow. "... but, the thing being sucked is someone's... uh, penis."

Granny's eyes grew big, "Oh! Well, Granny has done that, too." She let out a loud chuckle and then covered her mouth to avoid waking Billy. "Garret Peterson... hmm."

Cole recoiled into the couch. "Oh my god, Granny, I don't want to know." Both laughing for a moment, she turned serious.

"Sugga, kids are gonna pick up on things. Nothin' you can do about that. Stop worryin'. That sounds more like Ava than you. Listen to me, parenting doesn't come with a manual. Ya will mess up occasionally. Just don't kill them and you've done a good job. Pay no attention to Ava. She hasn't been the same since Jackie dying and she is strugglin' bad. She won't tell anyone, but she is hurting. And, that boy up there is the one thing she can attach herself to as part of Jackie. She doesn't mean it when she criticizes your care of him. She loves you, but she is still grievin' over her daughter. She knows ya know that they can't take care of that baby boy. But, when her emotions get bad she tries to tell herself that being a parent for Billy would be like caring for Jackie." She paused to let the words sink in. "And, let me tell ya somethin', the only one taking care of someone in that house is me taking care of them. Don't let them fool ya. This old lady is holding that place together."

"Yeah, but with everything in Atlanta, the kidnapper, Granny it isn't over."

She raised a brow to show her determination to not be crossed. "Grandbaby, this isn't my first rodeo. Someone coming after ya or that baby boy up there and they will have to get past me. So get that craziness out of your head, ya hear me? Cause you have called in Rambo-Momma and she is ready to kick some ass." She flexed a tiny bicep, making Cole smile. "But, before I get to that, I'm going upstairs and slipping off these shit kickers. It's one a.m. my time. I like my coffee like I like my men, strong and dark." With a wink she hugged Cole and went up to her room.

ALONE, HE STARED out the back window of the house. His concern that Pam's death and the attack on Finn had something to do with him only made the pain worse. Had Leas' investigation gotten too close to The Taker... prompting retaliation on Cole? Worse, had Cole's own digging caused their attack? Either way, Cole's craving to locate The Taker had now fully consumed him.

CHAPTER 57

D.C. CRYPTOLOGISTS TOLD him the symbol on Mr. Lasiter's chest was some type of code, shorthand. The carving was too rough to translate it precisely. Meadows agreed that without a lead, they were left pulling at straws. One of those was libraries. Perhaps someone had been looking into the symbol.

"Miss Kent, I'm agent Meadows, this is Agent Leas. We are with the FBI and are investigating a murder and attack that occurred recently."

"Oh my… here? In the library?" The old lady pressed her hand to her upper chest as if clutching a string of pearls. Her denim dress and red-framed bifocals suggested elementary school teacher.

The agents looked at each other before Meadows responded. "No ma'am. Somewhere else, but there was a symbol used in the murder that has been identified as a type of shorthand, Pitman's? We have visited several libraries in the area to see if there has been anyone mentioning or researching the symbols and just wanted to check."

"Oh my.. I… Not that I recall. Would you know when they may have come in?"

Leas shuffled his feet impatiently, "Ma'am, we don't know if anyone ever came in, much less when they would have come in." His words were cold, causing the lady to tighten her eyes at his rude tone.

Turning to Meadows, "Well, let me ask Lynette. Come with me." The two men followed as the woman approached another in a lemon yellow dress standing behind the library's help desk.

Speaking to a large mocha skinned woman, she said. "Lynette, these two men are from the FBI." The words were whispers. "They are investigating a murder and want to know if anyone has been around asking about shorthand." The first woman turned back to the agents. "Pitman's you say?" Meadows nodded as he noticed Lynette raise a gray brow.

The second woman pressed her hands into her broad hips. "I knew that boy was up to no good. Murder? No. But, no boy his age comes in asking about shorthand and then steals a book. Is he a killer?" Her gravelly voice accented the stern tone of her words as her large brown eyes focused on Meadows.

"We aren't really at liberty to say right now. You said he stole a book? Which one?"

Lynette slipped on her reading glasses and turned to the computer monitor. A few keystrokes later she looked up over glasses. *"Pitman's English and Shorthand Dictionary.* Our only copy, too. Up to no good, I tell ya. He had some book with him too, had all this writing in it. That's what he was trying to figure out...what it said."

Leas looked up to see a camera over the reference desk. "How long do you keep that security footage? We need a copy of that."

"That? Uhm, it's on its own cycle."

Leas interrupted. "When was the guy last in here? Would it still be on it?"

"Honey, slow down…. I want to say it records like a week's worth of video, but really don't know. I can have Floyd, our systems guy, burn a copy of that for you, though. But, you can watch it right now."

ALL FOUR CROWDED into the glass office directly behind the reference desk and stared at a monitor with a VCR like box under it. Lynette hit a few buttons and then turned a large dial making the video rewind. A desk bell rung from out front and she looked at the other woman. "Uh Lynette, you going to help that girl or what? Go see what that lady needs." The other lady shot a look of disappointment to the three and then shuffled off to the desk. "Damn woman. Always so nosy. You say 'killer' and she comes a running. Yet, you say anything else and she pretends to be hard of hearing." Lynette shook her head and then abruptly perked up. "Oh, there that lil' weasel is. Gotcha sucker. See, he brought that book in with him. I couldn't tell that writing from scribble. But, I referred him to shorthand." She stood up from the screen. "See, my sister-in-law… well, ex-sister-in-law, Rhonda was a court reporter over in DeKalb County and she would write that stuff out sometimes. Gibberish to me, but she could make sense of it. So, I figured it must have been something like that, you get me? Shorthand."

Paying no attention to the woman, Leas barked, "Freeze it right there." On the screen was the journal spread open on the reference desk. The two men leaned in to get a better view. "Can you zoom that in for us?"

"I can try, hold up a sec." A few turns of a smaller dial

and the picture zoomed in slightly before pixelating too much. "Take it back just a little bit." Meadows' cocked his head sideways to read the upside down text on the journal's page. "What... is... that?"

Leas tightened his eyes to focus and then turned to Meadows. "Mouzon. It says Mouzon."

"... well, I could'a told you that. It was the only word on the page that I could read. What's a Mouzon?"

The two men looked at each other and then Lynette. "Ma'am, we appreciate all your assistance. Please save this video and have it burned onto a disk today. I will send some agents over later to pick it up. Here is my card should you have anything else you recall or if the guy comes back here, but that is highly unlikely." Meadows handed the woman his card as Leas started out the office door. The video had just confirmed their suspicions; the deaths were all linked to Cole.

CHAPTER 58

JASMINE, THE YOUNG APD officer from the post-briefing romp session, rushed into Leas' and Meadows' shared make-shift office in downtown Atlanta. Looking up in surprise, Leas recognized the woman and then clicked off the video they had copied from the library earlier that morning. She spoke fast. "I think we figured it out... the connection." She waved the two men into the next room and pointed at the white-board in the corner. There, pictures of each victim lined the top with dry-erase marks with arrows pointing to one word. "Lowe's."

"What does it mean?" Meadows's impatience for the dramatic flashed.

"It was in their credit card records. I took the most recent, Celia Leigh's and reviewed it. Sanchez and White took the Macon and Athens victims. They all shopped at the Moreland Avenue Lowe's store a month or so before they died. Felicia Grubbs, the Macon victim, purchased a washer from her local store... but it was delivered from the Moreland Avenue location's stock because it was out of stock at the Athens location. Travis Rafferty, the Macon guy... lives here in Atlanta, but has been remolding his mother's old home in Macon. So he placed the order at Moreland as well." Jasmine paused with her eyes wide open, questioning for understanding of what she was saying. No one responded. "Celia was more difficult. She rents, so we found nothing other than a few plant purchases at Lowe's. But, when we saw that link between the other vics we gathered her apartment's records. Get this, Sanderson Management, her landlord, purchased a new stove that was delivered three weeks before her death."

Leas placed a hand on her shoulder. "Nice work officer. So, he's using his position as a Lowe's delivery guy to find his victims. Have you pulled their employee records yet?"

"The subpoena is being delivered to the judge now for signing. We hope to have the records in an hour or so."

Meadows' smiled. It was their first big break. The killer was like Rader, he was gaining access to his future victims' lives by being a delivery guy. He would be able to evaluate their life, their home and then plan his attack from there. Yet, the Mouzon friends were a divergence from that plan. "Okay, well we now know how he selected his last victims. But, unless you are telling me the museum boy and girl also shopped there, something has caused him to shift courses. What had changed?"

Jasmine looked back blankly. "We checked. They have no real ties to Lowe's. It seems they were killed for some other reason."

"Well then, we still have work to do. Don't waste anymore of my time until you have an answer." Meadows gave a cold look to those in the room and then returned to his office. Leas' eyes followed him until the door slammed shut. He looked down and shook his head before speaking.

"Officer, pay no attention to him. He's an ass, that about sums it up. That was good work." Jasmine rolled her eyes as she shifted her jaw in disbelief.

"Do we have all the coroners' reports? I want to compare them."

"Yeah, I think that White has them. White, do you have all the medical reports on the victims, including the two at the museum?" Jasmine looked at Leas to make sure that is what he was asking for. He nodded as White pulled sheets from a metal office tray on his desk.

"Yeah, I got them." He raised them in the air.

Leas walked over and grabbed them. "Thank you officer." Leas turned to the rest standing around the room. "Thank you all. You are doing great work. We appreciate it."

"YOU KNOW HOW to piss people off, don't you? Those officers are out there working overtime to help solve this and you are acting like a spoiled child. Might want to show some appreciation if you expect any assistance from them." Leas dropped into his cheap metal seat, placing the medical report in front of him. With no immediate response, he started to read.

"I really don't give a damn how they feel about me. I'm here to stop a killer, not to make friends. If they don't like that, they can leave."

Leas looked up to the man sitting across the desk from him. "Shit man, do you have any friends? I mean, have you ever even been married? Or, is this job your life?"

"Agent, the law is a jealous mistress. She demands all

of your attention if you want to do it right. Not that you would know about that." His eyes glared at Leas with disdain.

"Listen here you fuck, I may be saddled with you for this investigation, but I'm not one of those shy cops out there. I have no problem telling you that you are full of shit." Leas leaned back into his chair and crossed his arms while still maintaining eye contact. "You sit there like your shit don't stink, but you are no better than the rest of us mutts. We all have a reason for going into the law and they all usually relate to dark pasts. What's your shit story?"

Meadows went quiet with a look that suggested he was reflecting on something. Leas went back to looking at his papers when Meadows started to speak again. "My mom... when I was little she was killed by her husband, my step-dad, during one of his frequent drunk rages." He focused on a pen he was twisting between two fingers as he spoke. Then he dropped it and looked up. "What's your story? I mean, I know about your wife, but what got you in this game in the first place?"

Inhaling deeply, Leas looked up and pressed a smile to one corner of his mouth. "Shit, well... since I started it... for me, it was my brother. He was shot as a bystander during a convenience store robbery back in New Mexico. My parents and I were in the car and saw the entire thing. Kinda fucks you up." Leas relaxed his shoulders before continuing. "But, that doesn't give either of us an excuse to be dicks to those helping find this killer. And, this obsession you have about the Mouzon boy... it's stupid."

"Agent, you say that, but I think you are opening yourself up for disappointment and regret if you don't consider him. I should know."

Leas squinted his eyes. "What do you mean?"

Rolling his head as if he was trying to get a kink out, Meadows said, "Rader... I discounted his involvement initially. Looking back, my reasons were stupid. But, then... at that time... they made sense to me. I messed up. I had met Rader in 1979. I didn't suspect him and let him kill three more times before he was caught. Unknown to anyone, he had attempted to kill an older lady, Anna, at the time. He had watched her for months and determined her routine on Fridays. But, she went out with friends and didn't come home until well after he expected, he grew impatient and left. The threat to her life wasn't known until he sent a package to her with a poem titled, 'Oh Anna Why Didn't You Appear,' with a sketch of what he had wanted to do to her and several things he had stolen from her home. Scared, she called the police and I was invited to show." He lowered his head and attempted to twist out his neck kink again.

"Well, I took several statements from on-lookers that said they had information. One of those was a man named Bill Thomas Killman." He looked up. "That was the name Rader used in his 2004 letters. I didn't investigate him because he seemed nice, trusting. It could be easy for me to now say I was a young investigator and didn't know that those are usually the ones to watch out for, but it would be a lie. I was fooled."

The old man stood and removed his navy blazer and draped it over the back of his chair, leaving his gun holster tightly held against his ribs. He sat back down. "I didn't know about my mistake until March 2004 when he couldn't keep his mouth shut any longer. Eleven letters and packages were sent before he was finally arrested in February 2005. Most of those contained photos. One contained a draft autobiography called "The BTK Story" that mocked a truTV special that had aired in 1999. Another autobiography was delivered several months later that actually mentioned my interview of him. He was mocking my stupidity." He looked up to Leas and stared. "I won't make that mistake again. And, I won't let you make that mistake. I will not rule Mouzon out just because he appears nice. Those are usually the ones you never should rule out. We have set the trap for him. Either way, we are going to find out who this killer is."

CHAPTER 59

"HANNAH, THANKS FOR the invite." Cole looked around the remodeled ranch that sprawled out from the main entrance in both directions. Hannah pushed her gray hair over one shoulder as she welcomed Noel and Cole. "Well, of course. You're the new neighbor."

"This is a great place."

"Thanks, Noel. That's right. You haven't been here since the remodel. I've owned the place since the mid-80s and Nancy and I have wanted to change the place up since she was allowed to move in. Twenty years later we finally decided to just do it. She got a nice promotion last spring, so it was just time." The word "allowed" stuck with Cole but he was pushed towards the party before he could ask. He recalled his first meeting with Hannah and the insight into Denver's old co-habitation prohibitions.

Walking their way through the small circles of people dotting the kitchen and living room, Cole made his way to the bucket of beers.

Noel pushed forward into a crowded circle of people. "Oh, there you are! Nancy, tell Cole it's true about Cheeseman and the bodies." Noel was pulling Cole behind him. The tall, slightly gray-haired woman eyed Cole and then Noel. Her mocha skin was tight and smooth.

"Uhm, well hey Noel. Good to see you again, too. Cole. What do you want to know? It's true."

Noel turned to Cole. "Nancy works for the new History Colorado museum, she knows all of this crazy stuff." He sat on the arm of one of the couches like a child about to hear a good story. "Go on..." Cole had only met Nancy briefly since moving in next door and felt awkward putting her on the spot. He wasn't in the mood to hear ghost stories in light of the attack and slaughter of his friends just two days before. He and she looked at each other to suggest they knew this was more for Noel's entertainment than anyone's knowledge.

Rattling the ice in her glass, she started. "Well, I mean, the graveyard was called Mount Prospect, but the locals called it The Old Bone Yard or Boot Hill for all the outlaws that hung out in it in the mid-1800's. It was built on top of ancient Indian burial grounds – without removing the bodies. By the late 1800's the graveyard had been taken over by the Feds and was in horrible disrepair from vandals, grave robbers and just neglect. So Washington D.C. gave the survivors ninety days to move the bodies or they would move them. A guy named McGovern won the contract to move the remaining bodies. But, because he was paid by the box, he chopped the bodies into parts so each body filled at least three boxes. The locals went crazy when they discovered dead bodies all over the place. The plethora of bones and vandals pushed them over the edge. So the contract was yanked before the job was ever finished. It got much worse before the city just decided to plant trees and bushes in the open graves to spruce up the place. Eventually the headstones were removed, but it's estimated that over five thousand bodies are still under there. That's why there are all those depressions." She leaned in. "It's the caskets breaking down. Random bones and other artifacts are constantly rising to the surface and they say the place is haunted."

Cole looked at his host and tried to determine if she was making it all up.

Noel yanked on Cole's sleeve. "My friend Sam said he laid in one of those depressions one time and something grabbed him. He couldn't get up. It took two other guys to pull him free!" He cupped his hands over his face in feigned fear. Cole just rolled his eyes.

"Oh… Oh… Tell him about the Stanley. You know, The Shining hotel." Noel's excitement for story time made Nancy laugh.

"Okay, one more Noel."

"You really don't have to. You have a party to attend to." Cole felt Noel protest by nudging his ribs.

"The Stanley is pretty short. Stephen King learned about it during his visit to the hotel up in Estes Park. Lots of ghosts wandering around the old place including ghosts of kids, thus the scary girl twins in the movie, I guess. Nothing as dramatic ever happened there as the movie, but plenty of doors opening, rooms being trashed, you know… typical evil ghost stuff." Nancy looked down at Noel, "Was that what you were looking for?"

He looked back disappointed. "You totally flubbed that one. It's supposed to be scary, not read like a grocery list." Standing, he added with a hug, "I still love you though. Thanks for inviting us! This is pretty awesome."

"Sure thing, baby. I'm just glad you were able to come

to the city for the weekend. Not that Aspen sucks or anything. But, it is a haul."

"Cole, Nancy told me about your friends and that
stuff back in Atlanta and Charleston. If you need anything from us, just let us know, okay?"

Cole forced a smile. "Thanks. The law isn't being very
helpful right now. All they know is it seems the woman,
Poinsett, may have been successful in luring her father
out by killing all of us kidnapped kids off."

Nancy quizzically looked at him. "Poinsett? Was that
her family name?"

Her interest caught Cole by surprise. "Yeah, or... at
least her father's name. Why?"

"Are you talking about the Joel Poinsett clan? Because,
they came out here from Charleston in the late 1800's as
miners just as the Territory of Jefferson, now Colorado
and portions of Utah, was being created to set up free territory before the Civil War broke out. They ended up settling a lot of Denver and on up to Breckenridge."

Cole's stomach dropped. If the killer or his family
had ties to Denver, Billy and Granny were in trouble. He
needed to get next door and check on them, fast.

Cole's words were rushed. "I need to go. I'm sorry,
and thank you. Really, thank you for having me over. But,
I'm just not feeling well." Cole rushed out of the house.

CHAPTER 60

"NO MA'AM. NO. We just have some questions for him, that's all. Where would he run off to?"

"Like I say, that boy ain't been aroun' here in two… three days. I called the po-lease after he don't show up for breakfast. He's a good boy officer – what chu say your name is?" The large black woman squinted one eye.

"Leas, ma'am. Agent Leas."

Her voice grew skeptical. "Why the FBI all up in here investigatin' my son's missin'?"

"Just part of the job, ma'am. Would you have a recent photo of your son, of Kendrick, that we can have?"

She looked at him with skeptical eyes before responding. "Oh, I got one up in the house I can get you. Hold up." The woman walked slowly back into her house with her cane.

Leas turned and looked out onto the street from the old covered porch of Kendrick Monroe's home. An old model Ford Taurus drove by slowly, its driver peering through its driver's side window to inspect Leas. It came to a stop next door just as Miss Monroe opened up her screen door and walked out with a photo in her hand.

"Here's a picture of my baby. It's about a year old, but other than his height, not much change since then."

Leas looked at the photo and recognized the face. "Thank you, ma'am. I appreciate it. We will get this back to you."

"Jus fine'em, Mister Leas. Find my baby."

LEAS WALKED OFF the weathered porch and towards the front chain-link gate. "Excuse me, sir. Do you have a moment?"

The gray-haired man tilted his head in recognition. "As you can see, I've kind of got my hands full right now."

Leas looked down to the two pieces of luggage being toted. "Been out of town I see. I will only take a moment of your time. Your neighbor's boy, Kendrick, he's gone missing. You know much about him?"

The man kept walking slowly towards his porch. "Kendrick? He's missing? How long?"

Leas walked out into the street and over to the man's gate. "May I?"

"Sure, but, like I said... I don't know how much help I can be. I've been out of town for the past week."

Leas felt the man was just too relaxed for hearing his neighbor had disappeared. He walked into the man's yard and put a shoe up on his porch's edge. "Do you know Kendrick well?"

"Well? I mean he is a neighbor. But, he is a kid. We don't really spend much time together. Sorry... just don't think I can be of much help." The man was pushing Leas off.

"How long have you lived here?"

"Ten, fifteen years."

"Strange." Leas looked down to the ground.

The man took the bait. "Strange? Why is that?"

"Oh, I mean... don't get me wrong. It just seems strange that you have lived here that long. Your house is what... three feet from his and you say you don't know him."

The old man shuffled in his position at his open door. "Let me put these down." He turned and walked in, the screen door slapped shut. Leas pulled it open and stepped inside.

The small living room reminded him of something from the 50's, drab and old. A stand-up piano was pushed against wall. Small pieces of oak furniture and a worn couch made the room feel cramped. Several art prints littered the walls.

"Look, I don't want to get too involved. But, the kid comes from a pretty abusive relationship. His step-dad was pretty rough on him." The man leaned against the doorframe of what looked like his kitchen. "The step-father disappeared a year or so ago. But, the kid took the blunt of that. He would come over and mow the grass and we would just chat. I talked to him several times about it. I'm not surprised that he disappeared. Seemed pretty messed-up."

"Did he ever mention any place? Somewhere he may go when times got hard at his home?"

The man shook his head "no" slowly. "Nope. Like I said, I didn't know him that well. He more just vented when all that was going on. Things seemed to be improving since his step-father was out of the picture. He was certainly in a better mood."

"Well, if you think of anything, can you give me a

call?" Leas extended a card to the old man. Halfway out the front door he looked back. "I totally forgot to get your name."

"Smith Gilmore…" He looked down to the card in his hand. "… Agent Leas."

FUTILE

CHAPTER 61

A DAY LATER LEAS was surprised by a visit. "Agent Leas, either you tell him or I will. He deserves to know. He needs to know."

"He already fucking knows, okay!" Leas was pissed that Calhoun has showed up in Atlanta without notice and demanded the local police have Leas call him... like some valet driver. He was no one's call boy and he certainly didn't have time for yet another person trying to go behind him and investigate the murders. Agent Meadows and Mouzon were certainly enough. "Mr. Calhoun, what do you know about these?" He threw the photos of Cole at the graveyard onto a table. Cash picked one of them up and inspected it.

Cash looked up with a puzzled look on his face. "Where is this? When... is this?"

"Seems you two were in town a few weeks ago. He took a little detour and visited one of the crime scenes in my investigation. The one I called you about. Your little boyfriend has gone rogue and is fucking hunting The Taker."

From the appearance of Calhoun's face, Leas could

tell the he had no clue what he was talking about. "I… we aren't boyfriends. He and I… we don't talk anymore."

Leas softened slightly. "Look, he knows more than he is telling us… and you. We told him about the Audubon connection. So, you have nothing to offer him. But, my… my shit faced partner thinks he is actually in on it. Don't even ask what fucked up logic he is applying to get there. But, you and I know that isn't the case. Him visiting these sites, doing his own investigation doesn't help. I can't tell you what we know. But, please. You have to just stay out of it. If you go flying out there to help, it will only hurt him."

Cash leaned into the table. "I can't let him get hurt, Agent. I can't let him go." His head bowed.

Leas put a hand on Cash's shoulder. "He is safe out there. If you run to him now, you may cause the killer to follow. From what we can tell the killer is intentionally targeting Cole's friends – not Cole at this point. You being here is not wise. You are not safe in Atlanta. The killer somehow tracked Cole while he was here in Atlanta, followed him around, and now has attacked his friends. If your contact with Cole has stopped, leave it that way for your own safety and his safety. We will get this guy, promise. But you have to stay out of the way for right now. Promise me."

"But… Cole."

"Mr. Calhoun, I bet he will risk his life for you if he thinks you are in danger. If you truly care for him, don't give him a reason to place himself in danger. Leave him be."

CASH EXITED THE Atlanta PD's office and headed back

through the Atlanta Underground to the parking lot on its far end. The large underground market was at one time at street level, but the city built on top of the area, leaving over ten blocks effectively under the city, abandoned until the 1960's when they were rediscovered in relatively pristine condition. Someone caught Cash's eye as he passed one of the old gas street lamps. Leas' words were fresh in his mind. *You are not safe.* Cash ducked into a candied nut store and watched the man follow him in from a mirror on the wall. Reaching slowly into his pocket, he pulled out his phone and snapped a picture as the man pretended to look at a display.

Cash stepped towards the door and saw the man turn. He ran across the bricked walk and down the stairs leading to the garage. Several seconds later he heard the door slam shut from the level he had just left. He pushed faster until he reached the purple level and then jumped into the garage. Winded, he kept running until he reached his rental and jumped in, ducking below the dash.

Watching the door, it slowly opened but never fully. Someone was watching through it. Trying to see where he was. After a minute it shut in disappointment.

Cash stayed down for several minutes before sitting up and starting the car. He relaxed.

That's when the man struck, tugging on the door handle trying to get it to open. He must have walked from an upper level because Cash never saw him until that moment. The man then pulled out a black pistol. Cash hit the gas to escape, taking a hard turn around the garage and clipping another car. A shot rang out. From his rearview mirror he saw the man aim the gun a final time. But the shot never came.

CHAPTER 62

"WELL... WELL. WHO are you supposed to be?" Granny looked down to see Billy standing at her feet in the kitchen.

The small boy growled. "Err, I'm the Hulk, Granny. See, I'm all green. Don't make me angry. Arrr."

The woman threw up her hands. "Indeed." She stepped back for a better look. "I bet this will keep you from getting mad. We can't have that." She dipped her hand into a large plastic bowl and withdrew a handful of candy. "Here, let's get you started out right."

"Granny, save that for the kids that come to our door. He will get plenty out there." Cole had walked into the room and was now standing behind Billy.

She let out a long chuckle before asking, "And, what exactly are you supposed to be?"

Cole looked down at his costume. "Uh, Captain America. Shield and all."

"It looks like you put on one too many pairs of blue tights to me." Granny started laughing. Billy followed with a giggle. "Uncle Cole, I thought we were going to be the Avengers. We need Thor." Cole knew what his nephew was saying. He missed Cash.

"I know buddy, but Thor couldn't make it. But, we got Granny and she has serious butt kicking skills." Granny laughed and then did a karate kick. "Yahh."

Billy giggled again. "Awe, why isn't Mister Cash here? He promised he would be Thor."

Cole kneeled down to Billy's level. "Billy, Thor... Cash couldn't make it and I don't think we will be seeing him again."

Billy's face went sad. "Did I do something wrong? Is he mad at me?"

"Oh my gosh, no, Billy. You did nothing wrong." Cole told himself mentally, 'I did something wrong.' "It's just... well..."

Billy's voice went stern with disappointment. "It was you, wasn't it? You made him go away. You told him not to come. That's why Miss Ann was mad at you."

"Billy!" Granny scolded him.

"No, you did something and made him go away. I hate you... I hate you! Why did you make him go away?"

Cole rushed in to hold Billy, but he turned away and hugged Granny. Cole stepped back deflated. "Billy, he just... well, we aren't friends anymore."

Billy started crying in heavy wails. "I... hate you. Go away." Cole tried to fight the urge to cry himself, his eyes were red with unshed tears as he looked up to Granny for guidance.

Granny pushed Billy off of her and into Cole. She softly said, "Hug him. Just hug him." Billy fought and kicked as Cole wrapped his arms around him and then lifted him into the air. Billy's sobs continued for several minutes as Cole struggled to not join him.

Slowly the puffs of emotion dwindled until Billy lifted his head. "Can we still go twik-or-tweeting?

Granny walked over and rubbed the young boy's back. "Sugar, it has been forever since I've been out on Halloween. Why don't you and Rambo Mamma go trick-or-treating together? Let Cole go dry himself off and have a few hours to himself. What do you say?"

Billy pulled back to look at Cole who was still holding him in the air. "Is that okay?"

"Of course, mister. I think you will get more candy with Rambo Mamma, anyway." Cole grinned back at Billy.

Granny gathered her cheetah fur coat and feed-and-seed rain boots before heading for the door. "Uh, is Rambo Mamma a Russian hooker?" Cole grinned at his joke.

The old lady smiled. "Baby, with the skills I used to have, even a hooker would be jealous. By the way, you got some mail over there. Some packages, too." Granny pointed to the kitchen desk before walking out the door with Billy.

COLE FINGERED THROUGH the mail and saw nothing important enough worth tearing open immediately. The packages were both sent in soft plastic envelopes. The label indicated they were sent by Amazon Warehouse, but Cole couldn't recall ordering anything. He tore open the first one. *Pitman 2000: Shorthand Pocket Dictionary.* Cole turned the used paperback over and scratched his head. *Clearly a shipping mistake.*

The same occurred when he opened the second, larger and much heavier envelope. The large image of a blue heron stood out as Cole stared at the used copy of *Birds of America.* He flicked through its thick pages, each with some type of watercolor accompanied by what appeared to be a discussion of the painting's history. He had no clue why the book was delivered, but he was grateful. He needed to escape from his argument with Billy and the doubts that continuously circled his mind. Cole clutched the book to his chest and walked up to his room.

Cole drew himself a bubble bath surrounded by several candles and climbed in. Thumbing through the book he saw several images known to him from childhood. Charleston had an Audubon art store on King Street that Ava would take him to on the rare occasions she dared shop the peninsula. He recalled pulling through the stack of giant posters and prints of now extinct birds and wondering just how the artist captured all of their details.

Cole lost track of time as he found himself almost through the book by the time Billy knocked on the bathroom door. Cole wrapped a towel around his waist and opened the door. "What's up mister? Did you have a great time with Granny? Get lots of candy?"

"Yeah, but she keeps telling me she needs to test it for poison and stuff by eating it." Billy leaned in and whispered with a cupped hand. "She can have a few pieces, but I think she is just trying to eat it all."

Cole laughed. "Yeah, watch out for that Granny. She's a sneaky one. She used to do that to me, too. You better get down there and save it before she eats it all."

"Uncle Cole... I'm... I'm sorry. I don't hate you. I love you."

Cole's eyes beamed back warmly. "I know you do, Billy. And, I hope you know how much I love you, too. I will never let anything happen to you." Cole grabbed Billy and gave him a hug. "Now, go save us come candy before she gets it all."

Billy ran out of the room and Cole could hear him shouting from the top of the stairs, "Granny, don't eat all my candy!"

CHAPTER 63

L EAS HAD PICKED-UP Kendrick's trail after talking to several coffee shops around the library. One of the baristas had recognized the photo provided by his mother and indicated he had been a frequent customer and been hanging out a lot in the past few days to use the internet. It took most of the day and too many venti's to mention before Kendrick finally showed. The FBI had little more than him researching shorthand to tie him to the murders at this point, making an arrest impossible to stick.

Leas had a particularly rough run-in with local defense attorney Jimmy Berry back in the nineties. Nancy Grace was the assistant D.A. on the case passed-on by the FBI for federal prosecution. A circus of motions about the shortness of her skirts and depth of her blouses ensued, distracting everyone from the marginal evidence in the case. Leas rubbed his temples as he recalled reading somewhere that she was ultimately smacked with ethical violations by Georgia and Federal courts for playing "fast and loose" with the rules. But, by then she had launched into stardom and never looked back.

Leas watched from a few stools over as Kendrick

propped open a small laptop and started surfing the internet. He couldn't tell what was being accessed from his vantage point, but Kendrick kept referring to notes on a small yellow pad. Occasionally he would jot down something and then continued his research. About half an hour later he looked at his watch then abruptly packed up and walked out into the now dark street.

Leas slowly followed at a distance as Kendrick headed down Crescent Street and then jumped into a long line of twenty-something's standing outside a nightclub. For the large banner hung on the building, someone named Armin van Buuren was performing. Watching from the edge of the building, Leas noted from their interaction that Kendrick appeared to know the doorman enough to be permitted to slip in with his backpack.

Leas took a deep breath, stashed his jacket in the bushes and jumped into line. Inside he discovered the club's name, Opera, was apt. The space was a converted opera house or theater with the upper boxes connected together and now lined with a glass railing. The entire main room was packed making it impossible to relocate Kendrick. The DJ de jour was situated somewhere in an alcove above the entrance way giving you the impression that a thousand people were staring at you as you walked in. Leas pushed through and up some side stairs to access a private box area that overlooked the entire crowd. *Come on, come on… where are you?* There were several misidentifications before he found the backpack, Kendrick attached to it, pushing towards the back sections of the club. Leas raced down.

Kendrick was just feet away when Leas saw him whispering in one of the bartender's ears. A heated conversation ensued with the bartender finally digging into his pocket and pulling out his car keys. They were reluctantly passed to Kendrick just as he discovered he was being watched. He snatched the keys and ran.

"Hold up! Your mom sent me. Hold up!"

Kendrick didn't stop, looking back once before being lost again in the crowd. Leas pushed through until he made it to a dark back room. Looking around he was unable to locate him. Then he saw the back door slowly closing. He rushed out onto its deck just as Kendrick was climbing over the top of a large wooden fence. Leas, out of breath, shook his head. Kendrick had escaped.

LEAS CAUGHT HIS breath and went back inside to locate the bartender.

"Dude, dude... chill man. What did I do?" The lanky twenty-something spoke like he had smoked just a little too much pot before work. "Seriously, dude. Can you put me down?" Leas released his hold on the kid's t-shirt that he had used to push him against the wall.

"That guy you just handed your keys to. Start talking."

He kid looked around, "What man? I didn't do anything wrong. He just needed to borrow my car, that's all."

The heavy base of the club's speakers were making it hard to hear. Leas shouted, "What's his name?"

"Kenny, man. Kenny Montrose or Monroe or something like that. What the fuck, man. Why do you care?"

Leas flashed his badge and responded. "He's been missing. Where's he headed?"

"Dude, I have no clue. He said he needed the car for a few hours, that's all I know. I owed him a favor. Damn, man."

Leas shouted, "You didn't answer my question. Why does he need your car?" The kid just looked at him causing Leas to grow impatient. He grabbed the kid by his shirt again.

"Chill, man. He said something about needing to set things straight. That's all I got, dude. Can I have my shirt back now?"

Leas loosened his grip again and let the kid walk. What was Kendrick going to do to set things straight?

CHAPTER 64

"GRANNY, SO I don't mess this up, what all do you need for that pie you want to make?" Cole sat on a stool at the granite island in his kitchen staring at Granny in an apron, Billy next to her on a small stepping stool covered in flour. Billy was learning to cook, but it appeared that most of the ingredients were ending up on him rather than in the mixing bowl. Cole shook his head and laughed to himself.

"Baby, you know what I need. How many times have you helped me make that pie? Peanut butter, a pie shell, vanilla pudding... that's it."

"And, whipped cream!" Billy added.

"I think you are sweet enough, mister. Any more sugar and we are going to all have cavities."

"Baby boy wants whipped cream, get him whipped cream." Granny shook a wooden spoon at Cole to jokingly enforce her words.

"Yes, ma'am. I've also got... eggs, sausage.. uhm.. some pork chops for tonight. If you think of anything else, just call me. I'm going to run to the bank, too. Should be back in an hour."

THE FRONT DOOR was barely closed when he saw them walking up the home's brick path. Cole spoke cautiously. "Agent Leas, this is a surprise. I didn't know you were in Denver." Cole looked to the older man standing next to Leas and put out his hand. "Cole Mouzon. And, you are?"

"Agent Meadows, Mr. Mouzon. We are sorry for the surprise visit. But, we have some questions for you." Agent Leas was clearly not in charge. Cole looked back to the house and then the two men. "Sure, but not here. Coffee? You can ride with me."

The three men loaded into Cole's Audi and drove in silence for a few blocks. "So he's back right? I mean, you wouldn't be here unless he was back and he was coming for me. That's who killed Pam, right? The Taker or whatever he calls himself." The two agents sat silently. "Oh come on! Is my family in danger? Should they be home alone right now?"

"Cole, they are safe. We don't think he has gotten here yet. He stole a car in Atlanta a day ago. But, we suspect it's just a matter of time. And, it isn't your kidnapper. It's someone else. But, he seems to be working off your kidnapper's script."

"Mr. Mouzon, do you know a Kendrick Monroe?"

Cole looked at the man sitting in the front passenger seat. "Agent Meadows, you said? Monroe? No. Should I know him?"

"No, we are still piecing things together, but it appears he is the one who attacked your friends at the museum and killed three others. He appears to be another follower of your kidnapper, like the Winters woman."

Cole shook his head as they stepped out of the car and walked into Ink! Coffee. He hadn't heard Winters' name in months, preferring to refer to her by her murderous name – Poinsett. She had killed his sister in an attempt to kill him. Cole still hadn't figured out her theory for how he and the other kids kidnapped were The Taker's prizes, such that her killing them would draw him out. Daniel Page's sporadic drops of information from inside the FBI provided little to date, beyond what Cole had already suspected. The news had filled in a few more of the gaps, linking the newest Atlanta murders to Cole's experience in Charleston.

Sitting in the far corner of the modern-style coffee shop, Cole asked, "So, what's going on here? Do I have like a bounty on my head or something? Why are people signing up to try and kill me and my friends?" Cole looked to Leas for answers. But he remained quiet.

"This one is different Mr. Mouzon. We have found no connection with the first two murders in this latest killing spree. Moreover, there appears to be a shift. Your friends' attacker was much more careless. We think Mrs. Hemmer walked in on Mr. Lasiter's attack, surprising the killer. From all the evidence we have, there was a fight."

Cole's eyes welled up with tears. He suspected that Pam's attack had been his fault and the FBI was now confirming that. He felt toxic, dangerous to all around him. "You promise that my family is safe?"

Leas leaned in. "Cole, we will not be letting anything happen to them. I personally promise you that." Cole cut his eyes to Meadows for agreement, but instead he shot a look of disagreement to Leas who had apparently made a promise that the FBI could not keep. "Nothing will be happening to his family." Leas said defiantly.

"Is he here?"

"No. He hasn't booked any flights or been spotted by TSA. So, if he is coming this way, he will have to drive. All Greyhound offices have been notified just in case he tries to catch a bus. We know he was in Atlanta as recently as a day ago based on his mother. But, he has since disappeared." Meadows spoke like he was dictating a report.

"Why do you think he is headed this way, for me? Hell, why did he attack my friends?"

"Cole, we don't know why." Leas words were slow. "But, as to how he got on your trail… He has a book, some type of coded journal. We don't think it's his. He seems to have found it and de-coded it. Our guys at Langley have interpreted a part of that journal and… it appears to be about you."

Cole looked at Leas quizzically, "About me? What do you mean, about me?"

"Mr. Mouzon, someone… whoever's journal it is, has been watching you, documenting your movements… studying you."

Cole let the revelation of someone spying on him sink in before responding. *Studying him? Why?* "When? Like when I was a kid?"

Leas' look suggested the answer. "No. It appears you have been watched as recently as just a month ago. Notes taken document your movements to work, your exercise routines, even your nephew."

Chills ran through Cole's body. "Billy? Someone has been watching Billy?"

"Only when you are around Mr. Mouzon. It appears the focus is entirely on you." Cole took some comfort in that fact, but he was being studied nonetheless.

"So, two people are after me, not one."

"Cole, we have no indication of that. It appears that the killer is tracking you from the other's notes. We don't know if the journal's owner knows that, whether the owner is alive or dead. At this point we are only certain of one killer." It was obvious from Leas' tone that he was trying to calm Cole down. Cole took a deep breath and pushed out his emotions enough to throw up his mental wall. A calm came over him. He could see Meadows' skeptical response to the instant composure Cole exhumed. Cole was preparing to fight again.

CHAPTER 65

"GENTLEMEN, COME IN. Leas, you know Granny from Jackie's funeral. Granny, Agent Meadows."

"Oh, the drunk has a partner I see." Granny stood behind Cole and squinted one eye at Leas.

"Granny!"

"No, she has a right to be a bit angry. She…"

Granny interrupted, "'A bit?' Buster ya betta think again. I'm more than a bit angry. Because of you and your bottle, ya got my granddaughter killed. That boy up there is motherless. How dare ya come in…"

"Granny! Stop. They are here to help. Please go grab us some tea or something. You are going to wake up Billy with all that sass." Granny took a few steps back. "Go on woman. Don't make me put you in a home." Cole cracked a smile at the last few words. A few seconds later Granny smiled back. "Ain't puttin' me in no home. I'll tell ya that." Cole had defused the situation enough to get the men into the house before Granny started in on Leas with a cast-iron pan.

"Here, let's go into the dining room. We can talk in there without too much interruption."

Seated, Agent Leas started. "Cole, you know I've promised to be entirely on the up-and-up with you. So here is what we know. Winters had started an investigation into her father, your kidnapper, and the materials were found in her mother's home after the events in Charleston. It was just pieces of a puzzle, not much of it made sense. And, it still doesn't today. We are sharing this with you because you can, well, you may be fresh eyes to all of this."

Meadows opened a large leather satchel and pulled out some manila folders. Cole pulled one open and saw photos of the most recent killing in the cemetery. He had already seen the photos thanks to Daniel's sources in D.C. He opened the second folder. He had never seen this scene before. A bald man had been obviously wired to "perch" over a wooded creek, his naked body only covered by what appeared to be a black wool overcoat thrown across his back. The frozen look of fear in the man's eyes made Cole pause and think about what may have happened in the seconds before his death. The man clearly knew he was going to die. Cole looked up to see Meadows studying him.

"Not a pretty sight, is it? That man knew." Meadows was apparently trying to shake Cole, to get a response out of him. But, Cole's emotions stayed firmly behind the wall where they couldn't interfere.

After studying the pictures a few more minutes, Cole turned to the third folder, a woman was bound at her hands with wire and crouched at the knees as though praying. She was at the base of some dense bush dotted with white flowers. Her look, like the other two, was forced, manipulated. And, like with the others, the bodies were clean, no blood. Well, except for the marks.

Each body had been marked with various strokes, symbols at their lower back. From the lack of skin trauma, the FBI had opined the marks were etched into the body after death. From the report Cole had seen of the most recent murder, there was no indication of the marks' meanings.

"Have you figured out what the marks mean?"

The look on Meadows' face suggested they had. "Not currently, we are still trying to figure that out." Cole could tell he was lying. He looked over to Leas who was refusing to look him directly in the eyes.

"Huh? I would have thought that was the first thing you would try to figure out. I mean, the poses and all are interesting, but they are scripted, left for interpretation. Those marks, on the other hand, they are a message and intended to be clear." Cole's noticed Meadows staring at him with fascination. He knew Cole could tell they were lying, but he wasn't about to suggest otherwise. "Agent, I get the feeling that you suspect me in all this."

Meadows sat back. Cole knew the only people that sat back in interrogations were liars and sociopaths. "No, no, Mr. Mouzon. We are here to help. I'm sorry if I make you feel that way. Please continue. What do you see? Agent Leas tells me you are really good at this stuff." He crossed his arms as if he was about to take in a story. Cole could feel that he was being tested.

Closing his eyes, Cole circled the images he just saw in his mind. They formed the skin of a sphere, with him having the vantage point from the center of its interior. Slowly, he manipulated them, moving them around like jig-saw puzzle pieces until they made some kind of sense.

"The knots... They are all tied in the same style." Cole had already researched the knots from the graveyard murder and was now able to compare them to the other two killings. "All are 'two half hitches' for the hands, legs."

"Yeah, we already know that Mr. Mouzon. Tell us something we don't know." Meadows' tone suggested impatience causing Cole to momentarily open his eyes.

"Let the man think. Cole, please continue." Leas said.

Cole closed his eyes again. Something about the knots was different, wrong. His mind zoomed in on them and focused harder. "Shit. There are two... two killers."

"Why do you say that Cole?"

Cole opened his eyes and shuffled through the photos until he found the ones he had just seen in his mind. "There! Look at those two knots. The first killing in the park and the one from the graveyard. Look how that loop goes. That isn't messy; its left handed in the first shot and right handed in the latest murder."

Meadows leaned in. "I don't see it."

"See here that loop goes around that Franklin tree trunk at the hands? It's tucked opposite the first knot from the park. Two different people tied those knots."

Meadows sat back with a quizzical look on his face. The FBI already suspected two killers working together, but they weren't prepared to tell Cole that. But... something about what Cole just said had stumbled upon another clue.

"Franklin tree? Where did you get that from?"

Leas looked over to Meadows. "Why? Is that important?"

"Mr. Mouzon, please answer. Why does that tree stand out?"

"Huh? Cause that is what it is... a Franklin tea tree. A type of camellia, I think. My Granny had a few in her yard when I was growing up. Made the whole yard smell like honeysuckle."

Meadows stared at Cole for a second, clearly pondering whether to say anything more. Slowly he turned and withdrew something from his satchel and slid it across the table.

CHAPTER 66

S ITTING ON THE table between the three men was a weathered copy of *Birds of America*, by John James Audubon. Cole paused before reaching for the book. His mind flickered to the copy that had randomly arrived a few days earlier. The cover of this one was different but it was the same book.

"What is this?"

"Cole, we found that and several other books in Winters' stuff at her mother's old house in south Georgia. Do you know anything about this book?"

Cole quickly let go of the book and let it fall to the table. The thought of touching something of Winters, his sister's killer, made him sick. He lied. "I... uh, yeah. I've got a copy of it somewhere. It used to be on one of the coffee tables. What does this have to do with all of this? With the killings?" Cole pretended to look around the living room as if to try and locate the book.

His copy of the book had been delivered randomly without any indication of from whom it had come from. Someone had known about Winter's book. Someone was trying to tell him.

Meadows eyes perked up, but his tone stayed flat

with an obvious intent to avoid saying too much. "Mr. Mouzon, we really have no clue at this time. But, this book was found in her belongings, all related to her search for you, the other kidnapping victims, and her father. That Franklin tree thing that you just mentioned, it was written on a note tucked into this book. Winters had noted it after the first murder... the park murder in Macon. We have no clue why she noted that and how it relates to this book. Do you know?"

Cole's mind was too busy trying to process the idea of Poinsett and the book to answer immediately. Meadows suspected Cole of being involved. Identifying the tree fed right into Meadows' theory. "What? Give me a second." The two agents watched as Cole tried to gather his thoughts. "Nothing. I've got nothing. I mean... Audubon? Birds? Plants? What are we dealing with here?" Cole's words became rushed. "How is all this related to me? To The Taker?"

"Mr. Mouzon, we are working on that. That's why we are here. Agent Leas feels you may be the key to all this. You may just not know it yet."

Cole shook his head in defiance. "I am not the key, Agent. I am the victim in all of this." Sitting back, he continued. "Look, I can try to help. But, you are the experts. You are supposed to be helping me. You look at me, Agent, like I'm a suspect. I assure you that I have killed no one."

Meadows looked at Cole sternly before responding. "Mr. Mouzon, you have to admit that all this seems to be circling around you. I'm not saying that you are a killer. But, your insights were almost *too* convenient in the first murder to be disregarded."

Cole felt his skin tingle with heat from the accusation.

"Now hold on a second! You are coming into my house and accusing me of making this all up? It was my friends that were killed and attacked. It was my sister that was killed. You think I am some sick fuck that did that for attention? Well..."

Leas interrupted in an attempt to get the situation under control. "Cole, we don't think that. Forget what Meadows just said." He cut his eyes to Meadows before continuing. "Please... It's been a long day. It's two a.m. our time. Let's leave you for tonight and start back up in the morning."

Cole stared at the agents and then stood up. His words were cold, formal. "I think it is time for you to leave. Leas, you may call me in the morning. But, you..." Cole leaned over the table to direct his words at Meadows who was still seated. His irritation flared. "... you can go fuck yourself. You are not invited in this home anymore. And, if any more of my friends or family get harmed... it will be your ass I come after. Do you hear me?" Meadows just looked back unemotionally.

Leas stood and tugged on Meadows' shoulder to get him to stand. "Cole, you have my number if anything comes up, if you learn of anything." Cole just nodded as the two agents exited the home.

He stood at the glass storm door watching as the agents' black sedan drove away. No matter what happened next, he knew one thing. He had to figure out the mystery of the book before Meadows did.

Progeny

CHAPTER 67

A QUARTER MILE AWAY, Leas finally spoke. "What the fuck was that? That kid has nothing to do with those murders and you know it."

Meadows kept his gaze on the road as he responded. "Leas, you get too close to your cases. You are blind if you think that Mouzon guy doesn't have his hands dirty. He knows way too much. You think that magic show he just put on is deduction? Boy, he's playing games with you. Feeding you information just so he can be part of his sick game of cat and mouse. It's typical psycho shit. They insert themselves into your investigation to feel important, to get credit for solving their own damn murders. That boy is involved in some way and I'm going to prove it."

"Damn man, is this why they shelved your ass for so long? You turn the victims into the suspect? I don't know what you think you know, but there is absolutely no evidence that Cole Mouzon killed those three in Georgia, or anyone else for that matter. It's all in your head. Let go of your past, of Rader. Mouzon is not your guy."

"All in my head? Son, while you've been suckling from his teat as he spoon feeds you tips, I've been actually investigating him. Do you know he visited the graveyard in Atlanta after the body was found? What do you think he was doing there? Huh? I say he was reliving the killing. So, when he goes off talking about knots and duel suspects, I think he is talking about his own damn work."

Leas was thrown by revelation that Cole was seen at the crime site. "Uhm, well... that doesn't mean he is the killer simply because he visited the site after the crime. Do you have any evidence he was in town when the murder actually happened?" Leas waited for a response. "See... nothing. And, do you really think he would go as far as to murder and mutilate one of his friends?"

"Son, I'm telling you... that boy is involved. While we were being played by him I got an email from the guys in D.C." Meadows lied and continued. "Seems that sign etched into his buddy's chest has a meaning. *Progeny.* Someone is saying they are the second coming and I don't think that is a good thing. So you go on believing your buddy back there is innocent. But, I'm going to do my job and actually investigate and listen to what the evidence is trying to tell me.

Leas pushed his back into the car seat. He couldn't think. He needed whiskey and bad. *Progeny?* Who was announcing themselves as the son? *And, the son of what? The killer? Was the student becoming the master in this messed up game?*

Meadows continued. "Don't believe me? Take a look at these."

Meadows threw a folder into Leas' lap, several photos falling out.

Leas picked them up and immediately recognized the subject.

"He's been seen at the scenes. He's either involved

or interfering. Either way, he is not the innocent you figure him for. So, get your head out of your ass and start
investigating this file like any other. Mouzon is not your
friend."

CHAPTER 68

THE AUDUBON BOOK received just two days earlier was located on the bathroom counter where he had placed it Halloween night. The cover of Cole's copy was torn at its spine. The book cracked when opened, the glue too old to hold its pages in place. Cole carefully flipped through the book again for clues.

Cole knew enough about Audubon from his middle school science and history classes to win a few questions at trivia. According to Cole's annotated copy, the book was his attempt to paint every bird in North America. The original version was huge, at almost four feet by three feet. At some point, it became cost prohibitive because of the size and lack of sales for him to continue, so he produced a smaller version sold like an encyclopedia set. Cole recalled reading somewhere that the larger version was the most valuable printed book ever, selling recently for something like twelve-million dollars for a single copy.

Image after image of watercolor birds demonstrated the time Audubon dedicated to documenting every fine detail of the birds. A wild turkey, seen in the early 1800's as the national bird, was the first engraved plate in the

collection. Audubon tried to portray both sexes of a specimen as much as possible.

He needed to store the information. Since Charleston,
his ability to recall every image he had ever seen through
life, reading, etcetera, had grown unreliable. There was
just too much running through his head all the time now
to focus. His emotions leaked in now, clogging the cogs of
his mind.

He pressed a finger at his temple in a weak attempt
to shut out the distraction of emotions. He needed to concentrate...to stop this threat once and for all.

IT WAS ALMOST five a.m. on Sunday morning by the
time he flipped through all the mental images in his head,
mapping them and then locating the significant ones in
the book for comparison. He had discovered the reason
for Poinsett's interest in the book. It was there at Plate
185. *Bachman's Warbler*... and the Franklin tree, *Franklinia
alatamaha*. Two finch-like birds of yellow and olive green
were perched on the plant in bloom. Cole looked closer
and compared it with the mental image of the murder scenes he had been shown earlier by Meadows and
Leas. The more drab female was at the base... just like
the Macon victim. *Female. Pointing to the trunk of the bush.
Posed to look like she was "perched."*

Poinsett had discovered the most recent killings'
inspiration. Someone, The Taker..., was killing with
someone else to replicate Audubon's paintings. A rush
ran through Cole at his discovery. The plants were the
rosette stone. He pushed on, flicking through the images
in his mind, studying every painting with the crime scene
images stored in his head. He would find the plates and

re-confirm what he was seeing. The killers were acting out scenes from the book and he needed to figure out what scene was his before it was too late.

CHAPTER 69

"I KNOW YOU DON'T trust me. I know you think I am somehow involved in the murders. So, telling you what I found isn't what I should do. But, I need your help." Cole stood at his kitchen island in his charcoal gym pants and heather-blue T-shirt as Agent Leas sipped a cup of coffee. Though he had on his typical white button-down and jacket, it was the first time Cole had ever seen the agent without a tie. His hair was as disheveled as Cole's.

Rubbing one eye with his knuckles, he responded. "Cole, Meadows' is old school. He thinks everyone did it until he rules them out. He is having problems ruling you out because of everything. That's all."

Cole leaned into the island's granite counter, his own coffee mug between his hands. "I don't really care what he is. But, I cannot risk my family or friends. Are you going to help me?"

"Of course. What is it that you found?"

Cole stood and walked over to a china cabinet. He opened its drawer. Walking back, Leas recognized the book Cole was carrying toward him. "After y'all left I found my copy of the Audubon book... the book that

Poinsett had placed her note about the tree. Well, I studied the book and found..." Cole paused to check with himself as to whether to reveal his discovery. "... I found what I believe to be the link... what Poinsett had found." Cole opened the book to watercolor Plate 185 and turned the book towards Leas across the kitchen island. He pointed to the white flowers depicted in the painting. "That's a Franklin tree." He moved his finger. "And, that is your body in Macon... the pose anyway." Cole pulled back to see if what he had just said sunk in.

Leas inspected the painting and looked back up. "So... what you are saying is that someone is copying these bird pictures, reenacting them?"

"Pretty much. And, that isn't all. I think I've figured out the other two murders." Cole turned a few pages forward in the book and pointed again. "Plate 159, *Cardinal*. That's your graveyard murder. Note the tree, black cherry – the same as in the photos of the scene. And, the head pose is the same as the female at the bottom." Leas repeated his inspection, looking up with a grin. He was impressed. Cole flashed one back. "Good, no?"

Cole revealed his final find. Thump an index finger on another page in the book, Cole said, "The last one was the hardest. There was no plant to match it to, just the look. But, I think it's this one, Plate 426, *California Vulture*. The victim was bald, male like the vulture. The victim's nude body was covered by a black overcoat, similar to the black plumage of the bird. And the pose... from this angle is a perfect match."

Leas leaned away from the book and stared at Cole. He took a sip from his coffee. "Impressive as always, Cole. This definitely jives with my impressions to date – that someone is trying to celebrate the bodies' beauty. If you are correct, the killer is trying to play artiest, making his own gruesome version of these paintings."

"Yeah, but as I recall the pictures, they aren't gruesome visually beyond the fact that they are killing people. There is no blood. They are honoring them. That is some messed up stuff."

Leas paused before speaking. "Cole, I am under orders to keep a tight lid on what we know so far. But, I feel I need to tell you that these murders appear to be highly planned. The victims were watched for weeks, perhaps months before the killers moved in to play out their bird fantasy. Don't ask me how I know that – we just do. That said, we don't know when or even if someone may try to attack you again. There is a suggestion that one of the killers is now acting alone. As I told you last night, he has stolen a car in Atlanta. How that changes the game, we just can't say at this time. He may be just running. But, he may also be preparing to move on you."

Cole crossed his arms as he listened to Leas rattle on about what he couldn't tell him. "Then what can you tell me Agent? This is my family we are talking about. Is there a threat or is there not?"

"I honestly have no clue. The killer that has spun off... has disappeared. There is no indication as to where he has gone. But... Cole, he was researching you right before dropping off the radar."

Cole's skin began to tingle, preparing to spring at the slightest threat. Leas had confirmed what Cole had already figured out. *Why else would they be here?* "Then, the FBI is going to help, right? They are going to watch and wait, or what?"

Leas shook his head slowly. "No, Cole. They say if there is no movement here by tomorrow, they are turning it over to the local authorities to handle. They have ordered us back to Atlanta to keep chasing the tracks there." It was as Cole feared. He was being abandoned to deal with this threat alone.

CHAPTER 70

COLE HAD BEEN up for almost forty-eight hours straight since Leas' arrival. His mind drifted to the last time he recalled having any resemblance of good sleep, Atlanta with Cash. His mind flickered images of that night and the next morning. For a brief second he felt happy, but then reality made it all come crashing down. Feeling himself being watched, he moved to the kitchen where Billy and Granny couldn't see his stress.

Pushing up the wall at that moment was futile when it came to missing Cash. It refused to budge, subjecting his mind... his heart... to the onslaught of emotions stirred by his longing to just be held again. To feel safe and protected. He had fucked up, overreacted to what he thought he saw and then made it horribly worse with sleeping with Zander. Sex or no sex, he couldn't imagine Cash forgiving him. Cole covered his eyes with the heels of his hands as the tears leaked out and down his face.

A hand softly grabbed his shoulder. "Baby, you alright?" Granny had slipped in without him noticing.

Half-smiling, Cole responded slowly. "Granny, I think

I'm cracking... literally cracking. There is just so much right now."

Granny wiped away come of Cole's tears with her thumb. "Baby, ya can't do this all by yourself. Ya have to let those around ya, those that care for ya help, too. Have ya talked to that nice Charleston boy lately?"

Cole looked down and shook his head. "I messed up, Granny. I don't think there is much you or I can do about that. It just is."

The old lady grabbed a chair from the table and sat next to Cole, rubbing his back as she talked. "I wondered why I hadn't heard ya talkin' to him on the phone or anything, but ya know I'm no snoop." Granny smiled knowing that wasn't the truth. "He seemed to be a good one. And, if it's meant to be it will be. Ya hear me?" She paused before continuing. "Does he know how ya feel?"

Cole looked back to the old lady. "Uhm, well... I kind of ignored him until he stopped trying. I was stupid. But, that's because I messed up, did something that if he knew... he won't want anything to do with me."

"Baby, in my experience, men are like cats; sit still and ignore them long enough and they will come purring at your feet." She chuckled. "But, more importantly, whether he wants ya in his life or not isn't your call. Ya have to just get it out there and let whatever happens happen. Not doing that is just torture. And, he may surprise ya on how he responds. Ya want me to tell'em? What's his number?" Granny winked at Cole.

Cole's eyes grew big. "No. No. If it needs to be said, it needs to be said by me. I'm just scared."

Granny stood up. "Then do it. Tonight. Enough wastin' time on things that ya have no control over. Ya hear me?"

Granny was right. He had to just get it out there and then leave it to Cash as to whether he wanted anything more to do with Cole. As Granny walked away, Cole turned to the small kitchen desk and opened his laptop and began typing an email that told the entire story.

CHAPTER 71

WITH NOTHING HAVING occurred in Denver in the week since Leas and Meadows arrived, they were ordered back to Atlanta. Before they left, Cole had been introduced to the City of Denver police investigator assigned to monitor the investigation just in case something occurred in Denver, but the meeting had left Cole feeling abandoned. It was clear there would be no effort to prevent an attack, only to respond.

Cole sat at the dinner table and turned through the *Birds of America* book as Granny and Billy played a water sports game on the Xbox. The occasional squeal from either of them made Cole look up and laugh at the old lady shaking her butt in front of the TV to activate the Kinect motion sensor. Looking back down to the book, he had studied every page several times since first learning about its connection to The Taker and Poinsett. The connections to the other murders had come easily. Yet, he still hadn't figured out if any of the paintings related to him. Perhaps the mimicking of the painting was a new thing. After all, it had been over thirty years since his kidnapping and the murders just began a year ago.

The addition of a partner was certainly new for the

killings. *Or, was it?* There had never been any indication of a partner in the kidnappings that he was aware of. *Who was this partner, and why now?* Cole had twisted those questions around his head so many times that he couldn't sleep. They were even interrupting the nightmare that was always a constant in the depths of his nights. He just needed sleep.

CHAPTER 72

THE SMELL OF bleach and bed pans filled The Taker's nostrils as he walked through Grady Hospital in the middle of the night looking for room 357 C. Passing one security camera and another, he had no care about his face being seen, they had never and could never locate him when he hid. *Let them know who I am.* He was sure they already knew. Kendrick had been reckless, attacking someone and causing the authorities to zero in on him easily. Even if they hadn't already discovered the connection between Kendrick and him, it was just a matter of time.

He worked part-time at the Moreland Avenue Lowe's home improvement store as a senior customer service clerk showing idiotic twenty-somethings how to install a light switch or how to get the wife's wedding ring out of the garbage disposal. He had also got Kendrick his delivery job with the store.

The system had worked. Kendrick identified the next potential hits, took photos of them and their homes with his cell phone while conducting the delivery. Smith evaluated whether they were worthy of further watching for a potential kill. He watched, documented, and evaluated their worthiness. They had to be the right age, with the right look if they were going to become part of the story he was attempting to tell. Everything had to be perfect.

All that was lost. The FBI could be dim, but not enough to make it hard to now connect the dots between him and Kendrick. Smith's skin grew red as his temper flared thinking about how Kendrick destroyed his plan. Worse, Kendrick was now claiming to be The Taker... claiming to be him. *I am The Taker.*

ROUNDING THE CORNER of a nursing station on the third floor ICU wing, he saw the room. A single officer stood outside. The Taker walked back to one of the open rooms where a patient appeared completely out of it. He removed the pulse meter on the patient's finger and quickly stepped out of the room and into the one next door. Seconds later he could hear the high pitch of the monitor alerting the nursing station of someone redlining. The running footsteps into the room told him the overweight charge nurse had rushed to respond.

With her occupied, he slipped back into the hallway and casually walked toward room he had come to visit. The officer barely noticed the man walking past until he felt a warm heat at his abdomen. Cupping his hands over the area, red blood oozed between his fingers. The last thing he saw was the figure entering the room.

Finn was drugged asleep as The Taker walked in. He looked over him, inspecting his next victim. He found a pillow in the chair next to the bed and fluffed it. He switched off the oxygen being fed into Finn's nose. Holding the pillow at both ends, he lowered it and pressed it firmly over Finn's face. There was no struggle, no fight for a few seconds. Then Finn's legs kicked... his arms reached and grabbed for anything. They pulled for forty or so seconds at The Taker's hands firmly planted against the pillow before finally relaxing and falling to each side. The Taker slipped out the other end of the hall with just enough time to hear the nurse scream. *The time had come to clean up loose ends.*

CHAPTER 73

"GRANNY, I WON'T hear it. We talked about this. You are going to meet mom and dad in Florida. Billy has been looking forward to this trip for a while. It's a good time. I will join you next weekend."

The old lady squinted her eyes defiantly. "Boy, the safest place for Billy and I is right here. Disney can wait." She placed her hands on her hips to emphasize her position.

"Woman, you and Billy are getting on that plane or I will kill you myself. Do you get me? The FBI has abandoned the hunt here and I won't have you sitting around here while some killer from Atlanta comes knocking. So, please… if you love me, go pack your luggage. Your flight leaves in less than three hours." Cole turned and walked away before his grandmother could protest any further. She had always been stubborn, but the arrival and quick departure of the FBI had made her reluctant to leave as scheduled after her two week visit.

Cole still felt the best, safest way to deal with this threat was alone. He didn't want to be alone, but he was. Cash had been there before, by his side, against Poinsett. It was Cash that was injured, not Cole. But, he still wanted him in this moment to stand by his side and tell him everything would be okay.

Cole hadn't heard Cash's voice in over a month. There had otherwise been no response to Cole's email sent four days earlier. So, Cole had his answer. It was over. His heart sank at the thought of that.

The phone in his pocket vibrated. Withdrawing it, he saw that Zander had sent another text. Cole knew he needed to resolve that relationship, to set things straight. But, life had gotten in the way. He had pushed off Zander's requests for coffee three prior times. The last thing he needed to worry about was another man. He slowly typed his text. "2 nt – 6? Starbks?"

WATCHING

CHAPTER 74

MEADOWS LOOKED OUT the driver's side window across the street from a mini-storage unit facility. Meadows had been following Cole for three days and his gut feeling was now being confirmed. Cole Mouzon had something to hide.

Mouzon had parked outside one of the end units and stepped inside over thirty-minutes earlier. Meadows waited, reading the Denver Post until Mouzon reappeared and drove off.

Meadows stepped out of his car and ran across the road. The property was empty other than the front office manager who was too busy watching a college football game to note Meadows slipping into the fenced property. Finding the row of units where Mouzon stopped, he counted. From what he could determine, Mouzon had stepped into unit seven in from the end. Freshly disturbed dirt and dust on the garage door style entrance confirmed he was at the right unit.

A few twists of a pick and the padlock opened. The metal door rattled as it was pushed up into the ceiling of the unit and then pushed back down. Meadows flicked the light switch and stared. Mouzon had corkboard lined the walls of the unit. Pictures of kidnapping victims, victims of Beth Winters and the most recent murders in Georgia were all posted. The organization of the boards reminded him of how detectives worked up murder investigations.

A single wood bench ran half the back wall. Several books and papers were organized in different piles. Meadows walked the theory boards lining the three walls. From what he could tell, Mouzon had access to information never released to the public on several of them. But, they were all that... investigation photos and information. There were no prizes, no personal photos, nothing to suggest he was at the scene when the murders happened.

Looking down, he saw a copy of the Audubon book found in Winters' things. Several of the pages were dog-eared. Thumbing through, he noted the pages related to the links Mouzon had disclosed to Leas several days earlier. Numbers above the photos on the wall corresponded with the watercolor plate numbers of the book's pages. He was mapping out the murders.

Yellow Post-it notes flagged other pages, but their significance was unclear. A white slip of paper with some type of drawing of a finch-like bird had also been slipped into the book. Meadows marked down the page numbers, snapped a picture of the drawing with his cell phone camera and then slid the book back into place.

The stack of papers and print-outs on the bench all related to research on Audubon. Sections were highlighted, noting Audubon's link to Charleston and Bachman. Meadows recalled overhearing the conversation with Mr. Calhoun over a week earlier. He wondered if Mouzon learned about Bachman from the Calhoun man.

His attention was caught by a sheet of paper with different symbols scribed on it. Several of them had words next to them: "futile," "prey," "run," and "progeny." Mouzon had numbered each one, one through four. "Progeny" was struck out as if Mouzon had rejected it.

Meadows studied the list for a second without any understanding as to what Mouzon had stumbled across. It was only after he glanced back to the boards with the crime scene photos did he notice it. There, in plain sight, was a message. Holding the sheet up against the photos he noticed small ink where Mouzon had located the same symbols at the crime scenes. "Prey" was written in the dirt next to the body first body found under a bush. "Run" was etched into the stump where the man had been found. And, "futile" was etched into the tree trunk where one of the knots had been tied in the graveyard. None of the marks were larger than a quarter and all could easily be over looked as just random marks. The message was clear – *Prey, running is futile.*

CHAPTER 75

STILL THINKING ABOUT his research in the storage shed, Cole was startled as he felt an arm unexpectedly slip around his waist while standing inside the Starbucks. He jerked around, his elbow cocked to strike.

"Whoa whoa! Hold up, sexy. It's just me." Zander had his hands raised in surrender.

Cole relaxed and exhaled. "Shit, sorry. You just scared me."

"Damn. What has you so jittery?"

"Don't ask. It's just my fucked-up life. How goes it?"

"Great, now that I'm here with you."

Rolling his eyes, Cole turned and placed his order with the young clerk behind the counter. "Want anything?"

"I'll take tea. I don't do coffee."

Cole raised a brow. "Well, shit. You should have said something. We could have gone elsewhere."

"Nah. This is good. Plus, I figured I couldn't be picky since it took me like five times to get you to confirm anything." He smiled briefly and then turned to locate a table.

Seated at a small round-top table, the two men caught up briefly on mundane things before the subject turned to Atlanta. "Zander, about that... I, well... I wasn't in the right state of mind that night. I guess what I am trying to say is that I shouldn't have leaned on you like that."

Zander looked back at him with examining eyes. "Didn't we already have this discussion? I mean, we are adults and all. I didn't take anything away from that night other than enjoying seeing you naked."

Cole rolled his eyes. "Yeah, what a treat, right? I just don't want you thinking that there is something more than that. I was upset and shouldn't have used you that way. I am sorry."

"Ha. Used me? I only wish you would use me. I get it. I really do. It's that other guy, isn't it? Still 'complicated?'"

Cole nodded in agreement.

Zander leaned in to make eye contact. "Well, he is a lucky man. That is all I have to say. I hope he knows that."

"I doubt he is feeling that way. I haven't spoken to him since that night. At first, it was me ignoring him. But, then when I reached out it was his turn to not respond. It probably has to do with me telling him what happened between you and I."

Zander sat back, his brows lifted. "What? You told him about that? Shit. Why did you do that? Nothing happened. Just some naked play."

"I had to, Zander. I just needed to get it out there. 'Naked play' wouldn't be cool to me if I was him. And, I wanted to be honest. It was kinda making me sick." Cole could tell Zander misinterpreted Cole's description. "Well... not sick as in that it was horrible, you are hot. But.. you know what I mean... sick, as in I cheated."

"Cole, you have no clue what cheating is, do you? Any other guy wouldn't give a second thought to what happened, but you stress over it. It's adorable and all, but man, you have to relax. It wasn't that big of a deal."

"It was to me. And, clearly it was to him, too." Cole hung his head.

Leaning back in, Zander dipped his head to find Cole's eyes. "Look, if this guy is smart he will snatch you up. You are a catch. It sucks that you are stressing over that guy when I am right here trying to tell you that I want you and I don't just mean sexually. I want you in my life completely." Cole turned his eyes up and felt guilty at what he was hearing. "But... I get it. I've been there. When you love someone, you love someone. You've got to let this thing play out. You have to try your hardest so that there are no regrets. Can I ask one thing though?"

Cole smiled slightly and nodded. "When this guy fucks up, will you give me a shot?... That's all I am asking! Just a shot."

Cole stared at the man seated across from him with new appreciation. After a few moments he said, "Deal. In fact, I'll give you a shot right now... a shot to drive me home. I walked here and it's now dark outside."

"Ha. Sure enough."

CHAPTER 76

"YOU DIDN'T HAVE to walk me to my door, you know. I can handle this."

"What kind of gentleman would I be if I didn't? I'm just practicing for when I get my shot. I know how you love those southern gentlemen types." Zander made a grand bow and laughed.

"You are a dork. But, it's very nice of you."

Zander grabbed Cole's hand. "You know, you are stronger than this... all of this mess that has happened to you and what you were telling me in the car about some crazy in Georgia. You seem all timid and frail, but you are defiant and strong. You are an aspen."

Cole pulled back. "Huh? I'm a what?"

"An aspen. My people, the Utes, have this belief. According to legend, sometime long ago the Great Spirit visited during a special full moon. All of nature trembled in homage to the Spirit's arrival except the beautiful and proud aspens. They stood still, refusing to pay respect. The Great Spirit became furious and cast a spell on the aspens that their leaves shall tremble whenever anyone looked upon them. You are the defiant and strong aspen. Anyone would be a fool to think you were weak."

Cole gave a sideways smile. "An aspen, huh? I kinda like that. Thank you."

Cole pushed against the door he had just unlocked and took two steps inside. Turning back to Zander, he said, "And, again, I appreciate it. Perhaps we can do this as friends every once in…." Cole noticed Zander's eyes go wide as he talked. "What?"

"Uhm, is someone else home? I just saw someone move behind you." His head bobbed left to right as he tried to get a view past Cole.

"Where?" Cole turned quickly to see nothing there.

Zander pushed his way past him and pointed, "In there, a few feet behind you! Someone's shadow raced across. Hold up, stay there." Zander took several steps into the house towards the living room before heavy steps were heard running toward the back of the house.

"Shit!" Cole tried to grab Zander and pull him out of the house, but he was too strong. Zander chased after the steps and Cole followed. A man in some type of wind jacket and hoodie raced out the back glass doors of the house and into the unlit yard. "Zander! No!" Cole raced over to the light switch for the back flood lights and flicked it on. The yard was lit up like day. From the back door Cole could see the hooded man at the yard's edge, Zander on the ground at his feet. The man paused for a second to gaze at Cole and then turn and disappeared into the hedge.

Cole ran to the kitchen to grab a large butcher's knife and then ran out the back. Holding the blade in one hand, he rolled Zander's body with the other. Zander grunted. "Shit! The fucker stabbed me!" He smiled as if being stabbed were a good thing.

Cole let out a short laugh and shook his head. "Still alive, I see. My hero."

CHAPTER 77

COLE HAD BEEN interrogated by the Denver PD for over an hour before the first call was received by Leas. He was in Atlanta when they had alerted him to the home invasion. It was still unclear to them if the hooded man was just a random break-in or if it was part of the Atlanta case. Cole was certain of the latter. That or he had once again pulled the short end of the luck straw. "I'm telling you Leas, this isn't some random burglary. It's The Taker... or his partner." Cole felt relieved that Granny and Billy were somewhere in the air between Denver and Orlando at the moment, far away for this attack. But, having seen Zander carted away in an ambulance made him feel guilty.

"How is the guy that got stabbed, Zander? Any word?"

A heavyset Latino officer responded. "The cut was pretty deep, but he will be fine. Hell, I've been cut worse. Just stings like hell, that's all. A few days of hospital food and he will be running out of the place."

"Thank you, officer." Knowing Zander hadn't been too seriously injured calmed Cole slightly. He took a deep breath to recalibrate. The fight had finally come to him and he needed to be ready.

TRAP

CHAPTER 78

WITHIN AN HOUR of getting home, the phone rang. Ann was on the line. She told him that Finn had passed away in the night. A guard was dead. They both had been murdered. Cole wanted to break down. It was all his fault. Why couldn't he have just let things be? Why couldn't he have just kept his promise to Cash.

His body went rigid, cold as a sense of calm passed over him. His wall was going up, preparing him for what he knew he would have to do. His body was preparing for the fight.

That's when he discovered it. There, in the living room was a pad. Cole's mind flickered to where he had last placed it. It had been moved from the kitchen desk. He walked over and lifted it. It was blank. He looked away in thought as to why it was there. Had he placed it there and just didn't remember? He reached to lay it back down when slight ridges on the paper were caught by the kitchen light. Cole drew it back up and saw more ridges.

He stood and rushed to the kitchen desk to find a pencil. The words started to come together slowly as the graphite gray filled the paper. There was an area code,

"404." An Atlanta number. The first line of the short message made Cole pause in fear. "I'm here." *Who is here? … The Taker.*

Cole's thoughts turned to what happened with the original note. Someone, the police, had taken the note during their investigation into the home invader and hadn't bothered to tell Cole. He grew angry at the thought of being left in the dark again. He was being hunted. Someone had reached out. And, they hid it from him.

Cole's body buzzed with the adrenalin of anger. The killer was already here. If the law was going to leave him dangling out there as some sort of trap or lure, he was going to make sure that this hunt ended and now. Cole stood, dialed the number in his phone and followed with a short text message. The time had come to end this.

Carolina Parrot

COLE PULLED UP to the stables where he had agreed to meet the person on the other end of the phone number he had found a few hours before. The responding text had come with a simple message, "I will tell you everything." Cole sent him the GPS location of the stables because it was far away from anyone he cared about. Slipping the officers outside his home proved almost too easy. The snow storm made it impossible to monitor him as he snuck out of the house to the back alley garage and backed out the car, careful to not turn on his lights until he hit the main street.

Turning off the car, he wondered if he would make it out alive. It was an obvious trap, but luring the killer away from town in hopes of ending it all was the only option he had. He took a deep breath before opening the car door and stepping out. The snow had already started to build up on the ground but there was no evidence of another car or footsteps in the snow. Cole's heart raced.

Cole ran to the stables and pushed open the bay door. The lights were on with several kerosene heaters lining the walk down the spine of the building to keep the stables just above freezing. "Hello! I'm here!" There was no response. Cole told himself that he would walk the length of the stables and if no one was there he was heading back to the car. Halfway through, a young black male, perhaps twenty-two or three stepped out of the last stall. His face was hidden by the shadows casted from a light just behind him. Cole's wall kept his fear at bay. He felt nothing but a desire to attack.

"I'm here." His words were calm, calculated.

The body responded. "Yeah. Mouzon?"

Cole nodded. He eyes were fixed on the gun in the shadow's right hand. "What are you going to do with that?"

Kendrick looked down at the pistol and then pulled it up to aim at Cole. "Not sure yet. But, don't force me to make that decision right now. For now, walk over here real slow."

Cole raised his hands and took a few steps. "You got me here. Now what? You said you knew about me... about someone from my past."

"Just walk over here. You hear me?!" The young black man came into view. His face was drained of color. Heavy bags hung under his eyes. He was not The Taker as Cole had hoped.

Cole got within feet of Kendrick before being slammed face first against one of the stables. Kendrick patted him down. He sniffled before he spoke. "Turn around." Kendrick shoved the gun into Cole's stomach. "Why are you special? You're just some white dude."

Cole squinted in contemplation. He had heard that question before, but not by him. She... Poinsett had asked him that over and over again inside the battery just before she was shot by Leas.

"I don't know, man." Cole still had his hands in the air.

"He wants you. He's been watching you… like forever. It's all in here." Kendrick pulled a black journal out of the pocket of his navy wind jacket and waved it in Cole's face still firmly planted against the stable wall. Cole felt the need to snatch it from his hands, to discover what was in the journal. Kendrick saw Cole's response.

"Uh uh. Don't think about it. You know he's been watching you since you were a kid. Been documenting it all. Calls you a king, a parrot king. What the fuck is that about?"

"What? A parrot, what?"

"Yeah, what the fuck. If you're a king, I'm going to be a king killer." Kendrick pulled away. Cole pushed himself off the wall and then slowly turned to face him. "I told the old man I was ready. Damn, look at me now. Told him I could do this without him. I'm ready for this." Kendrick pulled up the pistol and aimed it, his gaze fixated on Cole.

Cole's body froze. He had seen the crazed look in Kendrick's eyes before, in rabid dogs… in Poinsett. Keeping his head still, Cole quickly glanced around the stables for an escape. His mind tried to map his surroundings.

Kendrick started rambling again. "I told the old man. I told him I was ready. He didn't believe me." Kendrick wiped some snot from his nose. "Shit, I can fucking do this. I don't need him anymore."

CHAPTER 80

COLE WAS TOO distracted to hear the steps next to him. "I knew better." The voice made Cole and Kendrick turn towards the open bay door.

"Hands up, both of you." Agent Meadows was standing there somewhere in the shadows. "Mr. Mouzon, you made it too easy. The idea that you weren't involved, that you just happened to figure out clues that no one else could… I never bought it."

Still keeping his eyes on Kendrick and the journal, Cole responded. "Agent, you have it wrong. I didn't have anything to do with this. I found a note and I…"

Meadows lifted his other hand. "You mean this note? How did you find out about it?"

Cole's face grew red. "You! You took the note from my house. You wanted me to just sit out there, to be bait."

Meadows chuckled. "Bait? Stop playing innocent, Mr. Mouzon. You've been in on this… this whole thing."

Shaking his head, Cole attempted to walk towards Meadows but Kendrick caught his arm and lifted the gun to his head. Cole looked back to Meadows. "Does it look like I'm fucking in on it?!"

"Seriously, is that the only thing you can come up

with?" Meadows paused. "Tell your partner to put his hands up, now!"

Kendrick shouted back. "Fucker, I'm not putting down my gun. I'm already dead. Cause, as I see it, either you kill me, or he will."

Cole didn't turn around as he rushed to ask, "Who? Who is going to kill you?"

Meadows interrupted before Kendrick could respond. "Both of you, shut-up and walk over here slowly."

A step in, Kendrick hit the light switch behind Cole before the first shot was fired by Meadows. Cole heard the bullet strike the stall next to him just as he leapt inside. A wood splinters hit his face. Several other shots followed between the two men before there was a pause. Cole could hear steps outside the stables racing around to the back bay door. The door rattled open just as new shots were released from inside. It went silent again.

Afraid to move for fear of being shot, Cole remained still as he heard steps outside the stall. Somewhere in the darkness he heard the light switch flip. The lights came on slowly, flickering as they heated up. Cole finally looked up to see Meadows pointing his gun at his head.

"Stand up, Mr. Mouzon."

Hands up, Cole looked at Meadows. "Agent, if you will just listen… I got this text. He… he texted me and told me if I wanted my family to be safe to come here, alone." Meadows swayed the gun to tell Cole to move from out of the stall. He slowly stood up and started walking.

"Mr. Mouzon, save it for your lawyer."

Halfway out Cole saw Kendrick shot in the stomach just outside the stall, lying on his back on a bale of hay.

Blood was bubbling out of his mouth. He tried to speak but gargles just came out.

Cole pled with Meadows. "Agent, please listen to me. I need to talk to him. He knows who The Taker is."

"Mr. Mouzon, if you say one more word, I'll…"

Cole didn't see the strike, but heard Agent Meadows go down with a hollow thud. Cole jerked back to see who was attacking and then relaxed. Standing there was the stables volunteer, Mr. Kennedy, with a heavy shovel in his hands.

"You alright Cole?"

Cole leaned down to inspect the agent knocked out on the hay lined ground. "Yeah, I'm okay. But, you shouldn't have done that. That's an FBI agent."

A gargled, low voice called out. "Help me." Cole rushed over to Kendrick who was still motionless but for his eyes. "Can you talk? Where are you hit?" Cole put his hand over the man's stomach and then slid the other around his back to feel for an exit wound. But the location of the warm blood on his back, Kendrick's spine had been hit by the exiting bullet. Cole felt Kendrick grab his hand and squeeze it tightly. Cole looked up to see the man's eyes intensify. He tried to speak but Cole couldn't make it out.

Cole turned to Mr. Kennedy. "Here, put pressure on this." Cole stood and ran out of the stables to his car.

Extinction

CHAPTER 81

"DID YOU REALLY think you could steal from me and get away with it? Did you really think you could be me?"

Kendrick was fixed on the gray eyes looking back at him. He had recognized him as soon as he walked into the stables. His fear pulsed out in bloody flows from his stomach. Smith had found him. The Taker had found him.

"Why were you so impatient? I treated you well, didn't I? Taught you how to be careful, how to plan." Smith removed his hand from Kendrick's wound and stood up. "I gave you those others to cut your teeth on. To learn. But, you got cocky. That attack on his friends... leaving my mark. Sloppy. They know who you are now. They know who I am!" He slapped Kendrick's face hard, throwing blood across the stable. "You sicken me. I tried to teach you, to prepare you for the hunt. Yet, you threw it all away. I should have never have pulled you out of that gutter you were in."

Smith leaned back in and flashed a knife blade in Kendrick's eyes. "You were never going to survive this. You know that, right? He isn't yours to kill." Smith turned the knife and thrust it deep into Kendrick's heart.

CHAPTER 82

COLE RUSHED INTO the stables with a large towel. "I called 911, they should be here soon. How is he?" The old man stood up and looked at Cole.

"I'm sorry. His injuries were too much. He passed away."

Cole rushed over to Kendrick. "What? No... No! He can't be. He was going to tell me. He was going to tell me about everything." He was about to hear all the answers. He needed to know. His family was at stake. It could have all ended if Meadows had just stayed out of it. Cole pounded his fist into the ground and put his head down.

The old man put a hand on Cole's shoulder. "I did all I could do. I'm so sorry." Cole lingered beside Kendrick for a minute or so and then stood. Walking over to Agent Meadows, he leaned over to check his pulse. *Still alive.* Cole collapsed to his knees and then looked over to Mr. Kennedy. "I'll take responsibility for this. It's my fault. You were just helping."

"Cole, you have called 911. Help is on the way and there is nothing else we can do. I don't know what you did to get involved in this, but I think we should leave. Let the cops deal with this." His gray eyes looked sincere.

"I can't do that. This is all my fault." Cole pressed his back against one of the stalls.

The old man rushed over and grabbed Cole's wrist, yanking him up and off the wall. "That won't do, son. We have to leave. Now!" He pulled Cole halfway down the stables before Cole forced him to stop.

"Mr. Kennedy, stop!" Cole jerked his hand away and then stared at the man. Something on Kennedy's forearm had caused Cole to flash through his memories. Flicking through image after image, his mind stopped. It was a tattoo… the bird tattoo he had seen during his visit with Meme in Charleston. Penny's hoodoo ceremony had found the memory of the night he and his mother escaped The Taker. Cole's heart pounded hard. Mr. Kennedy was The Taker.

COLE SLOWLY STEPPED backwards while keeping his eyes on The Taker.

"Cole, is there something wrong?" A mischievous grin came over his face. Cole just stared. With no response for several moments he continued. "Ah. So it seems I've been made." The man walked towards Cole. "I wondered if you remembered… if you knew my face when I saw you in here last month. You were always clever, too clever. That's why you were the first pick." Cole stepped back further, keeping his distance from his mother's killer.

Cole's thoughts flooded out in a rush. "Why? Why all this? Why the killings and kidnappings?"

"Boredom? Self-preservation? Vanity? You pick. I

wanted a challenge in the end. But, that seems to have been wasted on you."

Cole took a few steps backward, but tripped and fell over Agent Meadows.

The Taker rushed over and withdrew the knife from his pocket. Leaning over Cole, he said, "So, I guess this is checkmate." Cole kicked, landing a blow to the man's knee and causing him to fall backwards. Cole pushed himself up and ran out the back bay door and into the snow. *Run Cole. Run. Don't stop.* He heard a shout behind him. "That's right! Run Cole! Make this worth my time." The Taker's heavy laugh followed.

CHAPTER 83

"**Y**OU DON'T KNOW me, but I am…"

"Cash. I know who you are." Zander stared back from the hospital bed.

Cole had sent a text with an address, nothing more, in the middle of the night. Cole needed him. He caught the first flight between Atlanta and Denver at five a.m. when there was no response to his calls and went straight to Cole's new address where he found Agent Leas who filled him in on the last few hours. Agent Meadows had been found unconscious and a body of another young man found dead. Cole was missing, his car abandoned.

Cole had previously mentioned that Zander worked at the stables and Cash needed his insight even if he couldn't stand the guy. Leas had told him where he could be found.

"Cole… is he okay?" Zander's voice was weak, but hurried.

Cash wondered how much Zander knew. "He's missing. Something happened at the stables. The snow storm has made the search impossible. Please. If you know anything, where he may have gone, please tell me." Cash's plea for help was emotional, accompanied by tears.

Zander grabbed his hand weakly. "The cabin. Check the cabin."

"What cabin? Where?" Cash's voice was rushed again.

Zander pulled Cash's hand toward him. "Stables. Red mountain. Cabin." With each word he touched a different spot on Cash's palm. He had made a map.

"Thank you, Zander. You don't know how grateful I am."

Zander pulled Cash in. "Promise me you will save him." Cash wondered the extent of the two's relationship since Atlanta but Zander cut off his thoughts. "He loves you, you know?" A slight smile appeared on Cash's face. He nodded and then rushed out of the room.

AN HOUR LATER, Cash finally pulled up to the stables in Vail. Yellow police tape cordoned off most of the area. From what he could hear as officers talked nearby, the snow in the mountains hadn't slowed and was coming down too heavy, making it impossible to follow any trail Cole may have left.

He approached cautiously. "Sir, you are going to have to stay back. This is an active investigation." An older police officer pushed a hand against Cash's chest.

"Officer, he is with me." Agent Leas stepped out of the car's passenger side and addressed the officer. Leas had told him all that he knew when the met at Cole's house in Denver. They agreed to ride up into the mountains together with under one rule; Leas had to tell all that he knew. Along the snowing mountain pass drive Cash learned everything. Meadows. Kendrick. The Taker.

The officer raised the tape to let Cash and Leas dunk

under it and into the yard next to the stables. The snow was deep, already six or so inches up the side of mud boots Cash snagged from Cole's home. It was white-out conditions. He struggled to decipher the ground from the air because the snow was coming down so thick.

Walking into the stables, Cash looked around at the last place Cole was seen. *What had made him run?* From what Leas told him, Agent Meadows was at the hospital and wasn't alert. Cash walked over to a blood stained bale of hay and stared.

"The snow storm up here has made it impossible to track him. We found two other cars. One out back linked to the dead guy and another out front with local tags. DMV advised the car has been reported stolen from Denver for over four months, about the same time of the Charleston events."

Cash turned to Leas for answers. "Someone followed him here?"

With an officer still whispering in his ear, Leas responded. "Perhaps, we aren't quite sure yet. But, it sounds right. We never told Cole this, but someone was watching him, documenting his every move. We don't know for how long. And, we only learned about it a week and a half ago."

Cash's face flashed anger. He grabbed Leas' shirt at the chest with both hands and slung him into a wall. "You led the guy to him. You used him as prey." Several of the officers looked over to see the ruckus. Leas waved them off.

"We fucked up, okay? We didn't think the kid would lure him out like that. He had been careless with the other attack. So we watched and waited. Well… I watched and waited. I had one of the local guys following Cole and keeping me in on the loop." Leas still didn't know how Meadows ended-up at the stables but suspected that he was pursuing his own investigation on Cole. Leas had tried to convince him that Cole was clean, but Meadows refused to listen. To him, Cole was a killer.

Cash released Leas' shirt. "We have to go get him. He could be freezing or worse..." Cash looked around the stables. "Help me find the keys to that four-wheeler out there. I have to go find him. He is in danger. How far is that cabin I told you about... that that Zander guy said may be where Cole ran to...?"

An officer interjected. "A four-wheeler won't get you very far in this storm. There is a layer of ice underneath it all. You'll slip off the side of that mountain trail. And, that cabin is at the very top based upon what the owner says. Best to just wait for it to clear and then we can try to search from the air. You are doing him no good if you get yourself in trouble."

Cash cut his eyes to the officer. "Sir, that isn't an option. He is out there. We have to find him, now!"

Walking away, the officer said, "Boy, accept it. Until that storm stops we are all stuck waiting."

Leas went to place a consoling hand on Cash's shoulder, but he swiped it away. Cash looked around until his eyes landed on a large horse. Leas watched him as the man walked over to the stall and slid open the door. The brown and gray speckled horse snorted at the disturbance. "Whoa. Hey fella." Cash placed his hand between the horse's ears and scratched.

Leas approached. "Cash, I don't know how to ride a horse and as an officer of the law I have to recommend that you not do this. You could get yourself killed." His voice lowered. "But, I won't stop you."

Cash's face still stern, he turned back to the horse and started talking in a soft tone. "Hey buddy. I need your help." Cash grabbed the bridle and bit from the stall wall and attempted to place it over the horse's head. The horse nudged it away. Cash tried again, and again the horse pushed it away. Cash's eyes grew sad and wet. Holding the bridle in his hands, he saw where someone had scribed the word "Thrasher" with a marker.

He spoke softly on the edge of tears into one of the horse's ears. "Thrasher, huh? Please help me. Cole is out there somewhere, alone. I promised him he would never be alone again. Help me keep my promise." The horse shook his head and then slowly bowed it slightly. Cash pulled back and then approached again with the bridle. Thrasher finally let it fall over his head as Cash slipped the bit into his mouth. Cash scratched the horse's head again. "Thank you."

Leas looked on and finally spoke slowly. "Go get our boy." Cash grabbed the large horse's neck with one arm and slung a leg over its back. A slight kick sent Thrasher racing out of the stables.

CHAPTER 84

COLE WAS DISORIENTED from the snow. Everything was white. The ground, the sky... everything. Attempts to call for help were futile. His iPhone kept shutting down saying the battery was dead because it was too cold – he was barely functioning himself.

He knew the cabin that Zander previously mentioned was on the south side of the mountain. His watch said eight a.m. meaning south east was the direction of the sun. So he kept walking up and slightly ahead of the sun. The cold was seeping into his jacket by its sleeves, forcing Cole to shake his hands constantly to keep warm blood flowing into them.

He couldn't know for sure if The Taker was still pursuing him. In this snow he could barely see three feet behind him, much less see if he was being followed. So long as the killer was staying away from his family Cole didn't care. He needed it to end. The entire game that The Taker had put in place thirty years earlier just needed to stop. If that meant he died he didn't care.

PATTING OFF THE flakes collecting in his jacket's zipper, he felt the journal. He had grabbed it when the young man was shot at the stables. Whatever it contained scared the man and drove him to seek out Cole. He didn't know whether the man intended to kill him when he first decided to meet him. He didn't care. Cole wanted to know either way why Mr. Kennedy, The Taker, thought he was so important. Why was he being hunted?

His mind drifted to the text he had sent to Cash just before leaving Denver to meet the killer. If felt natural to reach out to him in that moment. After all, it was Cash he reached out to in Charleston when he discovered his sister had been attacked. It was Cash that had gone with him to the island battery to confront Poinsett. And, it was Cash he wanted with him in this moment.

Cole stumbled in the snow, tired from the four hours of hiking in the snow. He pushed himself up and looked ahead. It was there, covered in snow. He had found the cabin.

The snow had piled up against the door making it impossible to get it open. Cole trudged through the snow and started to shovel with his hands until they were too cold to respond. The wind howling covered the steps behind him until it was too late to respond. Everything went black.

PARROT

CHAPTER 85

"I HAVE TO SAY, you are resourceful. I didn't know about Beth Winters' attack on you until the news went crazy with the story. By then, you were back here in Denver. It didn't take long to relocate you." The Taker sat in an old chair across the room as Cole woke up and rubbed his head. Looking around, he discovered he was inside the cabin, thrown into a corner against an old wood stove. The cold iron of the stove burned against Cole's cheek from the frozen air that filled it.

"You know, I've been watching you forever. You have impressed me with your ability to deduct, to figure out things. So, one last riddle...." Cole watched as the man walked across the room and looked down at Cole. Scratching his forehead with his index finger, he asked, "How do you die?"

Cole stared back for a second before blurting out, "Why all this... this stuff with the birds? Why did you kidnap me?" Cole craved to know the truth, but he also hoped to buy time to figure out how to escape. The Taker grinned. He knew what Cole was trying to do.

"Let them come. They will only find one of us." He

walked backwards and settled back into the rusted chair. "But, know this… you have your father's eyes."

COLE COULD MAKE out through the shadows what appeared to be a wink. His mind raced. *What was he saying? That he was my father? Insane. He's too old and my eyes look nothing like his.*

A demanding shout came out. "Stop it. I am not your father if that is what you are thinking. I *knew* your father. Quite the specimen physically and intellectually. We killed together." He watched as those words sink in. Cole refused to speak though his mind churned with questions. The Taker pushed. "What? Not surprised?"

The question came out with hesitation. "How… how did you meet?" His shivering was making it impossible to speak clearly, slurring his words.

"Hmm, see you do care." He paused before continuing. "Prison, 1979. After you were born. We were cellmates…got out in 1980 and worked together until he was shot while breaking into a home in Florida. He was a loss." He twisted a large hunter's-style knife in his hand as he talked. "He was the best I had ever seen."

The Taker paused and scratched his leg with the knife's blade and exhaled. "That's when I crafted all of this… based on the pitiful selection of books in the prison library. It was Audubon, history books… evolution. Such an interesting idea that things can change both genetically and through adaptation to survive. If they don't… they die, go extinct."

His speech hastened with excitement. "What if… what if the desire to kill could evolve, be fostered to flourish. As wonderful as your father was, could you be even greater?"

Cole's stomach churned in disgust. The Taker had chosen him to see if the need to kill could be perfected. Re responded defiantly. "You're 'eory has fail. I don't desire to kill." His words slurred from the cold. He pulled the collar of his fleece up over his mouth to hold some bit of warmth to his face.

The Taker chuckled and then leaned in. "Oh? Not even now?" The Taker twisted the handle of his knife until the blade was caught by the light and flashed. "You have already showed a great ability to survive. But, I agree. You are a disappointment. Your downfall is the very one that I was testing."

Cole refused to show emotion as the man spoke, to respond in fear or anger. His face stern, he looked into the light that blinded him from seeing The Taker's full face. "Plate twenty-six."

The Taker stood. "What?" He was impressed.

Cole repeated himself. "Plate twenty-six, the *Carolina Parrot*."

"Ha. Ha ha." The Taker turned and reseated himself. "Very good, Cole. Yes, your plate is the *Carolina Parrot*. I thought it was fitting for my game when it was dreamt up before I started kidnapping... when I was killing with your father. He is the one that selected it." Cole continued to fight for clarity, pushing his wall up higher at the news that his father may have offered him up for this horrible game.

Cole felt calm as he spoke. "What... what's special about it?"

The Taker studied Cole's face before answering.

"Hmm, what's special about it? Do you know the story of the bird?"

Cole shook his head feebly "no" as he shivered.

The old man grinned. "Okay. Well, like the little ants that are people now, the bird was widespread, covered half the country in flocks said to black out the sky. And, like people, they were noisy, devouring everything in their sight. They were... pests." The Taker rubbed his palms together, the knife still held loosely by his fingers. "I despise people. Their stench fills my nostrils. Sharing my air with them makes me sick. They should be extinct, like that bird."

Getting no response from Cole, he continued. "Humans and that bird share the same weakness – they care. That stupid emotion was used against the parrot." The Taker leaned in from his chair. "Imagine this. A hunter would shoot a few of the birds and hope that one survived just enough to scream out in pain. He would grab the bird, tie it to the ground and then wait. Slowly one bird and then another came to help. The hunter shot them down. Then, the whole flock would swarm in to try and help, to free the injured. Apples in a barrel. The entire flock was dead in a matter of minutes because they cared... they cared!" He released a heavy laugh. "What a wasted emotion."

CHAPTER 86

C OLE REMAINED SILENT as The Taker focused on trying to see through the bright light flooding into the small cabin attempting to see Cole's response. "My theory, humans can be unhinged from caring. When put in the right situation, when exposed to the right stimuli, their capacity to care is snuffed out. And, when that happens... well, watch out world." His arms lifted in reverence. "You have a killer. So slowly I collected you... and the others, exposed them to their parents' murders, and then released them into the wild. I sat back and watched, keeping tabs on each of you. Some of you were more disappointments than others. Winters was impressive. She wasn't an intended part of my little experiment. Don't get me wrong, she sufficed for sure, but she was certainly disruptive. She changed my little game– turning on the other subjects. That seems to have been repeated. But, you survived. Why do you survive Cole?"

By the twist in the shadowed face, Cole could tell The Taker was studying him. "I have my suspicions." He tapped the blade's tip against his forehead. "That little mind, those things... tricks you are able to do is pretty interesting. I bet its working overtime right now trying to figure out how to escape. Or, better yet, kill me. I can hear it in there. Click, click, click, clicking along… analyzing." A grin crossed his face as he tightened his eyes.

Cole's heart raced as he saw The Taker stand again. Story telling time was over. The room was too dark to see, but he saw the shadow creeping closer.

Cole closed his eyes and prepared. Calm came over him as the edges of the room glowed blue in the darkness of his mind. He was safe in this place. He mapped out his movements in the space just as he did his morning routine. *Three steps here, two there, turn.*

With his eyes still closed he pushed himself up quickly, swinging a small log that had been under him. From the cracking sound he heard, the log had broken a rib. Cole released it and grabbed the mop of hair leaning down. He connected his knee to The Taker's face. A loud moan was followed by an angry yell. Cole finally opened his eyes, but was disoriented by the sudden flash of white from the small window. He stumbled toward the door.

The heat of a blade stabbing into his abdomen was sudden and overwhelming. The Taker had landed a blow. Cole retaliated, his fist collided into the old man's face but the momentum caused both of them to topple to the weathered wooden floor. Cole pushed himself back up and tried to make another run for the door but was pulled down. The Taker had his foot and was twisting it. Cole kicked towards the man's head and landed another blow to his jaw. Cole scampered again, finally making it to the door to fling it open. Overwhelmed by the white light, Cole covered his eyes with the bend in his arm, focusing on his feet.

He was only ten feet outside the cabin when he was

tackled to the snowy ground. The Taker pinned his arms into the snow with his knees. "You fucking kid. I am going to show you what I did to your mother. Remind you of her pain."

Cole's anger welled up inside him. He shoved his feet under him and pushed, throwing the man off and over him. There was no immediate attack. Cole rolled over to see a steep ledge, with The Taker dangling over it with nothing to hold but a thin pine branch. Cole stared down at him.

The voice was panting but calm, almost proud. "Bravo, Cole. It seems I have discovered why you survived." Cole just stared back, his hand on his stab. The Taker looked down and then back to Cole. Sounds of shoes scraping against rock, trying to find a grip, could be heard. "So… what happens next Cole? You let me fall? I don't think so. You care."

Cole just looked on quietly trying to figure out what to do. He was torn. This man had killed his mother and put in place a chain of events that would take his sister's life. Saving him risked letting that threat remain. Leave the man and he will fall. Cole slowly extended his hand halfway.

The Taker grinned. "As I thought… you *are* one of the parrots."

Cole pulled back his hand and kneeled in the snow. Pulling his hand away from his wound to see the damage, he grimaced. His hand was covered in red. He looked back to The Taker. "I do care. I care for my mother you killed…my sister that was killed by your daughter…my friends murdered by you and the kid. I admit it. I care. It is over. Done. I don't want to be part of this anymore."

Cole stumbled several times as he tried to stand. Erect, he turned to walk away.

The Taker's hand slipped and he twisted on the branch trying to get a better grip. The Taker shouted. "It isn't over, Cole. But, my money is on you." Cole squinted as he attempted to understand what the man was saying. He turned to The Taker. "It was always on you." The Taker's hand suddenly slipped and Cole rushed forward, his hand out, to grab the man. But, he fell into the white abyss below. Cole fell to his knees and looked down cautiously. There was no sign of the man.

UNABLE TO STAND, he stared at the whiteness until the soothing dizziness of blood loss and hyperthermia caused him to topple to one side. He rolled to his back and looked into the sky watching the heavy flakes float down as he contemplated The Taker's last words. "My money is on you." *What did he mean?* Calm came over him as his eyes grew heavy. He was dying. The sound of snow falling sounded like a conch shell or the ocean, a soft white static. His thoughts drifted to the white sand beaches of his childhood just as a large shadow crossed over him. And, then all was dark and quiet.

REGICIDE

CHAPTER 87

COLE WOKE AND slowly rubbed his eyes as they adjusted to the light flooding into the hospital room. Looking over, he saw Cash asleep in the chair next to his bed. The air went out of him. He had to be dreaming.

"Well, welcome back sweetie." A cheery stick of a nurse walked up to the bed and grabbed his arm to examine the I.V. inserted under the skin.

Cole's voice was dry, scratchy. "How long... how long have I been here?"

Busied, she responded. "Two days. You lost a lot of blood from that wound. That fella over there donated most of it." She raised a chin in Cash's direction. Cole looked back over to the man covered by a thin blanket. He had no memory of Cash's return.

Cole spoke softly. "How did I get here?"

"I wasn't here when they brought you in, sweetie. But, one of the other nurses said that cowboy over there went out into a snow storm and found you. Brought you back half dead and frozen." She winked at Cole. "He hasn't moved from this room since you arrived other than when we forced him to go grab coffee. If you ask me, that man is crazy for you. He's in love." Cole inhaled deeply at the woman's words.

HE HAD BEEN staring at the ceiling trying the piece together the last few days when Cash finally started to rustle in his chair. Cole watched as he yawned with his eyes still closed. The moment reminded him of their morning in Atlanta. Stretching out in like a waking cat, feet and arms in all directions, Cash finally opened his eyes and then jumped up. "Shit! You're awake. Oh my god, how are you feeling?" Cash grabbed Cole's hand while he waited for a response.

Cole smiled back warmly. "I've been better. But, right now... this is pretty good." He rolled his thumb over the back of Cash's hand. "Cash... I'm... I'm so sorry for everything."

Cash stood and leaned over Cole. Looking him in the eyes, he said, "Hush. There is nothing to be sorry for." He pushed a strand of Cole's hair off his forehead. "I love you. And, that is all that matters." A slight smile appeared on his face. "Well, that and... you look like shit."

The laughing hurt Cole's ribs. He buried his face against Cash's forearm and took in his smell. "When do you head back?"

"I ride in like the prince, give you half my blood and you want to know how quickly you can get rid of me. I see how it is."

"You know that isn't true. I just want to know how long I get to enjoy this."

"In a few days." Cash leaned in and nuzzled his nose to Cole's. "That is, until I move here in the spring."

Cole jerked his head to refocus. "What?"

"I got the job. I start the spring semester." Cash smiled warmly.

Cole wrapped his arms around Cash's neck and pulled him halfway into the bed. "Ouch." Cash looked down to Cole's wound. "Hold up there mister. We don't want you hurt any further. There will be plenty of time for that later."

Cole tightened his hug around Cash's neck. "I think after everything I can handle that little thing." Cole pushed his lips against Cash's. He felt whole again.

CHAPTER 88

O N THE DAY of Cole's hospital release, Agent Leas visited. "Cole, I'm glad to see you are still doing well. Based on what you told me yesterday, I have talked to Agent Meadows and he has begrudgingly confirmed much of your story as to what happened in the stables. But, don't expect him to apologize for suspecting you. Seems he isn't a fan of eating crow." Leas briefly cut his eyes to Cash. "Seems what happened on the hill wasn't much better. They found Smith Gilmer's body this morning at the base of the mountain. The journal you found has been sent to D.C. for decoding, but our initial inspection suggests he was watching not only you, but all of the kids he kidnapped. From what you have told us, this was his sick version of a petri dish experiment that he watched play out over the past thirty years. The young black man, Kendrick, seems to have been the newest addition to the dish, added to move things along. It will take a while to work through the journal, but Cole, it is all over."

All over. Cole didn't know whether to believe those words. Something felt unsettling in believing that the shadows no longer posed a threat. "Agent, thank you. Thank you for believing in me when others did not."

"Of course. But, it wasn't me that found you. Mr. Calhoun is the one who refused to give up on you."

Cole looked up to Cash standing by the hospital bed. "Anyway, I have a two p.m. back to Washington. The local guys will collect any other information we need from you. Cole, it's over. You are safe."

Looking back to Cash, Cole thought to himself – *Yes, you are safe.*

CASH WALKED LEAS out of the room and into the hall-way. "Take care of him, Mr. Calhoun. He is tough, but he has also been through a lot."

"I will." Cash paused. "Are you sure… sure that I…. we are doing the right thing? It just seems like a lie."

Leas paused when he saw the conflicted face of Cash. "We discussed this. Telling Cole will do nothing but pro-long his healing. Look, if anything changes, I will let you know immediately. Agreed?"

Cash nodded in reluctant agreement. He looked back into the hospital room and saw Cole watching. Cash flashed a smile and looked back to Leas. "Agreed."

ABOUT THE AUTHOR

ROBERT REEVES WAS born and raised in and around Charleston, South Carolina where his family still resides. He currently lives and practices law in Denver. Accompanied by his dog Cooper, Robert frequently treks the Rockies searching for inspiration for his next novel. To inquire about a possible appearance, please contact him directly at:

Facebook: https://www.facebook.com/a.robertreeves

Goodreads: http://bit.ly/161XAjI

Twitter: https://twitter.com/CRobertReeves

Web: Robert-Reeves.com

COMING SUMMER 2014

GOOD PEOPLE:
A Novel.

HALLOWEEN NIGHT 1958, a man is bludgeoned to death with a brass candlestick by a young Air Force airman. On its base: Jesus, Joseph, and Mary. The normally hushed city of Charleston, South Carolina reacts with shock and horror, but grows conflicted as the murderer pleas self-defense. On the courthouse steps, his young catholic lawyer claims his client was preserving his innocence. As the trial commences, it quickly becomes an indictment of the victim – not his killer.

Based on true events, *Good People* tells the untold story of a murder trial and its lasting impact on the city and its people. Occurring in the shadows of the brewing racial tensions about to engulf the Nation, the novel follows a young man as he attempts to find quiet acceptance within himself and his newfound home. When he is called upon to testify against the airman, he and the city find themselves having to choose between their own peace and justice.

COMING FALL 2014

BLOOD PINES:
BOOK THREE OF THE COLE MOUZON THRILLER SERIES.

THE FINAL INSTALLMENT in the series, Blood Pines finds Cole and Cash attempting to settle into life together in Denver. But, their peace is short-lived as family dynamics threaten to tear his nephew, Billy, from the home. Distracted, Cole doesn't realize that The Taker's last words have come true and a new hunter has come for one final kill… killer that Cole has known since Charleston. Attacked on all fronts, Cole must find the strength to survive and finally end the game put in place as a child before he loses anyone else.

www.ingramcontent.com/pod-product-compliance
Lightning Source LLC
Chambersburg PA
CBHW051326250626
47155CB00007B/2467